THE TIME TRAVELLER'S MURDER

ANDREW S. FRENCH

NEONOIR BOOKS

ALSO BY ANDREW S. FRENCH

The Arcane Supernatural Thriller Series

Book one: The Arcane.

Book two: The Arcane Identity.

The Ella Finn Fantasy Novella Series

Ella and the Elementals

Ella and the Multiverse

Ella and the Monsters

Ella and the Dreamers

Supernatural Short Stories

Dead Souls.

Writing as A. S. French

Crime Fiction and Thrillers

The Astrid Snow series

Book one: Don't Fear the Reaper.

Book two: The Killing Moon.

Book three: Lost in America.

Book four: Gone to Texas

The Detective Jen Flowers series

Book one: The Hashtag Killer.

Book two: Serial Killer.

Book three: Night Killer.

Book four: The Killer Inside Them

Northern Crime Fiction

Where The Bodies Are Buried

Go to www.andrewsfrench.com for more information.

1 THE CLUB

Detective Inspector Harry Hook flexed his fingers in anticipation of strangling a man.

The music was bouncing off the walls when he entered the Vixen nightclub, the girl at the desk too busy chewing gum to acknowledge him. When she took his payment, she let out a silent yawn and blew strawberries in his face.

'What have you come as?' she said.

Harry glanced into the mirror behind her, seeing two days of stubble and eyes borrowed from Lucifer. He gave her his best smile.

'What do you mean?'

She twirled her hair through her fingers and pointed at the poster next to him.

'It's an 80s revival night – everybody gets kitted out for that. So, who are you supposed to be?'

'The 1980s?' Harry said. 'Who listens to music from seventy years ago?'

She shook her head and turned to the queue building up behind him. He glanced at them, men and women dressed as pirates, clowns, or beauty queens. Then he stumbled forward into the club and straight into the middle of the dancing horde. The music burnt his ears, so loud he couldn't hear himself think.

But he heard the roar when the crowd went wild. For one second, he thought it was because they'd realised there was a police officer with them. However, once his misguided arrogance vanished, he understood what all the fuss was about – someone at the Vixen had turned on the latest hi-tech musical accompaniment: the holovideo.

Harry didn't recognise the song – some group singing about a love shack – but the video sprang to life around the revellers, appearing so real that the people might have been standing right next to him. Instead, he was inside a shimmering forest watching a car drive through him as a man and woman belted out the lyrics. It was catchy enough for everybody but Harry to go crazy with dance routines well beyond his ageing bones. Dancers pushed and prodded him as he forced his way through, ignoring the music and the holovideo in search of the bloke he'd come for.

It didn't take long before he located him on a balcony, dressed like a harlequin and sipping champagne – Jackson Vine. When he entered a room, it felt as if his hands were around your throat, even at fifty feet away. Muscled bodyguards and scantily clad women surrounded Vine, but Harry ignored them as he made his way up the steps and stood before him.

Vine shook his head. 'Detective Inspector Hook – has the Met's worst copper come to harass me again?'

The holovideo enclosed Harry, so real he thought he'd been transported to that place. He was inside a shack as people long dead danced around him while he peered straight into Vine's twisted eyes.

'The judge let you off on a technicality, Vine. I'm only

here to remind you that justice will catch up with you, eventually.'

Could he drag Vine away from the bodyguards and get his hands on his throat before anybody could stop him?

Vine laughed before drinking more fizz.

'A technicality?' He removed a phone from his pocket. 'You mean when you burst into my apartment and took this without reading me my rights?' He waved it at Harry. 'You'll never see the videos again, DI Hook. You'll be better off enjoying these old music clips swamping us. There are plenty of pretty women for you to gawp at. Just because you've got no joy in your life, don't make everyone as miserable as you.'

Harry inched closer to him. 'Do these people know what you did to your wife, Vine, how you put her in the hospital?'

Vine's teeth glittered under the illuminated shiny balls.

'It doesn't matter, copper. You should scuttle off to your fellow pigs before I get the boys to show you how to breakdance.'

'You're too little to make that big a mistake, Vine.'

Vine grinned at him. 'Are you ill, Harry? You look like a vampire waiting for a shaft of light to hit them.'

Harry reached into his pocket for his phone.

'I made copies of your videos, Jacko. Did you know that?'

Vine scratched at his face, dislodging silver stars from his cheeks.

'See, I knew you were like me. Do you watch them late at night so you can hear her scream? Is that what you enjoy?'

The music and the holovideo changed around them. It was a tune Harry recognised, finding himself in sunny

Australia as David Bowie encouraged everybody to dance – not that anyone needed prompting. It was such a good song Harry hated interfering with it, but once the holovideo had kicked in, he'd known what to do when confronting Vine. On his way to the club, all he'd thought about was dragging Vine out to give him some of his own medicine, but this was going to be better.

And it shouldn't get him into trouble with his colleagues at the Met.

This time, Harry waved his mobile at Vine.

'If you like your home movies so much, Jacko, you won't mind everybody else seeing them.'

Harry used his phone to cut into the Vixen's wireless connection, overriding its video feed and replacing it with the clips on his device. The last thing he wanted to see was Vine abusing his wife again, but the legal system's failure had left him with little choice.

'Don't!' Vine screamed as he lunged for Harry.

But he was too slow.

Harry fell back into the crowd as Vine's video filled the venue, hearing his foul voice as he exploded into violence for everybody to witness. The courts may have failed Angela Vine, but Harry knew this community wouldn't as he observed their faces.

He didn't hang around to see what they did to Vine, slipping outside so the wireless connection would break. A multitude of stars glittered above him as the night settled over his face, chilling his flesh, but not enough to ruin his evening.

And then his phone rang.

'Why are you ringing me at three in the morning, Caroline?'

Caroline Diaz, Harry's partner at the Met, sighed down the line. 'You need to meet me at the morgue.'

'A murder victim?'

'It looks like it.'

He walked away from the Vixen, across the road towards the Thames.

'It can't wait another five hours?'

'I don't think you'll get the chance to see her if you delay that long.'

The smell of the river invaded his senses, bringing back memories he'd tried to forget.

'Why not, Caroline?'

She sighed again. 'Our murder victim – she's a time traveller.'

2 THE MORGUE

Detective Inspector Caroline Diaz was waiting for Harry at the morgue. Apart from the stainless steel autopsy tables, equipment, and freezers, it was just like any other office.

And the dead bodies.

The facility had a CCTV viewing area with a live link to the post-mortem room to witness the pathologists at work. With DNA and fabric transfer issues, the fewer people present, the less chance of contamination and the more reliable the evidence.

'The forensic pathologist isn't here,' Diaz said. 'I don't think they'll do the post-mortem until the morning.' She nodded at the entrance to the mortuary. 'An anatomic pathology technologist is inside, but they won't be a problem.'

'What's this about, Caroline?'

She glanced around as if a thousand eyes were scrutinising them, even though they were the only people there.

'Do you believe in time travel, Harry?'

He leant against the wall, letting the chill spark his

weary bones into life, wondering if this was a wind-up by his colleagues since he was leaving the Met in two weeks.

'You could have just bought me a watch, Caroline. And a bottle of wine.'

The stern look in her eyes told him this wasn't a practical joke.

'We haven't got long. I'm only here because of a tip-off from one of the paramedics who brought the body in.' She kept staring behind Harry as if they were being observed. 'SD officers will be here soon.'

SD – the Special Division of the Metropolitan Police, created to deal with – in their words – "crimes relating to temporal disturbances".

'Why am I here, Caroline?'

She put her hand on the door and pushed it open. 'Follow me.'

Harry took a deep breath as he went inside, letting his nose get used to the smell: an aroma of strong cleansers and preservative chemicals. The pathology technologist greeted them with a dull smile. There were no introductions as he led them towards a body on a gurney, a plastic sheet covering it apart from the head – pale skin, sculptured cheekbones and a dark bobbed hairstyle.

'Damn,' Harry said.

'Do you know her?'

That cold face wouldn't let him go. 'I know who she looks like.'

Caroline's phone pinged. 'And?'

He leant in closer to the dead woman. 'She's the spitting image of Louise Brooks.'

'Who?'

'She was a movie star in the 1920s.' He only knew this because his father's obsession with old movies had also infected him. But then, a crazy idea hit him. 'Perhaps it's her if she's a time traveller.'

Caroline shook her head. 'You can only travel back in time, not forward.'

Harry ran his fingers over the plastic sheet, a chill rushing through him that was nothing to do with the temperature in the room. Considering where he was, he shouldn't have laughed, but he did.

'That's if you believe what we've been told the last ten years by the so-called Time Authority.'

The TA – the organisation created in 2040 when three women, all renowned physicists, announced they'd discovered the secret of time travel.

But you could only go back, never forward.

So they claimed. But they also made other claims, ones they'd never proved.

'Her name is Amy Croft,' Caroline said. 'She drowned in the Thames sometime late last night or early this morning.'

Harry couldn't take his eyes off her, this Amy Croft. He'd always been obsessed with Louise Brooks, spending hours watching her movies or reading about her. And gazing at the photos. He knew he'd fallen in love with her on his fourteenth birthday when he'd rejected a night out with his mates to watch a double bill of *Pandora's Box* and *Diary of a Lost Girl*. Harry thought he'd outgrow the obsession, but he never did. It was one reason he could never maintain a relationship for more than a few months. For who would want to compete with a dead woman?

And now he was staring at her dead doppelgänger.

Murdered?

The noise outside drew his gaze away. The doors burst open and two uniformed police officers strode in, followed by a man and woman in dark suits. Harry didn't need to see their identity cards to know who they were.

'You shouldn't be in here,' the woman said.

Caroline grabbed Harry's arm. 'We were just leaving.'

The bloke in the suit blocked their way. 'Who are you?'

Harry wriggled out of Caroline's grasp. 'DI Hook and DI Diaz from the Met.'

'Why are you here?' the woman said.

The answer evaded Harry because he didn't know himself.

'We were misinformed,' Caroline said. 'We thought the victim was one of our informants.'

The SD officers scrutinised them, glancing at each other before allowing them to leave.

Harry followed Caroline from the morgue and out of the building. She went to the car and removed a cigarette from her jacket.

'You know they'll kill you,' Harry said as she lit it.

'Everything in this world will kill us eventually.' She blew smoke into the air and he flinched from the smell. His father had been a heavy smoker before his obsessions got the better of him. 'But at least I can enjoy this.'

The car was damp to Harry's touch. 'Now, can you tell me what's going on and why you brought me to see a dead woman who looks like a movie star from the last century?'

She reached into her pocket, removed a card and handed it to him.

He read the information on the front.

'Amy Croft – Time Authority Operative.'

Caroline pointed at the text. 'Check the back.'

Harry turned it over, seeing his name handwritten on it. He couldn't take his eyes off the words as the clouds burst and the rain came.

They scrambled into the car, spots of drizzle dotting the card.

'You took this off the body?' Harry said.

She shook her head. 'It was in her hand when they dragged her out of the river. My friend saw it and called me.'

Harry peered at her. 'Why?'

Caroline laughed. 'Because I've told him all about you – how you're the best homicide detective in the city. And you still haven't explained why you're quitting.'

He ignored her jab. 'The forensic pathologist won't be able to determine the cause of death until after the post-mortem. So it might not be murder – it could be an accident or suicide.'

Caroline retrieved the card from him and handed over her phone.

'Somebody murdered her, Harry.'

There was no sound on the video and the quality was grainy, but it was Croft in the clip, standing on a bridge above the river and gazing into the water.

Harry eyed the screen as she put her hands on the railings, the Thames glistening in the video as the moonlight bounced off the water. Croft didn't move as if waiting for something or someone.

'Where is this from?' Harry said.

'CCTV,' Caroline replied.

He watched as Croft turned to the camera, her face illuminated for a second, thinking once again he was looking at Louise Brooks. The screen was silent, but the noise was everywhere around him: birds fluttered in the trees, crickets created peculiar music using their bodies, while low-flying planes drifted over his head, humming as they jetted off to places unknown.

Amy Croft turned from the lens, speaking to somebody Harry couldn't see. He examined the perfect sculpture of her face, watching her say the words he was desperate to hear, but couldn't. She appeared relaxed as if she knew the person off-camera, which made the pain Harry felt for this woman even worse because someone she trusted was about to take her life. They had taken her life.

He reached for the screen to warn her, an involuntary response he had little control over. A hand hidden in the shadows was on her shoulder. Then her head turned to the CCTV as if she knew the camera was there and what was coming next.

He struggled to breathe, felt the bile in his throat as he turned away and coughed. When he returned to the clip, the screen was empty and he knew someone had thrown her into the river.

Harry rewound the video, freezing it at the start as Amy Croft's face stared at the moon.

Do time travellers know when they'll die?

It was a question he kept running through his mind, but the investigation wasn't his. The Time Authority and the Metropolitan Police had a special relationship set up by the government that didn't involve him. Some other officer would lead the search into her death, but he couldn't help it. He was about to watch the murder of a time traveller again, knowing he'd never have the chance to save her.

But Harry was wrong.

3 PRIVATE INVESTIGATIONS

Six months later, Harry was out of the force and running Hook Security and Detection. Yet Croft's murder continued to haunt him. Her face was burnt into his retinas day and night, and he didn't know why.

Of course I do – she looked like Louise.

'Wake up, Hooky. You'll never pay back what you owe me at this rate.'

That was the voice of his not so silent partner, Chuck Connors. Harry brushed haze from his eyes but still saw Amy Croft staring at him.

'So much for the promise of an interest-free loan, Chuck.'

Chuck laughed and slapped him on the shoulder.

'You know it's not me, mate, but my investors.'

His smile couldn't betray his nervousness. Harry's silent partner had other partners he'd neglected to mention when floating the idea of them going into business once Harry had quit the force. Chuck reached into his jacket, removed a holodisk and placed it in the middle of the desk.

Harry waved his hand at him. 'I don't want another

replaying of your drunken night in that so-called gentlemen's club you frequent.'

Chuck rolled his eyes in mock horror. 'You need to get out more, partner. Anyway, that's not what this is about.' His fingers hovered over the top of the holodisk. 'What we need is a new client, a marquee signing to broadcast our name across the city and impress potential suitors. That's what this will do.'

He pressed the button and a hologram sprang to life, showing a tall, shiny building that every citizen and their dog would recognise unless they'd been living under a rock for the last six months: the headquarters of the Time Authority.

'You want us to handle the Authority's security?'

The light of the hologram animated Chuck's face into maniacal glee.

'Think what it would do for our standing in the City. There'd be no stopping us then, and the investors might stop hounding me.'

Harry didn't like the sound of that. When Chuck had initially mentioned the business idea, Harry had assumed it would be just the two of them: combining Harry's vast experience with the Met and Chuck's family finances, which were considerable. Instead, Chuck had failed to mention there would be other investors – something that only came to light with their recent struggles. Harry needed to have a long conversation with Chuck about it, but that was a conversation for another time. First, he had to nip in the bud this ridiculous idea of working at the new Authority building.

'Even if I gave you a badge, Chuck, that would mean there are still only two security personnel on our books. I don't think that would be enough for the Authority's tenth-anniversary celebrations.'

All the good intentions Chuck had promised Harry at the beginning – how they'd be the premier security service in London within six months – had ground to a halt with Chuck's father's death and what that did to the Connors financial empire. Apart from the two of them, there was only one other employee – Agnes, who did everything they didn't, which was a lot – and Harry was the only investigator.

Not that they were swamped with cases, with only one on the books: a missing teenage girl who Harry was searching for as a favour – so even that wasn't bringing money in.

Chuck moved his hand through the shimmering hologram, making the building wobble like jelly.

'Once we get the contract, then we can employ more people. So it's a guaranteed win.'

Harry's shoulders slumped into the chair, his brain aching and wondering where Chuck had got this marvellous idea.

'This is all redundant, Chuck. You, I and the rest of the planet know the Authority deal with their own security. Better firms than ours have tried to worm their way into their good books and failed.'

The day the world discovered a group of British scientists had worked out the mechanics of time travel – when one of them let it slip during a BBC interview – was the start of a mad scramble by every government and private institution across the globe to acquire the secret. But the Crucial Three, as the media nicknamed them, were determined to stay autonomous from everyone, regardless of how good-natured they claimed to be. Having their financial independence helped them do that.

Chuck twisted his fingers through the hologram, waving it around like a magician.

'That may have been true before, Harry, but we have an ace in the hole now.'

Confusion must have consumed Harry's face. He picked up the tiny snow globe on the desk, a gift from his sister a long time ago.

'What do you mean?'

'I've spoken to them and they've asked for you by name.'

Harry nearly dropped the globe. 'They know who I am?'

Chuck held out his hands like a carnival barker about to announce the star turn.

'You must be more famous than either of us realised.'

Harry peered at him, assuming this was a wind-up. Since he was a kid, Chuck had played practical jokes on him and others – most of which were more harmful than humorous. For some poor bloke's stag night, he and his posh university mates had got the prospective husband drunk and left him in a coffin for twelve hours.

'You've acquired a few more stress lines across your face since yesterday, Chuck.'

They were the same age, but he looked ten years older than Harry.

'I'm still having problems with my father's estate.'

Bruce Connors had been a difficult man when he was alive, never a great husband or parent or even general human being, but he'd proved more of an irritation to his only son after his death. The debt he'd left was considerable, and he'd passed it on to Chuck, which was another reason he needed the business to work.

'Is it that factory?'

In the last few years of his life, Bruce Connors had switched from the things that had made his fortune, which were all debt-based, into more practical products to sell. He moved from producing parts for the motor industry into selling second-hand goods online, all of which he stored in a large factory on the other side of the city. But the building now stood empty and the rent and the rates were crippling Chuck's personal and family finances. He'd been trying to sell it since his father's death, but with no luck.

Chuck waved a hand in the air.

'No, I've got a buyer for that. But, unfortunately, a few other things are taking more time and effort than I expected.' He gazed at the hologram of the Time Authority building as if it was real and Harry was the shimmering illusion of light in the room. 'This contract could be the answer to all of our problems, mate.'

What he meant was it might solve his problems. Harry had plenty of his own to worry about, but they didn't concern the business or his partner's private life.

'I'm busy at the moment, Chuck. Why don't you work with the Time Authority?'

Chuck laughed. 'Busy? What, looking for that girl we're not even getting paid for?' He shook his head. 'What's her name again?'

'Same as it was before: Christine Kerr.' Harry reached across the desk and opened the computer file he'd created on her. Not that there was much in it. 'Imagine how worried you'd be if Kelly disappeared, and then you can put yourself in Christine's parents' shoes.'

Kelly was Chuck's young daughter and Harry's goddaughter.

Chuck pulled at the top of his shirt. 'Don't even think of

such a thing.' He peered at the back of the computer screen. 'Are you getting anywhere with finding her?'

Harry blew out a sigh of frustration. 'The police have classed her as a runaway. So I got little joy when speaking to my former colleagues.'

Chuck grinned at him. 'Perhaps you're not as likeable as you think.'

'It doesn't matter. Her parents gave me the names of her friends, so I'm going to speak to them this afternoon.'

'Okay, okay,' Chuck said. 'The meeting with the Time Authority is tomorrow morning, so you'll have plenty of opportunities to do your research on them before that.'

'And what if I get a lead on Christine today so I can't go to the TA tomorrow?'

Chuck slumped into a chair and pulled his mobile from his pocket.

'Is this about Lily?'

Him saying her name was like a punch into Harry's gut.

'No, Chuck. Why would it be?'

He showed his phone to Harry, the screen displaying a photo of the three of them together not long before Harry's older sister vanished twenty-six years ago.

'You know why, Harry. What happened to Lily drove you into the army, and then into the police. Of course, you pathologically need to protect people, especially children – and I admire you for that – but sometimes it clouds your judgement.'

Harry gazed at the photo on the phone, saddened by his sister's deep brown eyes and glittering smile.

'We don't know what happened to her, Chuck. Nobody does, but at least I can try to find Christine and ease the burden on her parents.'

Chuck put the mobile into his pocket. 'What if she

doesn't want anybody to find her, Harry? If I'd had the guts to run away when I was sixteen, I would have. And I wouldn't have wanted anybody to come looking for me, especially my parents.'

Chuck's relationship with his late father had been a troubled one, and Harry was sure Chuck hadn't told him the whole truth of what he'd had to endure from such a cold, unemotional man.

'You could have joined the army with me. I asked you to.'

Chuck shook his head and laughed.

'Yes, that's what I should have done – gone from one strict regimented life straight into another one.' He waved a finger at Harry. 'And you didn't last that long, did you?'

Three years Harry had lasted until the army let him leave because of his fragile mental health. He was surprised the Met accepted him less than a year later, but they didn't seem concerned about why he'd left the army. It didn't take him long in the police to realise having a healthy mind wasn't one of their job requirements.

'Well, we're here now. I'll go to this meeting with the Time Authority, but only if it doesn't interfere with my search for Christine.'

Chuck nodded. 'Great.' The phone pinged in his pocket and he removed it. He gazed at the screen for twenty seconds before getting up. 'I've got to sort out more of my father's mess of an estate, but make sure you ring me as soon as you finish with the TA tomorrow.'

Harry said he would as Chuck left.

Then he stared at the computer, looking at the photos he had of Christine Kerr, but only seeing his sister again on that day she'd disappeared so long ago.

4 THE CRUCIAL THREE

Harry spent a frustrating afternoon talking to Christine's friends, understanding why they were reluctant to tell him anything useful. None of them appeared too concerned she'd left home a week before her sixteenth birthday. That made him think they knew she was okay somewhere.

Perhaps she's staying with one of them.

He sent a text to Agnes with the addresses of the four teenage girls he'd spoken to.

Can you take a subtle look around these places tomorrow to see if Christine is living in any of them?

Agnes Kaminski was the first person they'd employed at HSD. Harry had met her while working for the police during a chance encounter with an organisation laundering millions through several electronic accounts. HSD needed an expert in computer programming and hacking, and she was the best, so Harry didn't hesitate to hire her. She wasn't a trained investigator, but was as good, if not better, than most coppers he'd worked with.

Do I get a pay rise? she replied.

Have we paid you anything yet?

We'll I didn't want to mention it, Harry, but since you did...

Then he told her about his meeting with the TA and how they might be rolling in money soon.

The Time Authority! Wow! You better tell me all about it tomorrow.

Harry said he would and signed off.

When he got home, the wine was chilling in the fridge. Opening the bottle as he warmed up yesterday's food, he drank half a glass, letting it wash down the pasta and prepare him for the night's work. Then, as he set the automatic sink to clean the dishes, the virtual assistant technology built into the apartment informed him it had found more than one hundred million references to the Time Authority online.

'Thanks, Bob.'

Harry had disabled the visual option when he'd bought the flat and changed it from female to male. The idea of him coming home – living on his own – after a day of investigating murder, rape, and child abuse to be greeted by the holographic appearance of an attractive woman was too much for him to take. There were multiple displays to choose from, including the shimmering visages of long-dead celebrities. Still, he'd settled on the gruff Yorkshire twang of Bob, hoping it would keep him sane and kill off that niggling desire he had to set it to play random holographic images of his favourite female actors.

He grabbed the laptop and slumped into the sofa, staring across the room at the reproduction vintage film posters on the walls: Humphrey Bogart and Mary Astor peered at him from *The Maltese Falcon*. Veronica Lake and Robert Preston advertised *This Gun For Hire*. The wine chilled the back of his throat as Harry remembered all the times he'd sat in the family home wanting to see those movies and others while Lily had told him off for being too young.

'When you're older, we'll watch them together,' she'd always say to him.

Yet they never got the chance.

Before the alcohol and his memories transformed him into a sentimental wreck, he turned to what Bob had discovered about the Time Authority. He ran the details through the computer, displaying them on a holoscreen in the middle of the room.

The Time Authority.

Such a grandiose name for the unassuming women he stared at on the screen: Dr Rose Adler – born 2000; Dr Sally Cohen – born 2001; and Dr Mary Hazell – born 2001. As the media named them, they were the Crucial Three, all renowned physicists. It was ten years ago, but Harry remembered it as if it was yesterday, the eventual uproar at Dr Hazell's claim of discovering the secret of time travel. Few people saw the TV programme when it was first broadcast on a live late-night science show, but the clip was soon all over the internet and social media.

But it was one thing to say you could travel through time and another to prove it. Once Dr Hazell had dropped her little nugget on national TV about going into the past to see her grandparents, most of the chatter was disbelief and ridicule, mainly from other scientists and physicists, as well as the odd conspiracy theorist throwing in their two cents. The story might have withered away as an internet hoax if a reputable news site hadn't posted a piece online about the Crucial Three.

The post said the claims of time travel were true, and

the British government, with the science community's help, had suppressed the news to stop the public from panicking. There was a theory Dr Hazell had let slip her claim on purpose. She was only on the TV show to talk about her family and how her great grandparents had been spies during the Second World War when she'd dropped her bombshell. There were other claims that she was drunk and that's why the information had slipped out of her.

Harry flicked through the search list, finding the original video and playing it. He'd seen it before, not long after its first broadcast, but had never given it much attention. Now, he gazed at Mary Hazell as if she was a suspect in a serious criminal investigation.

'People say that science has reached its limit on this planet,' the interviewer said in the clip. 'There's nothing we can do to stop the changing environment and we should concentrate on leaving this world in the near future.'

Dr Hazell peered at the man, her eyes rigid like a black hole. She was about to reply when Harry paused the video. He rewound it a few seconds and moved closer to the life-size hologram shimmering in front of him.

Her fingers are trembling. Only slightly, but they're moving.

Was it because of alcohol? Or was she afraid? Perhaps it was something else.

He restarted the clip, so close to the hologram he could imagine Hazell's breath on his cheeks as she spoke.

'Humanity's future lies not in space, but in time.'

'What do you mean, Dr Hazell?' the interviewer said.

She hesitated with her reply, one hand going to her face before gazing straight into the camera – and into Harry's eyes.

'Two other colleagues and I have discovered how to go back in time.'

The silence in the TV studio engulfed the flat. Harry could hear his heart beating, feeling its thrust against his ribs as his blood appeared to move through him like lava seeping out of a volcano. He paused the video to pour another glass of wine. The static from the hologram pricked at the hairs on his arms, so he moved from it to the sofa. He sipped at his drink as he watched the end of the clip, observing as the interviewer gently mocked Hazell's claims of going back in time to see her grandparents.

'I viewed them from afar, knowing they would die two days after I saw them.'

The programme finished before the man could ask Hazell why she hadn't saved them.

Harry rewound the video, freezing it at the point where Hazell made her astonishing claim. Then he opened another web browser and searched for any links related to the immediate aftermath of her words.

What were people saying right then, immediately after her TV appearance?

Not much from what he found and most of it was more ridicule, mainly from her peers in the scientific community. He scanned through the comments before returning to the list of videos, locating the next one of Dr Mary Hazell. Two days after her first appearance on the TV, she was back on the same show, but this time with her colleagues. Now, all three of them repeated the same claim. Time travel was possible and they'd all done it.

Dr Rose Adler spoke with a northern accent, gazing into the studio audience.

'My mother died when I was too young to remember her,' Adler said, 'so I travelled back to see what she was like.'

Dr Sally Cohen seemed nervous, her freckled face twitching as she glanced between her colleagues. Then she removed a photograph from her pocket.

'This is my brother, George. Twenty years ago, I found him lying in the street with a fractured skull. He's lain in a coma ever since and I needed to know how it had happened. So that's what I went back to observe.'

Harry expected the interviewer to ask Cohen what she'd discovered, but he asked something else.

'Extraordinary claims require extraordinary proof. Do you have any?'

Harry froze the video as the three of them glanced at each other, moving his head closer to the hologram. There was a silent acknowledgement between them as if they knew this was coming and they'd prepared for it, which would make sense if you could travel through time.

Harry started the clip again as Dr Hazell answered.

'Stonehenge,' she said.

The interviewer looked surprised. 'What about it?'

'The ground inside the stones has been scanned many times, so a complete map of it exists. Cameras have focused on the site twenty-four hours a day since a group tried to blow them up ten years ago. So we'll go back a thousand years and place a capsule in the middle, six feet underground, and inside will be a copy of this interview and other items from this year, 2040.'

A hush fell over the audience before loud clapping erupted from everyone. The interviewer appeared disappointed as if he'd wanted something fantastic to happen there and then, perhaps wanting one of the women to pull a historical person out of a hat.

This time, the public reaction was greater, with half the people disbelieving, while the other half believed.

Why would respected scientists, renowned physicists, invent such an outlandish claim? That was what many said. Yet others said it was nothing but a hoax, promoted by the women because they sought fame.

Harry scrolled under the clip, seeing the link for the Stonehenge incident. Then he clicked on it. He watched as a group of selected archaeologists scanned the area inside those famous stones. They discovered the box immediately. It was out of the ground and opened five minutes later in front of the cameras. Photos from the TV interview were next to a computer disk that contained the video from the previous TV appearance Hazell had made. Testing on the wooden capsule showed it had been underground for over a thousand years. Some people still claimed the box must have been placed there days or weeks earlier, but nobody could explain how the videos and photos from the day before were in it.

The wine warmed his insides as Harry flicked through the media reaction to the Stonehenge Event, as it became known. Worldwide headlines followed, but many claimed it as a hoax. The Crucial Three said they didn't care; they only wanted to be left alone with their research. But those who believed them needed to know the nature of that research. Were these women changing history? Who was controlling them? Which government was behind this? Was it the military?

We need more proof, the world said.

So the Crucial Three provided more.

Adler, Cohen, and Hazell returned to the same TV studio, this time to a live worldwide audience, including a collection of their doubting colleagues sitting opposite them – scientists who'd ridiculed and mocked the women for their claims. The presenter showed the Stonehenge footage again to a familiar mixture of gasps and snorts of derision. For many, it seemed that wasn't proof enough. Harry wasn't sure if Dr Hazell was the group leader then, but she came across as the most assured and confident. The camera moved into a close up of her, glued to her face. Ten years ago, her hair was long and dark, draped over her shoulders as she sat there like a queen. Even though she was a hologram, Harry could sense her presence.

Hazell got up and addressed the audience and the cameras. And Harry.

'If the three of us can't convince you, maybe six can.'

The camera lingered on her face until distracted by the murmuring in the audience. Then every lens panned out to see three people emerging from the spectators, women removing wigs and glasses to reveal replicas of the Crucial Three. Later, the media would nickname them the Secret Six, three older versions of them who had travelled from two days in the future to now. The six of them stood in the middle of the studio, every eye and lens focused on them, as the noise grew into a cacophony where nobody could be heard.

When everything calmed down, the Secret Six took questions from the interviewer and the other scientists.

'How can you travel through time?'

They wouldn't reveal that.

'Who do you work for?'

Only themselves. They'd created the Time Authority three months ago, a company owned by all of them.

'Who funds you?'

They had their own money. Later investigations would show that family money had started their initial experiments – financed by Rose Adler's inheritance.

'Can you change time?'

No. The past can't be changed.
'What will you use it for?'
Observation only. Historical research.
'What happens in the future?'
We don't know. Travel to the future is impossible.

The video clips were on the official Authority website, with biographies of the three women: they'd met at Oxford University in 2018. Mary Hazell and Sally Cohen were in their first year; Rose Adler was in her second. Their time there appeared to be uneventful, all three of them leaving with First Class degrees, and then moving on to research opportunities in the capital. However, nearly twenty years later, they discovered the secret of time travel together, a secret many had tried to repeat or uncover in the subsequent ten years, but had failed so far.

The lack of personal details on the official site sent him scurrying through the outer reaches of the internet, plodding through rumour after innuendo after conspiracy theory. No idea was too ridiculous: it was a hoax; a government ploy to distract the masses; an alien invasion; a cloning experiment; and on and on. The proliferation of theories was hardly a surprise considering none of the Crucial Three had been seen in public since the attempt on Hazell's life five months after the appearance of the Secret Six on the TV.

The Authority website made no mention of it, but there were descriptions and reports all over the internet. They all repeated the same details – Dr Hazell was attacked near the river by anti-travellers, as they came to be known. She only escaped when people leaving a gig stumbled upon the attack. Grainy CCTV clips of the incident accompanied most reports, where frames had been scrutinised in intimate detail. Some sites claimed it as another hoax, a false flag event created by the Authority to garner sympathy from a confused public. The anti-travellers gained greater notoriety from it, using the violence as a spur in their attempt to create a national movement opposed to the Authority and the idea of time travel. For a moment, the disparate opponents to time travel came together in unity, but like all groups of their type, in-fighting led to splits.

Harry read the online posts, discarding them as the rantings of those fearful about the implications. Instead, he found other comments more interesting, from scientists – other physicists – who claimed what the Crucial Three said they'd done was impossible.

But even though Harry scanned through another two dozen articles, there was no evidence these remarkable women had done what they'd said. Apart from the Stonehenge revelation and the trick with the "doppelgängers" in the TV studio, they'd provided no proof of the existence of time travel.

There was no law against claiming you could travel through time and not prove it. But, after another hour of online browsing, it seemed to Harry that the people who believed it the most were those against it: the anti-travellers.

Whether it was true or not, the three of them had the money to pay for that shiny new TA building he'd be stepping inside tomorrow.

And then there was Amy Croft.

There'd been no mention of her murder anywhere on the TA website; no links to someone with that name working for the Time Authority.

But he'd seen the reports and watched that video numerous times in the police station.

Harry typed Amy's name into an internet search, already knowing what would come up since he'd done this before: a singer, an artist, a lecturer, chef, and even a road with that name in Canada.

However, there was no mention of the woman who'd died or an image of her. So he went to the official website of the Metropolitan Police, searching for a link to Special Division, but not finding one. But, he knew they existed – he'd seen their officers.

But what did they work on, apart from Croft's murder?

That's if it even was murder.

Harry finished the wine and settled into the comfort of the sofa.

Tomorrow, at his meeting with the Time Authority, he'd have a few questions of his own to ask the Crucial Three.

What had they been doing for the last ten years?

How did their future selves know to travel back to that TV studio?

If travelling to the future was impossible, what had happened to their future selves?

And who was Amy Croft?

5   CELLULOID HEROES

Harry took the Tube from his flat in Islington to the Authority headquarters in Westminster. It was a thirty-minute journey and he spent most of it watching *Blade Runner* on his phone.

It was re-watching since he'd seen it dozens of times before. It was near the top of the list of his favourite films – he could never decide what number one was, his decision changing with his mood, but it was the film he'd watched the most since he'd fallen in love with movies as a kid.

Yeah, even more times than Pandora's Box or Diary of a Lost Girl.

His father was to blame for Harry's celluloid obsession.

Lily got her love of books from our mother, while I inherited a cinema obsession from the old man.

Oliver Hook's addiction to the silver screen meant the only time he spent with his son was when they were inside some dusty cinema in the dark or curled up in the back room of their house, peering at a screen covering most of the wall.

A double feature of John Carpenter films at the Electric

Cinema in Notting Hill was the gateway drug that had led Oliver Hook down a relentless path of devouring movies and cataloguing them in a diary and online blog. His work and relationships suffered as he couldn't relate to other people's everyday interests that didn't involve films. He rationalised his behaviour by thinking it would give him the insight to make a great film of his own. His descent continued until he hit rock bottom after seeing *Fifty Shades of Grey*.

Harry always figured his father's obsession was his way of dealing with his daughter's disappearance, but they never talked that. Or her. Neither of his parents mentioned Lily to him beyond the vague promise she'd turn up some-day. It was only three years later, on the eve of Harry's thir-teenth birthday, that he thought about talking to them about it.

Then his mother abandoned them and Harry's relation-ship with his dad started on a downward spiral it had never recovered from. He hadn't seen the old man in two years, leaving the family home as his dad sat glued to a flickering TV screen, gazing at Humphrey Bogart clutching on to the Black Bird for the thousandth time.

While Harry hadn't chased the celluloid dragon as hard as his father did, he was always thrilled to kill an afternoon at a special showing of *The Hidden Fortress* or spend the better part of a day in a Sigourney Weaver marathon. Not that he'd had many opportunities to relax in front of the screen as a copper. When he was a police detective, his colleagues had mocked him for his obscure movie obsession, wondering why he wasn't spending his free time like most of them did, chasing ephemeral relationships or diving headfirst into a bottle.

Harry had smiled at their jokes, unable to tell them that

peering at the depravities of human behaviour meant his only relief came through falling into shimmering neon fictional worlds.

Six months after leaving that life, he continued to gaze into silver screens of all sizes. As he got off the Tube and stepped into the light of day, Harry peered into the sky, putting his phone away and feeling disappointed he couldn't see any flying cars above him.

It's the middle of the twenty-first century and I'm still waiting for a hovercar.

He dodged the tourists and headed for Victoria Street, enjoying the irony of the Authority building standing on the spot where the old New Scotland Yard headquarters used to be. Thirty years ago, it had been flats, offices and shops, but the economic collapse of the mid-2020s had left that part of London empty for a long time. So now, the HQ of the world's only time travellers stood there like a modern church, all sparkling and angular.

I guess this could be the start of a new religion.

Harry scrutinised the building, still surprised it wasn't one of the city's latest mega skyscrapers. In the last decade, London had appeared to be desperate to acquire the title of the city with the largest buildings in Europe. It reminded him of his time spent in New York, of that year between leaving the army and joining the police force. It had allowed him to wallow in all those memories he had of the Big Apple from the movies his father had introduced him to.

While in New York, he'd gone to the ballet and imagined himself as an extra in *Black Swan*. He'd visited Manhattan to spend hours sitting on a bench while listening to the soundtrack from the film with the same name. One afternoon he'd witnessed the police foiling a bank robbery – it was the spark that drew him to the police force when he returned to London – and thought about *Dog Day After-noon*. He'd spend nights in pool halls, imagining he was Paul Newman in the *Hustler*. Harry won more money that way. After a month in the city, he rented a place in Brooklyn and got a job in a cinema that showed *Do the Right Thing* every afternoon. It was around this time that hip-hop became his musical genre of choice.

Each time he took a taxi, he'd expected Robert De Niro to be driving the cab. He saw the ghosts of Orson Welles and Burt Lancaster everywhere he went, and his local corner store was owned by a woman who was the spit of Bette Davis in *All About Eve*.

However, that was all behind him now, just like his time in the Met.

An aroma of exhaust fumes mixed in with something rotten coming off the river settled over him as he stared at the building. Then he took a deep breath and crossed the road. He walked up the steps and put a hand on the door. The lack of security intrigued him as he entered.

Hold on, Harry, it's going to be a bumpy ride.

He stepped into the lobby and checked the surround-ings. Art deco decadence permeated the space, with chequered flooring, shimmering mirrors and metalwork sculptured to represent exotic or extinct animals. Hundreds of flowers brought vivid colours and aromas to the building as if he was in the middle of some magnificent garden.

A young woman in her mid-twenties approached him with her dark hair tied into a swaying ponytail. Her ocean-blue eyes spoke of a curious mind searching for knowledge.

She smiled at him. 'Detective Hook? I'm Bronwyn Cromwell.'

He returned her grin. 'Just Harry. I quit the force six months ago.'

'Oh.' She pulled out a phone and gazed at the screen. 'You have a ten o'clock appointment with the Executive Officers?'

He nodded. 'If you mean am I here to see Doctors Cohen, Adler and Hazell, you'd be correct.'

Bronwyn Cromwell fidgeted with her mobile as she scrutinised him.

'But you are a detective?'

'Yes,' Harry said. 'But not with the Metropolitan Police anymore. I run Hook Security and Detection with my partner, Chuck Connors. It was him who organised this meeting, though I'm unsure what it's about.'

He hoped she'd provide him with more information, but she only seemed more confused.

'Right, okay.' She put her phone away. 'I'll take you to the top floor.'

She turned and led him towards the lift.

'I thought there would be more people, considering it's the only time travel building in the world.' He inhaled the aroma of the roses as he went. 'I'm surprised you have no security here, with all the protests against your organisation.'

He didn't mention the attack on Dr Hazell by anti-travellers.

Bronwyn Cromwell stopped outside the lift.

'We have security; you just can't see it.' Harry didn't know if he was irritated or attracted by her grin. 'The front door wouldn't have opened if we hadn't encoded your details into the digital lock. And all the windows can withstand the strongest of explosions.'

He followed her into the lift. 'What details of mine are programmed into the security?'

The brightness of her teeth relaxed him as they went up.

'Why, all of them, Mr Hook. Fingerprints, retina scans, blood work and DNA samples.'

His stomach lurched as the lift did. 'Where did you get those?'

Bronwyn Cromwell's laugh was enough to make him light-headed.

'From your former employers, of course.' She appeared to be enjoying his confusion. 'You joined the army at eighteen in 2032, correct?' He nodded. 'Leaving the military in 2035, and then you were in the Met for fourteen years, 2036 until now?'

The metal of the lift chilled his fingers. 'I was.'

'Did you read the fine details of your contract when you became a police officer?'

Harry shook his head. 'Nobody ever reads that stuff.'

The lift stopped with no indicator of which floor they were on.

'Perhaps you should have. But what you did was sign away any rights you had to what the government then sold to us.'

The lift opened and she stepped outside. He followed her into the corridor and towards the room at the end. He didn't know how to reply to what she'd told him.

She took him inside, leading him to a comfortable seat near the window. He peered through the glass at the London skyline, surprised at how high up he was. A narrow wooden door led on to the balcony and a patterned rug covered most of the floor. Three chairs surrounded a table; with a water jug and glasses on it.

'Would you like a hot drink?' Cromwell said.

Harry sat and poured himself a glass of water.

'No thanks. This will do.'

She continued to smile at him. 'I'll let the Execs know you're here.'

He sipped at the water and watched her leave.

I wonder if the Crucial Three will appear out of nothing, like one of those transporters from an old episode of Star Trek.

But not from the future, only from the past.

He peered through the window at the River Thames, thinking of time as resembling the river below him, flowing forward, but never backward.

Until these remarkable women cracked that code.

Apparently.

Then he glanced beyond the Thames, at the rows of tower blocks that had sprung up in the last five years. Harry remembered when his mother used to take him on trips around the city as a kid. She didn't do it to show him the usual tourist locations, but to introduce him to what she called Hidden London. Behind locked doors and lost entrances, he discovered a secret world of dilapidated Tube stations, overgrown pathways, empty lift shafts, and echoing ventilation ducts.

As well as taking him deep underground, his mother also showed him several high-rises abandoned by the owners or which only had a few remaining occupants. One of these had included his mother's brother, Uncle Sammy. There were more cats than people in the building and the place stank of piss every time he went there.

Uncle Sammy was the only extended family he had. His father was an only child, and his parents had died long before Harry was born. There was never mention of his mother's parents, so he always assumed they were dead.

Harry never understood why his mother took him to see

her brother since there appeared to be no love between them. It was only later, after she'd left, that he realised she'd done it as a warning to him, implying that Sammy's life of loneliness and poverty might be Harry's if he didn't make the right choices. It was one reason he'd joined the army, but that hadn't turned out how he'd expected.

He pushed the thoughts of his childhood from his head and focused on the room. The walls were bare, painted a soothing pink. A single vase of plastic flowers stood on shelves against the far wall, next to a large cabinet. It was a lifeless environment, the opposite of the vibrant colours and nature that had greeted him at the reception.

Harry finished the water and removed his phone. He was about to text Chuck and ask him why he was in this building when the door opened. The glass chilled his fingers as he watched the three women who'd changed the world stride towards him.

6 ONE MOMENT IN TIME

Harry stood as they approached, recognising the three most famous women in the world.

The three most famous people in the world.

Dr Rose Adler spoke first as she shook his hand. She had perfect cheekbones, short blonde hair, brown eyes and a winning smile.

'We're glad you could make it, Mr Hook. Did Bronwyn offer you something stronger to drink?'

'Please, call me Harry,' he said as he let go of her. 'It's a bit early in the morning for me, I'm afraid.'

He watched as Dr Mary Hazell went to a cabinet. She removed a glass and a bottle of rum. She wore a glove on her right hand, but not the other. He'd never seen that in the videos and photos. She poured herself a consider-able measure with no ice or mixer. Then she raised it to him.

'It's after five somewhere in the world, Harry.'

She didn't shake his hand, but Dr Sally Cohen did.

'Don't mind Mary. She's always grumpy about something.'

Hazell downed half of the rum. 'Maybe it's because I can't get used to death as easily as others, Sally.'

Cohen let go of Harry. From under long brown bangs shone eyes the colour of a shimmering sky. Below that was a nose so freckled, the spots tumbled over to cover her cheeks. Her smile was warm with a hint of shyness. After peering at their ten-year-old holograms the previous evening, he felt strange to be near them like this.

The three women sat, so Harry did the same. 'Why am I here?'

Hazell clutched her glass, sitting opposite him. Her eyes were the shade of acorns, bright enough to highlight the intelligence she refused to hide.

'Didn't your partner tell you?'

Harry's gut wanted what she was drinking. 'I'm in the dark, ladies.'

Hazell laughed. 'You must be used to that, surely, having worked for the Met for so long.'

Harry's legs tensed as he thought this was all a setup, another one of Chuck's practical jokes. He was about to stand when Dr Adler spoke through that winning smile.

'You were a homicide detective with the Metropolitan Police?'

His brain told Harry to go, but he was intrigued now.

Why are the inventors of time travel interested in my career?

'I was. There aren't many specific homicide detectives in the UK since murder rates outside the big cities don't warrant dedicated homicide teams, but there is in the Met.'

'Can you tell us about your work?' Adler said.

He shook his head. 'I might not be a police detective anymore, but I can't reveal anything that isn't already in the public domain.'

Is that what this is about? They're trying to get murder case details from me.

'We don't want specific information from you, Harry. Just a general idea of what you did for the Met,' Cohen said.

Harry stared at them. 'Why?'

Hazell finished her drink. 'Didn't you realise this was a job interview?'

He fought the urge to leave and gave them what they wanted.

'I worked under a Senior Investigation Officer as part of the Major Investigation Team dealing with homicides and other serious crimes. When a murder landed on the MIT, we gathered much of the evidence in the early stages of the investigation – the team identified witnesses, took prints and DNA from the scene, captured any CCTV footage, and many people knocked on doors, conducted interviews and trawled through intelligence reports.

'After this initial stage of enquiries, the more detailed work occurred. Exhibits were examined and sent for analysis; witness statements were scrutinised; CCTV examined; post-mortem reports were read. We'd review the past of the deceased, suspects and witnesses. Finally, the Lead Officer collated all this information to create a case to present to the Crown Prosecution Service to show who did it, how, when and where.

'The difficulties in this would vary a lot. Sometimes a corpse would need identifying first. In others, the initial call to the police would have all the information. I've been involved in cases where a person called us and said, "Come over, I've just murdered my wife." Other times, there were weeks or months before we'd identify a suspect.

'Most of the work, though, was about going through the evidence with meticulous attention to detail to make sure the case could get to court. There was no point going to trial if we didn't think there was enough evidence for a conviction. Then the team had to consider any defence so it could be countered to convince twelve people that the version of events the prosecution was presenting was accurate.

'What it's not like is the TV or movies. There's very little in the way of car chases, running after suspects, jumping over cars, splashing through puddles, or wrestling masked criminals wielding an axe. That said, I know coppers who've done all of those things.'

Hazell grinned at him. 'What was your success rate?'

He smiled back. 'Pretty high.'

She removed a phone from her pocket and placed it on the table. He recognised the photo on the screen.

'But you couldn't solve her murder, could you?'

Harry glanced at the image of the dead time traveller.

'Amy Croft's case wasn't one of mine.'

'Would you like it to be?' Adler said.

Her words surprised him. 'What?'

Hazell stood and went to pour herself another drink. He wondered where the nearest pub was as he watched her.

Cohen reached over to him. 'What my colleagues are saying, in their clumsy way, is that we at the Time Authority would like you to investigate the murder of our employee, Amy Croft. Do you understand that?'

He nodded. 'I do, Dr Cohen. But as far as I'm aware, Ms Croft's murder is still under investigation by a dedicated Met team – the Special Division. My understanding was that SD dealt with all incidences of temporal crime.'

Hazell laughed like a hyena. 'There's no such thing as temporal crime, Mr Hook.'

Harry peered at her. 'Are you saying you'd like Hook

Security and Detection to run an investigation parallel to the official one?'

Hazell retook her seat opposite him.

'No, that's not it.' She sipped at her drink. 'What Rose, Sally and I are offering you is the opportunity to become the first and only time-travelling detective.'

He nearly fell out of the chair. 'You want me to travel through time?'

All three women nodded, but Adler spoke.

'Yes, Harry. Would you be interested in that?'

He didn't know what to think, staring at the rum in Hazell's glass and wondering if he'd look unprofessional if he asked for a drink to calm his nerves. But then again, he thought this was Chuck playing the most audacious of practical jokes on him.

'Why me?' he said.

Dr Rose Adler leant towards him. 'I can see the disbelief in your eyes.' She gave him another one of those winning smiles. 'I guess it must be your detective training telling you not to trust us.' She glanced at her colleagues. 'And that is understandable since you know nothing about us.'

He laughed. 'I did my research before coming here, Dr Adler. So I know plenty about the three of you.'

It was Hazell's turn to laugh. 'Let me guess. You trawled through the internet last night and devoured every bit of gossip and rumour you could find regarding us. And you probably spent hours watching those videos of our TV interviews, didn't you?'

Harry eased into his seat. 'I'm all ears if the three of you want to tell me your secrets.'

Adler touched his arm. 'I'm from a family of demolition experts and grew up in a poor northern suburb of

Manchester. I spent my youth climbing up mill chimneys and blowing them up. However, somewhere along the way, I went from knocking things down to wondering what would happen if I could recreate time.

'I watched buildings crumble, seeing how the rubble and stones crashed to the ground, not as they once were as a solid connected thing, but as scattered parts of a former entity. Then I realised that's how time works as we move forward through it. The past has been knocked down behind us – only held together as memories or nostalgia – but I believed those broken parts of time had to be still around somewhere, as entities we couldn't see. And I was determined to reveal them.' She turned from him to stare at her colleagues. 'And then I was lucky to meet two like-minded souls.'

Cohen spoke next. 'I've never been to Manchester, but we bonded over something far more important than our shared interest in physics when I met Rose at university.' She smiled at Adler. 'As a girl, I enjoyed playing with dolls, computer games and climbing trees, which soon transformed into climbing buildings. I became an expert at buildering, or as I preferred to call it, skywalking. I loved clambering up old churches and mausoleums. Rose and I spent more time at these places than in the lecture hall.' She peered into Harry's eyes. 'You're no stranger to danger, Harry, so you know how addictive it can be. When you go skywalking, gazing down at the world below you, you get an appreciation of how precious life is. As you steal over each structure, the whole of your body, except your hands and feet, is over black emptiness. Your feet are on slabs of stone sloping downwards and outwards, only inches from your doom. Your fingers and elbows make the most of what you grab and touch. You know at any moment your grip might give way and, once you fall, you'll only have seconds left to live.

'My extracurricular activities prompted the spark in my brain which led me, with the aid of the others, to discover the greatest secret of the universe. And now we need your help to ensure it isn't lost to those who want to use it for selfish ends.'

Harry stayed silent, knowing they were telling him only what they thought he needed to hear. He expected Hazell to go for her third drink, but she didn't.

'Unlike my colleagues, I'm not a climber of buildings, Mr Hook. I had to scramble over people to get to where I am today. There was no help for me to be accepted at university, no financial or emotional support. I had no time for frivolous things; too busy fighting to keep my place. We are women, so our brains and discoveries have been ignored and underestimated, undervalued and patronised, but it's been far harder for some compared to others. Without a fight, I won't give up what we have at the Time Authority. It wasn't my idea to call you here; I argued against it.' She glanced at her partners. 'But I was outvoted, so here we are, but I don't care if you agree to help us or not. Ninety-nine per cent of the population would gnaw their hand off to get the opportunity we are giving you. If you decide to reject it, that's okay with me.'

Harry was unmoving, processing their words.

'You don't need me. You're time travellers. You can go back to see who killed Croft.'

Adler shook her head. 'It's not that easy. Since our announcement ten years ago, we've told the public little of what we do and how we do it. This is for good reasons, but I'll reveal now that time travel is not a precise science. We've tried to do exactly what you said, to travel to that point of Amy's murder, but we can't get to there or even close to it.'

He observed Adler, scrutinising her body language and words, analysing whether she was telling the truth. Fourteen years as a police officer, plus his period in the army, had given him specific skills in that area. She'd provided no details about why they couldn't travel to the murder scene, but she'd been confident when speaking, with no hesitation or playing with her hands.

'How close can you get to Croft's death?' Harry said.

'Six months,' Adler replied.

Would that be enough?

'So, let me get this straight. You want to send me back in time to six months before the crime in the hope I'll find the murderer?'

Hazell shook her head. 'You need to pass several assessments first, Mr Hook. Only then will you become an operative of the Time Authority. Even then, you won't be travelling on your own. We'll provide you with an experienced TA partner.'

'Okay,' he said. 'And if I discover who the killer is, what will you do with that information?'

'That's our business,' Hazell said, 'and not for you to worry about. Your assignment will be to reveal the identity of the person who murdered Amy Croft and return here with that.'

Harry smiled. 'Is that what you call them, assignments? Not missions?'

Hazell's crooked grin revealed her chipped front tooth. 'Are you interested or not, Mr Hook?'

He nodded. 'Of course, but only if you call me Harry.'

Adler stood. 'The tests start tomorrow at nine. I'd

suggest you get sufficient rest, Harry.' She held her hand out to him and he shook it. 'And good luck.'

He watched them leave the room, the hairs standing up on the back of his neck like they'd done when he'd got too close to their holograms in his flat.

Bronwyn Cromwell returned and escorted him out of the building.

Then he stepped outside and imagined travelling through time.

7 TEMPTATION

The nearest pub to the Time Authority headquarters was two minutes away. The Neon Bible was an unusual name for one of the city's watering holes, but its insides were the same as every other drinking establishment Harry had frequented: a circular bar in the middle and booths around the sides. He took the one closest to the toilets and perused the holomenu. He ordered a pint of cider plus an all-day breakfast and settled into his seat.

The place was half-full, with most of the seats taken by pensioners availing themselves of the BOGOF deal on the meals. However, Harry had nobody to share a Buy One Get One Free meal with. As he waited for his food, he wondered if he should have invited one of the Crucial Three to join him so they could explain more about their offer.

Which one would I want to spend more time with?

He considered the options as a server brought his drink over.

Adler has perfect cheekbones and a smile to die for – I could imagine spending a few enjoyable hours getting to know her better. Cohen's freckles are cute, but I think she'd rather be outdoors than inside a darkened pub. Then there's Hazell. I'm guessing she'd drink me under the table, but it might be fun if she lost that grumpy demeanour the more she drank.

He sipped at his cider and used his phone to go online to check if the things they'd told him were true.

Adler's family had come from poverty in Manchester, with her father working his way up to owning one of the biggest construction companies in the country. Harry wondered if it was the Adler family business behind the construction of the Time Authority building, but he couldn't find that information online.

Cohen, like her colleagues, was a renowned physicist, but that was all he discovered about her on the internet, with no personal details anywhere.

Hazell was another matter. There were photos and posts about her going back to her days at Oxford University, where she'd met the other two. She appeared to have been something of a party animal in her youth, and there were even details people had reposted of times she'd got into trouble with the police: protest marches and affirmative action against the government had given her quite the reputation.

Harry stared at a photo of the women on the screen, taken ten years ago just after they'd made their historic announcement, with the three of them standing in front of the statue of Queen Victoria in Kensington Gardens. Hazell and Cohen were thirty-nine then, Adler forty. None of them was old enough to be his mother, but he'd received a motherly vibe from two of them during the meeting.

His food arrived as he switched browsers on the screen and checked the day's news. Harry slurped hot beans into his mouth as he read about rising fuel costs and the increase in unemployment. The government blamed the opposition for both things, even though they'd been in power for a decade. He scanned past them and last night's football results before spotting a headline that interested him. He clicked on the link and peered at a photograph of a woman standing outside Harry's local Tube station.

He read the first paragraph while chewing on a burnt sausage.

Mary Boleyn becomes the leader of the Unity Party. She wasted no time in promising to do everything in her power to force the government to disband the Time Authority and to make time travel illegal.

The loose collection of anti-time travel groups had formed one collective. That wouldn't be a good thing. But what surprised him the most was Boleyn's involvement. She'd been a popular actor a decade ago – one of his favourites – but had disappeared from that world overnight.

'The media are going to love her.'

A piece of bacon dripped from Harry's mouth as he looked up to see the woman who'd slipped into the seat opposite him. She had a shock of bright red hair, nose piercings, and tattoos covering her arms and hands.

He wiped brown sauce from his top lip. 'I'm not looking for a girlfriend.'

Her purple lips quivered as she laughed. 'Don't worry, mate, you're not my type.'

'Too old?' he said.

'Too male,' she replied. 'I'm Ruby Red and you're Harry Hook.' She put her phone on the table and he noticed it was recording. 'Would you like to tell me what you were doing inside the Time Authority headquarters, Harry? Have they employed Hook Security and Detection because they're worried about Mary Boleyn and the Unity Party?'

Harry drank cider and peered at her. 'You're a journalist?'

She nodded. 'Are you going to give me a scoop?'

His laughter came out of his nose. 'Do people still use terms like a scoop?'

Ruby stole a mushroom from his plate. 'The English language is constantly rediscovering gems from forgotten times.'

He put the glass on the table. 'I know all the crime reporters in the city, but I've never seen you before. Who do you work for?'

'I'm freelance. Only fools make themselves a wage slave to masters only interested in their own profit.'

He shook his head. 'You're an internet journalist with no qualifications or experience, trying to make money off other people's misery. Isn't that right?'

Ruby removed lipstick from her bag and applied it to her lips.

'Academic qualifications are meaningless, Harry. You, of all people, should know that.'

He scrutinised her face, searching for some sign she was unstable.

'What does that mean?'

She grinned at him. 'Well, you went straight from school into the army, right?' He didn't reply. 'I'd guess you learnt more from active service than any papers they put in front of you. And I'm betting it was the same in the Met.' She glanced over his shoulder at the old man and his dog at the bar. 'You must have learnt more on the street than from any training courses they gave you.'

He finished his cider. 'Perhaps. So which streets did you gain your education from?'

She laughed in his face. 'Is that a dig at me, Harry, an implication I spend my time standing under a red light when not frequenting dodgy boozers talking to ex-coppers?'

'You said it, not me, Ruby Red.' His smirk hurt his cracked lips. 'What sort of name is that? You sound like you're from an escort agency.'

Her smile disappeared and she wagged a finger at him.

'Quit that before I decide I don't like you.' She picked a piece of bacon from his food and threw it to the dog at the bar. The mutt stared at the morsel with contempt before snapping it up. 'My journalistic education, like my name, came from my mother. She was a freelancer for thirty years before she retired, and she passed on a wealth of knowledge to me.'

Harry pushed the plate away. 'What do you want from me?'

Ruby Red's grin returned. 'Tell me what you were doing with the Crucial Three; give me a little snippet to get my readers hooked. No pun intended.'

'Did you follow me here?'

She shook her head. 'You have a high opinion of yourself, don't you? No, I was on the other side of the road opposite the Time Authority building when I saw you go inside. I've been watching the place since the announcement of who'd be using it and you're the only person I've seen enter.'

'How do you know who I am?'

She grabbed her phone and showed him a photo.

'I took this of you, and then ran it through an online facial recognition app.' She flicked on the screen to show him a page of details, all about him. 'I probably know you better than you know yourself, Harry Hook.'

He grabbed the device from her and scanned the information. Then he handed it back to her.

'They've spelt my sister's name wrong. It's Lily with one L before the Y.'

She put the mobile on the table. 'Is that why you went to see the Crucial Three?'

Harry knew he should have just got up and left this woman to her own devices, but the strangeness of the morning had withered away his usual reluctance to speak about his personal life.

Maybe she can give me information about the Time Authority I couldn't find online.

'What?'

'Are you going to become a time traveller? I've heard they're running a testing session for applicants tomorrow.'

He saw the frustration in her eyes. 'You applied and they turned you down?'

Ruby shrugged. 'It was a long shot.' She moved the phone closer to him and continued to record their conversation. 'So, is that why you were there?'

Harry pulled up the holomenu to order a dessert. He settled on apple pie and ice cream before returning to her gaze.

'Why are you so interested?'

She lifted both hands. 'Come on, Harry. Secrecy surrounds everything those three women do. There's a reason Mary Boleyn and her backers are collecting followers by the hundreds every day. People want to know what goes on behind those walls. How does the time travel technology work? What are they doing on their little jaunts? They claim to be only observers of history, but how do we know if that's true? They could mess with all our lives by changing points in time.'

'History can't be changed.'

She laughed. 'And you believe that because they tell you?'

Harry shrugged, wondering if it was too early to have a gin and tonic.

'What would you change if you could, Ruby?'

She puffed out her cheeks. 'Where to start?' She thought about it for ten seconds. 'Go back and kill Hitler, obviously. And Stalin.'

'Who?' he said.

Ruby's eyes narrowed. 'If we can't get rid of the greatest mass murderers of the twentieth century, then what's the point of having the ability to travel through time?'

His dessert arrived. He took a bite of the pie and chewed on a piece of apple as he spoke.

'What if those actions led to consequences that stop you from being born?'

Defiance seeped out of her. 'I can live with that if it saves millions of lives.'

Ice cream slipped down Harry's throat, leaving a chill inside his mouth.

'But that's the whole point, Ruby; you wouldn't be living with it. You wouldn't exist.'

She narrowed her eyes. 'You know what I mean.' She gazed at him and he knew what was coming. 'Don't you want to go back and find out what happened to your sister? To discover where Lily is after all this time?'

Harry dropped the spoon on the table, his appetite in retreat.

'Some things shouldn't be tampered with, no matter how much we might want to.'

He stood, leaving the pie half-eaten. The man and the dog stared at him from the bar, their faces as old as Harry felt. Ruby Red murmured something as he left, but he didn't hear what it was or give her another look.

Once outside the pub, he returned to the Tube station, trying not to stare at the Time Authority building as he went, but finding it impossible.

If I pass this test tomorrow – if I take it – then what?

Discovering who killed Amy Croft should be easy.

But what about discovering what happened to his sister?

8 VANISHING POINT

Harry went to the office before going home. It was twenty minutes from his apartment, which he had no desire to return to in a hurry.

It was an old structure, built during the later years of Queen Victoria, and only the cheap deal Chuck had got on the rent had kept them there once the work didn't come in. They were on the fourth level and he meandered up the stairs past the other businesses in the building. He smiled at the florists on the ground floor, who appeared to be flourishing, but it was the only one doing well. The second-hand bookstore had reduced its opening hours to only the weekend, while the toyshop had closed last month.

He lingered outside Geiger Books, hoping to glimpse the older woman who worked there even though it was shut. Harry didn't know her name, but she must have been in her late sixties. He peered through the glass, staring at the leather-bound volumes standing on a table. Harry examined the logo stencilled into the glass, how the Os in "Books" looked like cross-eyed spectacles scrutinising him.

'Is there something I can do for you?'

Harry turned to stare at her, the woman whose name he didn't know.

'Could you do me a tiny favour?' The words tumbled out of him like stones falling down a hill.

She opened the door. 'Maybe. It depends on the favour.' She stepped inside.

Harry didn't follow until she invited him in. 'Do you order books?' he said.

There was a glint in those brown eyes as she dropped the key on a table.

'It depends on what they are.' She sat on the edge of the desk behind her. 'Aren't you one of the detectives from the fourth floor?'

He held out his hand, but she ignored it. 'Yes, I'm Harry Hook.'

'What book are you after, Harry?'

Harry removed his phone and showed her the webpage he'd saved earlier.

'I tried to find it online, but I guess it's scarce.'

She grabbed a pair of glasses from the table, put them on, and leant towards the photo.

'*The True History of the Time Authority.*' The spectacles slipped down her nose and she pushed them back up. 'This is what you want?'

Harry nodded. 'From what I understand, it was self-published ten years ago in small numbers and has been out of print ever since.'

She got up and went behind the desk, turning on the computer and peering at the screen. Then, after two minutes, she looked up and stared at him from over the top of her glasses.

'It might take a while and be expensive.'

He moved towards her. 'That's okay. Thank you for your help...'

She removed her specs. 'Mrs Geiger.'

Harry nodded his gratitude and left. The stairs smelt damp and he wondered if he should complain to the landlord.

Let Chuck do it; he knows the bloke.

He entered the office, expecting to see Agnes, but it was empty. Harry stepped into the main room and strode to his desk. He checked his work emails, finding nothing but junk and bills, ignoring the rumbling in his stomach.

Those beans are coming back on me.

He opened another browser on his screen and went to the website of the Unity Group. He didn't read any of their so-called "Mission Statement", instead staring at the picture of Mary Boleyn. He ran an internet search on her, scrolling past the first dozen results, which focused on the sister of King Henry VIII's second wife, Anne Boleyn.

For a moment, he had the crazed idea that the Mary Boleyn in charge of the anti-time travel movement may even be a time traveller herself from sixteenth-century Tudor England.

He pushed that notion from his head and found the weblinks for this Mary Boleyn, the thirty-seven-year-old former actor. Born and raised in Newcastle, Boleyn had wanted to be an actor from an early age and first appeared on stage in a local play as a child. She made her film debut in the fantasy *Elric* (2023) and gained recognition for her parts in the comedy *Frick and Frack* (2025,) and *The Cat Conundrum* (2027). She shifted to adult roles in 2032 with performances in *Jude the Obscure* and *The Big Sleep*. Boleyn quit acting in 2040 to raise her twin daughters, Emily and Charlotte.

Harry searched for photos of the kids, surprised he couldn't find any.

She peered at him from the screen through enigmatic green eyes. He was about to search for movie clips of her when Agnes walked into the room.

'You're not answering your phone, Harry.'

He shrugged. 'I didn't hear it. Do we have a new client?'

She shook her head. 'Your dad called. That's why I've been ringing you all morning.'

'My father?' He stopped looking at the computer screen. 'What did he say?'

Harry hadn't spoken to the old man in a while.

Agnes moved towards the desk. 'He was bewildered, slurring his speech so much it was difficult to understand. The only thing I could make out before he put the phone down was this.'

She handed Harry a piece of paper with five words on it. Harry read them aloud.

'Tell the boy I'm going.' He stared at the text. 'What does that mean?'

Agnes shrugged. 'I don't know. He hung up before I could ask. Maybe you should see him.' Harry dropped the note on the desk. 'Isn't your family home nearby?'

'It's a five-minute walk from here,' Harry said.

She folded her arms. 'So, what are you waiting for?'

He grabbed the paper and tossed it into the bin.

'The old man and I don't exactly get on. I haven't seen him in a while.'

'How old is he?' Agnes said.

Harry thought for a second. 'Seventy-six, I think.'

She narrowed her eyes at him. 'You don't know? When was the last time you saw him?'

'Two years ago. He threw me out of the house.'

'That doesn't matter now, Harry. He sounded distressed on the phone. You should visit him.'

He tried to change the subject. 'Do you know where Chuck is?'

'He's doing something in Shoreditch.' She put both hands on the desk. 'It's five minutes from here, Harry. Do you want me to see if he's okay?'

Harry got up. 'No, I'll go.' He switched off the computer. 'I won't be back today, so you can go home.'

'Will you ring me later and tell me how you get on?'

He nodded and touched her shoulder. 'Of course.'

Harry left the building without looking into the book-shop, his mind focused on visiting the man he'd thought he'd never see again. He turned right and strode past the houses. Then he kept on going, glancing at the derelict pub where he'd had his first alcoholic drink twenty years ago. Then he reached the neighbour's house, outside of which had been the last sighting of his sister. Lily was fourteen when she disappeared, four years older than Harry. He stopped near the garden wall, avoiding the place where he grew up, and gazed at next door's row of gnomes standing in the grass. Then, on cue, Mrs Robinson came out of her house.

'You were always fascinated by those figurines, Harry. I'm sure you thought they were real.'

For an eighty-two-year-old woman – a widow for forty years – she looked livelier than he felt.

He smiled at her. 'You mean they're not?'

She approached the wall and he noticed her limp.

'Have you come to see your dad?'

Harry nodded. 'He rang me earlier. Has he been okay?'

Mrs Robinson shook her head. 'I'm afraid not, Harry.

He's been confused for a while. That's why they took him away this morning.'

'Took him away? Who did that?'

'The district nurse used to visit your father every day. I think it was her who finally realised he was having problems with his memory.' She glanced at the house. 'He'd forget to eat and was struggling to keep everything clean, including himself. The ambulance came for him about two hours ago. Do you still have your keys with you?'

'They're at my apartment. Do you know where they took him?'

She pointed across the road. 'The nurse told me he was going to stay at Redhill Care Home. What will happen to the house?'

Harry couldn't look at the place where he'd lived for the first eighteen years of his life.

'I don't know.' He didn't feel like smiling, but he did anyway. 'Thanks for your help, Mrs Robinson.'

He left her in the garden and crossed the road. He knew where Redhill's was; it had been there long before he was born, and all the kids used to call it Gerry's House because it was full of old people who couldn't remember who they were.

The building was impressive, standing on its own surrounded by a field, and it took him ten minutes to get there. He guessed it was Victorian, with its faded red brick-work and ornate windows. He went up the steps and inside, striding over a patterned carpet and to the reception. Nobody was there, so he grabbed a little bell from the desk and rang it. The sound echoed around the room as he waited.

Harry glanced at the walls as he stood there, wondering if the framed pictures of mountain views and oceans were there to help the residents relax. The large clock on the wall told him it was nearly two in the afternoon, and he thought how strange his day had already been, and there were still hours to go.

The door opposite opened and a tall woman wearing a blue suit strode towards him.

'Can I help you?'

When she smiled, he noticed the gold tooth in the corner of her mouth.

Harry didn't return the smile. 'I was told my father was brought here this morning.'

She went around the desk and fiddled with the computer.

'What's his name?'

'Oliver Hook.'

The woman peered at the screen before moving a finger over it.

'We have an Oliver Hook here.' She scrutinised him as if he was an escaped convict. 'But our records show his next of kin is a daughter, Lily. There's no mention of any other children.'

Her hand hovered over the desk and Harry assumed she was one wrong answer away from calling security. He took his wallet from his jacket and removed his ID. Then he placed it in front of her.

'I'm Harry Hook, Oliver's son. There's a contact number on the back of that card for the Metropolitan Police. Ring them if you'd like to confirm.'

She peered at the card as if it was infected with a virus.

'The Met? Why do you have their number?'

He sighed loudly enough to make sure she heard it.

'Until six months ago, I worked for them.'

'Were you fired?'

Harry picked up his ID. 'I retired to run a security agency. Is there anything else you'd like to know, or can I see my father now?'

The veneer of frost covering her face disappeared and she smiled at him again.

'Please accept my apologies for the questions, Mr Hook, but I'm sure you appreciate we have to ensure the safety and privacy of our residents.' He nodded. 'I'm Ms Ward and I manage Redhill's.' She stepped out from behind the desk. 'What have you been told about your father's residency with us?'

'Nothing,' Harry said. 'I only found out about it from a neighbour less than half an hour ago.'

'Okay, well, social services informed us that your father couldn't look after himself. They had no contact details for any relatives and he told them his daughter was living in Australia.' She peered at him. 'Do you have a sister?'

'Lily disappeared when she was fourteen, twenty-six years ago.' The words hurt his throat and he wanted to be back in that pub.

'I'm sorry,' Ms Ward said. 'Because social services couldn't contact any next of kin, the local council signed the documents to transfer your father from his home into our care. But, of course, you'll be able to contest that if you wish. Do you want to look after him yourself?'

Harry glanced at the calming pictures on the walls.

'Does he have dementia?'

'Yes,' Ms Ward said. 'The brain scan confirmed his doctor's diagnosis four weeks ago.'

'He's unable to care for himself?'

'That's correct, Mr Hook. If you wanted to contest the council's decision to place your father here and take him home with you, he would still need constant supervision with all of his needs.'

Harry remembered her gold tooth. 'I'm assuming it's not cheap, living here.'

'The council will cover some of your father's costs, and the sale of his house will pay for the rest,' she said. 'Do you have a claim on that property?'

Do I? I'm not sure.

'No, it's okay. I'm happy for them to go ahead with that. Is my dad settled in yet?'

Her smile returned. 'I'm not sure, Mr Hook. Perhaps you'd like to return in a few days when your father has got used to his new surroundings. It can be unsettling for new residents with his condition if they keep seeing reminders of where they used to live.'

Harry needed little convincing.

'I'll call you at the weekend, Ms Ward. And thank you for your help.'

He shook her hand, noticing how firm her grip was. Then he left Redhill's and stepped into the London air. He could see the smog drifting over from the other side of the river as he made his way back to his flat.

Harry tried not to think about his father, instead focusing on what he was about to do tomorrow. If he passed the tests, he'd be able to travel through time.

Then he'd be ready to solve Amy Croft's murder.

Bronwyn Cromwell greeted Harry outside the Time Authority headquarters at quarter to nine.

'Am I the first here?' he said.

'Hardly,' she said as she showed him inside the building.

Whereas yesterday he'd stepped into an empty reception, now it was full of people, dozens of whom were wearing white uniforms with the letters TA stitched into the front. Bronwyn was in a smart blue suit.

Harry studied the staff ushering who he assumed were candidates like him into various rooms.

'How many applicants am I up against?'

She smiled at him. 'Sixty-four.'

He shook his head as she took him into the closest room. It was empty apart from a chair and a table with gym clothes piled on it.

'Am I going running?'

Bronwyn did something with her phone and a large screen descended from the far wall. When it flickered into life, Harry stared at the Time Authority logo, the letters T and A merging into each other.

'There will be a short presentation to explain the assessment process to you first. Would you like to sit down?'

He did that while wondering if they'd got the correct size of clothes for him.

Bronwyn stood in the corner as Harry watched Rose Adler appear on the screen.

'Welcome to the Time Authority application process.' She sat on the front of a desk and beamed into the camera. 'Whatever happens today, you should be proud of the fact you've made it to this stage, considering we receive thousands of applications and take very few candidates. You will undertake four types of assessment: physical, psychological, intellectual, and emotional. There will be no breaks during the tests, with no food consumed. You'll be allowed fresh water at all times, but only have access to a bathroom halfway through the procedure. Please address them to the staff member with you if you have questions.' She got up. 'And good luck.'

The video finished and the screen returned to where it had come from.

Bronwyn smiled at him. 'Are you ready?'

Harry pushed the clothes away.

'How did all the other candidates get to this stage? I'm guessing they're not all former police detectives.'

'They completed one hundred questions and we assessed their answers.'

'What type of questions?'

'Why do you want to be a time traveller?'

'I don't.'

'Then why are you here?'

He'd thought about that all night.

'Did you know Amy Croft, Bronwyn?'

She didn't answer and walked to the door.

'I'll return in five minutes to take you to the gym.' Her smile had disappeared. 'Unless you've changed your mind?'

Harry removed his jacket. 'No.'

He was wearing the clothes two minutes later, impressed with how well-fitting they were.

Perhaps they'll let me keep them afterwards.

'You look good in them,' Bronwyn said when she returned.

She led him down a corridor to a bustling gym full of other candidates, taking him to an exercise bike. He glanced around the room, seeing men and women of various ages going through a variety of routines.

'I haven't cycled in years,' he said as he got on the bike.

She handed him a small metallic disc. 'Place this over your heart, please.'

He did as instructed. 'Will this send my vital signs to one of your machines?'

Bronwyn held out her phone. 'I'll get them on here. All I want you to do is cycle gently for two minutes as a warm-up. Then the resistance will increase on the bike and you have to keep pedalling and not allow the wheels to stop turning. Okay?'

He nodded as he put his feet on the pedals and moved his legs. He observed the others around him as he rode, checking if he knew any of them.

Perhaps I am only one of sixty-four former coppers here.

He prepared himself for the increase, but it was still a shock when it came. His leg muscles strained against the pressure while a spasm trickled down his back.

He lasted three minutes. The sweat dripped from him as he got off the bike.

'What's the average time for that exercise?' Harry said as he puffed out his cheeks.

'Don't worry about that,' Bronwyn said. 'Are you ready for the next assessment?'

He wasn't sure he was, but he didn't tell her that.

'I can't wait.'

The following thirty minutes were like hours for him as he used a cross-trainer, a treadmill, a rowing machine, and weights that nearly snapped his arms.

She handed him a glass of water as he sat on the floor.

'Have a quick drink, and then we'll move on to the psychological assessments.'

He drank the water in one go. 'Don't I get a shower and a change of clothes?'

'No breaks, Harry. You know that.'

He rubbed at his nose. 'I stink to high heaven.'

She laughed. 'Oh, I've smelt worse.'

He followed her out of the gym and into another room. Twenty others were in there, all like him covered in sweat and looking like they were desperate to sink into a Jacuzzi. There were no chairs, so everybody was standing, wearing headphones while holding a phone.

Bronwyn gave him one.

'Am I making a call?' he said.

Then she handed him a set of headphones.

'You'll get a series of questions and you answer them on the screen.'

Harry slipped the headphones on and stared at the device.

We're all tired and can't sit down. The psychological assessment has already begun.

He peered at the first question on the phone while a woman read it to him through the headphones.

The test comprised fifty items he had to rate on how true they were about him on a five-point scale where one equalled Disagree, three equalled Neutral, and five equalled Agree. He'd taken a similar test when joining the army at eighteen.

It took him ten minutes to complete.

The sweat was still dripping off him when he removed the headphones.

'Did I pass?'

'There is no pass or fail here, Harry.' She peered at the information on the screen. 'Out of a hundred, you scored in the nineties for four of the five factors, and in the seventies for the other one.'

'What are the factors?'

He thought she wouldn't tell him at first, but she did.

'They are extroversion, emotional stability, agreeableness, conscientiousness, and intellect/imagination.'

He had enough strength left to smile at her.

'Let me guess – the one in the seventies was agreeableness?'

She nodded. 'Is it true you like to insult people?'

Harry laughed as he glanced at the applicant nearest to him, who looked like he'd stepped out of a recruitment poster for the army; he was wider than a door with a bodybuilder's physique, crew cut and steel-blue eyes.

'Only those who deserve it. What's next?'

'Do you want another drink or a toilet break?'

'I'll have a pint of cider if you've got one.'

Bronwyn shook her head. 'You shouldn't have alcohol twenty-four hours before a trip through time.'

'Okay.' He didn't ask why.

'Are you ready for the intelligence assessment?' she said.

He nodded. 'Bring it on.'

'Put the headphones back on and the questions will be on the phone again.'

Harry did that. He'd taken IQ tests in the army and the police force, so it was nothing new to him. He knew it would take at least an hour to complete, so he was glad when staff brought chairs for all the candidates. A short-haired blonde woman smiled as she sat near him and he realised he'd seen her in the gym earlier.

The voice on the headphones told him he'd be taking the Raven's Progressive Matrices nonverbal test. The questions comprised a visual geometric design with a missing piece. Harry was given six to eight choices to pick from and fill in the missing piece.

When he finished, he knew he needed to take a leak. Bronwyn must have seen it on his face.

'Toilet break?'

He nodded. 'My eyes are aching from staring at all of those shapes.'

He expected her to give him a hint of how well he'd done, but all she did was lead him out of the room and to the bathrooms.

'I'll wait here for you.'

The blonde woman and the army man were waiting outside the cubicles when he stepped inside. He smiled at them both. She returned his grin, but the bloke only scowled.

'Don't worry about him,' she said. 'I think he's been busting for a crap since he got off the exercise bike. I'm Ellie. What's your name?'

'Harry,' he said as a nervous-looking man stepped out of the last cubicle. The army bloke went into it while the other guy washed his hands. He left while Ellie continued to talk.

'How do you think you're doing, Harry?'

He shrugged. 'I could do with a pint.'

She laughed. 'Gin and tonic for me.'

'It should be over soon,' Harry said as a young woman came out of the middle cubicle.

Ellie moved towards it. 'I'll meet you outside when it's all over and we'll go for a drink. There's a pub around the corner.'

He was about to speak when she closed the door behind her.

Five minutes later, he was taking the last assessments. He was already thinking about the cider slipping down his throat when he looked at the first question. Harry raced through them, and within fifteen minutes, Bronwyn was showing him to the showers.

'Your clothes are here. When you're done, I'll give you your results.'

She left him as he entered the locker room. A group of other men were there, including the army bloke. Most of them talked amongst themselves, wondering if they'd passed or not. Harry didn't get involved in the conjecture, relaxing as the hot water engulfed him. All he heard from the others was what they'd do if they could change time. He guessed that none of them was time-travelling material.

Bronwyn was waiting for him as he stepped into the corridor.

'Are you hungry? There's food for those who made it into the final three.'

The rumble in his stomach wasn't only from hunger.

'There's a final three and I'm in it?'

'Of course. You'll see the other two now.' She took him into another room, and he knew who would be there before he stepped inside. 'Harry, meet Ellie and Captain Cronin. Help yourself to food and drink, and I'll be back soon.'

She left as Harry watched Ellie devouring a colossal

sandwich. Cronin stood beyond the table of refreshments, not looking at either of them.

Was that meeting between the three of us in the bathroom a setup? Why were these two the nearest ones to me during the assessments?

'Eat up, Harry,' Ellie said. 'This food is great, and you'll need to put a lining on your stomach if we're going to the pub after this.' She nodded at Cronin. 'I invited him as well. I hope you don't mind.'

He went to the table and grabbed a plate of chicken wings. They were still warm.

'Did he reply? I thought he was mute.'

'Oh, he's just the shy and retiring type,' Ellie said. 'Can't you tell by looking at him?'

Harry watched her eat. She was five foot ten and built like a long-distance runner, slim enough to crawl through a ventilation shaft.

'Why do you want to be a time traveller?' he asked her.

She sat next to him. 'I was fifteen years old and sitting in the TV audience when the Secret Six made their appearance. Do you remember that?'

'I've re-watched that clip dozens of times since yesterday.' He stared at her. 'But I'll have to watch it again and look for you.'

A bit of tomato dropped from her lip as she spoke.

'You can't miss me. I'm right next to that version of Dr Hazell before she joins the others in front of the camera.'

'And that inspired you to come here?'

'She wants to change the world, don't you, Ellie?' Cronin sounded like one of Harry's old army instructors. 'Even though history can't be changed.'

'And what about you, Cronin? Why are you here?' Harry said.

Cronin took a bottle of water from the table.

'I want to make sure the world doesn't change. So why are you here, Hook?'

He was about to say he was there to solve a time traveller's murder when Bronwyn returned.

'Okay, it's time for the final assessment. Each of you will join one of the women who invented time travel and you'll visit the past. Then one will be chosen to become an operative of the Time Authority.'

Harry stared at her and knew which of the Crucial Three he'd be stuck with.

10 ULTRAVIOLENCE

Bronwyn led them through an exit at the back of the room. Harry had expected to step into another sterile environment, was amazed to find himself surrounded by flowers and trees: it was a vast botanical garden infused with many tropical aromas, like an exotic jungle.

'When you travel through time, do you move location as well?' he asked no one in particular.

'The Time Authority can do both,' Bronwyn said. 'As you're about to see.'

She led them through the greenhouse, past a flowing waterfall and the sounds of nature. Harry saw three lifts looking out of place in such natural splendour when they reached the other side.

Ellie sniffed at the large yellow flowers near her. 'Can't we stay here for a while? I never get out of the city, so this is a pleasant surprise.'

Bronwyn smiled. 'If you pass the final assessment, you can spend as much time as you like in here. I might even show you where we keep the dinosaurs.'

Ellie's eyes bulged. 'What?'

'I'm joking,' Bronwyn said. 'Travellers may not bring anything back with them from the past.'

Harry stared at her. 'Think of all the extinct species you could save during your trips.'

Bronwyn shook her head and he wondered if he'd already failed the final test.

'The lift on the left is for you, Ellie. The centre one for Harry and the right is for Cronin.'

'And these will take us to our guides?' Harry said.

'Yes,' Bronwyn said. 'Are you all ready?'

Cronin answered by striding towards his lift. Ellie and Harry followed suit. When all were lined up together, the lifts opened simultaneously.

Ellie gave Harry one last smile. 'The first drink's on you, Hook.'

He stepped into the lift and it closed behind him. The walls were blank, with no buttons or indicators to go up or down. He looked at the ceiling and saw there was no way out there, either.

Then the lights went out.

Great.

It shuddered into action, dropping at a tremendous speed as Harry tried his best to stay on his feet. His shoulder smacked into the side, sending pain through every inch of him. He couldn't see anything in the pitch-black but sensed something else in that confined environment.

As he felt along the walls, with the cold metal chilling his skin, the stink of sulphur filled the place. He clasped at his throat as he coughed like an exploding chimney. Harry fell to his knees, dragging at his neck as the gas attacked his nose and mouth.

When the lift stopped, he was spluttering for air as the

door sprang open. He rolled outside and threw up over a thick carpet.

'You'll have to clean that up before we go.'

Harry's eyes watered as he saw Dr Mary Hazell sitting at a table opposite him.

'What?'

'We can't leave anything in the past, Mr Hook. Not even vomit.'

He crawled backwards like a crab, finding a wall to rest against as the taste of spew slipped down his throat.

'The lift was the time machine?'

'I'd explain the quantum mechanics to you, Mr Hook, but I'm not sure you'd understand.'

Harry rubbed the blur from his vision and peered at her. She was dressed for a business meeting, wearing an expensive suit and waistcoat. Then, when his eyes returned to normal, he saw the pistol next to her on the table.

'Where are we?' he said.

Her grin unnerved him. 'Don't you mean when and where are we?'

'Sure.' He pushed his back into the wall. 'Is the gun for protection, or are you going to kill me?'

Her laugh was more disturbing than her smile, sounding as if she was chewing on broken glass.

'I'm not your greatest fan, Mr Hook, but why would I want to murder you?'

Harry got to his feet, his legs trembling as he did so.

This is perfect assassination tactics – disorientate and then kill the target.

'I don't know. Maybe it's something to do with my career in the Met. Perhaps one of my cases involved you or your family.'

She rubbed at her chin. 'Don't you think it's more likely

to do with those you killed during your involvement in foreign wars?'

'Is that what this is, just an elaborate plot to get revenge on me for imaginary crimes?'

Hazell placed a hand on the weapon. 'No, Mr Hook, it is not. My colleagues believe you can discover who murdered Ms Croft. That remains to be seen, but I have a more pressing engagement for you.'

He spat something horrible onto the ground.

'And what's that?'

She pointed the gun at him. 'I want you to kill the person in the next room.'

Harry studied his surroundings, glancing at the plain furniture with no signs of twenty-first-century conveniences.

'What year is this, Dr Hazell?'

She continued to hold the weapon. 'It's 1889.'

He gazed into her eyes and knew who she wanted him to murder.

'I thought time couldn't be changed, Doctor. You and the others have always claimed the Time Authority were only observers. Is that a lie?'

She nodded. 'A necessary one, Mr Hook. We have enough people protesting against us, not to mention continued government interference. Can you imagine what it would be like if the world knew we could change history?'

Harry gripped his stomach to stop from throwing up again.

'Is that what you've done, changed time?'

She returned the gun to the table. 'It wasn't by design, I assure you, but it happened on the first trip the three of us made together.' She removed the single glove she wore and, even with the distance between them, Harry saw the burn marks covering her flesh. 'The others want me to wear the glove – I tell people I have a skin condition – but I want to show it to the world as a reminder to me, Sally and Rose that going into the past without a proper plan will lead to terrible consequences.'

'What changes have you made?'

Hazell ran a finger over her scars. 'There are far too many to mention, Mr Hook. But, if Sally and Rose decide to let you into our inner sanctum, no doubt you'll get to view the records we've kept hidden from everybody else.'

Harry twisted his head from her when he heard noises coming from the next room.

'So, it's 1899. Should I assume we're in Austria?'

Bits of dead skin fell from her fingers. 'That's an astute assumption, Mr Hook. I can see why you're a detective. But do you know who you're here to kill?'

He moved forward, placing one hand on a rickety wooden chair.

'You want me to murder Adolf Hitler?'

Her grin grew as wide as her face. 'It was my idea to throw that question into the personality test – who would you kill and why if you could go back in time?' She shook her head and laughed. 'Hitler is still the most popular choice, but there is a disturbing number of applicants who nominate one of their parents or even both.' She peered at him. 'You left the answer blank, Mr Hook. Few people do that. Is that because you have too many murders on your conscience?'

He ignored the question. 'You've been going back in time for ten years. Why haven't you already killed Hitler?'

She stretched out her hand to stare at her palm.

'What makes you think we haven't?'

That surprised him. 'Have you?'

She closed her scarred fingers into a fist. 'Today will be the fifty-first time.'

The knot in his gut grew larger. 'Why so many times?'

Hazell sighed. 'The first was the easiest. I was the one who wanted to do it, but my colleagues thought I wouldn't be calm enough. So Rose volunteered. She wore a nurse's uniform and travelled to the Ypres Salient in Belgium on October 14, 1918, where a British gas shell temporarily blinded Hitler. That's where she strangled him.' She peered at Harry as if she was sitting in that hospital more than a hundred and thirty years ago. 'When she returned, she told Sally and me she felt no remorse for what she'd done. But, of course, the changes to history were worse than before.'

Harry monitored the door as he spoke to her.

'What was different?'

She unfurled her fist and he saw the blood where she'd cut into her skin.

'Rose had changed history, so Hitler never became the leader of the Nazis. Instead, that fell to Anton Drexler, a German far-right political agitator for the *Völkisch* movement in the 1920s. This led the party down a new path, one where their vile rabid antisemitism wasn't as public up to the war, which meant several important German Jews didn't flee the country. This included Albert Einstein and others who the Nazis forced to build an atomic bomb before the Americans did. I'm sure you can guess what the consequences of that were.'

'So you went back and altered your changes?'

'Yes, the older Rose visited the younger versions of us and told them what had happened, so stopping that first murder.'

Harry scratched his head. 'My brain hurts.' The noises

next door were getting closer. 'But that didn't stop you from trying again?'

'Yes,' she said. 'We knew we could go back and redo everything if the changes were worse. And they always were, no matter at what point in Hitler's life we killed him.' She glanced at the other room. 'Now we're at our earliest juncture.'

'How do the three of you remember what history was like before you meddled in it?'

She smiled at him. 'We sit inside a time sphere and wait for the traveller to return. The spheres exist outside of history, so our timelines remain the same.'

'And what gives you the right to play God?'

She laughed at him. 'God doesn't exist, Mr Hook.'

The door opened before he could reply and a pale looking woman with narrow eyes entered. She dropped the clothes she was carrying, but didn't shout at the strangers in her home.

Hazell pointed the gun at her. 'Don't move and stay quiet.'

Harry stared at the startled woman, unable to take his gaze off her large stomach. It looked like she might give birth at any second.

'You want me to kill a pregnant woman?' he said to Hazell.

She got up. 'You'll do future generations a huge favour while proving to me you have what it takes to join the Time Authority.'

If his guts hadn't been empty, he'd have thrown up again.

'What you've admitted to doing is monstrous, and I'm no monster.'

He saw the confusion on the terrified woman's face and tried not to think about the baby she carried in her belly.

'What if I told you she's not Maria Schicklgruber and this isn't nineteenth-century Austria?'

Harry's mouth was like sandpaper. 'What?'

Hazell turned to the trembling woman. 'Tell him your name and where we are.'

Her lips quivered as she spoke. 'I'm Hannah Rider. This is my house in Camden. The father of my baby left me with his debts, so this is the best I can do for now.'

'Rider?' Harry said.

Hazell moved towards him. 'It's 2001, Harry.' She placed the barrel of the gun on Rider's belly. 'And lurking inside there is Ronnie Rider. You haven't forgotten him, have you?'

Harry stumbled into the chair, clutching at his throat as the taste of sulphur returned to his mouth.

'It can't be.'

Hazell put her burnt hand on his arm. 'But it is. This is the beauty of time travel. You can go to any time and place and discover how history's monsters were born.'

'What... what do you mean?' Hannah Rider said.

Hazell rubbed the weapon over the unborn child.

'Growing inside you, Hannah, is the future Camden Ripper, serial rapist and killer of several women.' She glanced at Harry. 'And one time suspect in the disappearance of Lily Hook, aged fourteen.'

Hannah Rider pushed Hazell away from her. 'No, I don't believe you.'

Hazell offered the gun to Harry. 'So, Mr Hook. How would you like to change history and save your sister?'

Harry's fingers trembled as he took the weapon from her.

11 WORLD IN MOTION

'Nobody will know it was you, Harry. One shot and think of all the lives you'll save.'

He gripped the gun as Hazell's words burnt into his brain.

Hannah Rider trembled as she held on to her stomach and the unborn child in there.

He turned to Mary Hazell. 'You said the Time Authority has altered history too many times to mention.'

She nodded. 'That's right.'

'And how many times have you changed things for the better?'

Hazell puffed out her cheeks. 'That's hard to say.'

Harry refocused on the terrified pregnant woman. Hannah Rider was dead before her son Ronnie began his reign of terror across London, but Harry had seen photos and videos of her during the investigation. He wasn't the lead on the case, but he'd worked it, and after Rider was caught, he had to step aside while his colleagues explored the link between Rider and Lily Hook. Rider never admitted to anything, including the dozens of missing girls and women the police were convinced he was involved with, so Harry never got to speak to him. But he could never forget the times he'd stared at the serial killer through the glass in the interview room. Rider's glare was unique, a hollow stare that cut right through you even when you were on the other side of a window. Harry had seen the same thing with the mother, Hannah, in the clips he'd watched.

And this woman didn't have it.

He threw the gun to the floor and moved towards the door Rider had come through.

'This is your last chance, Harry,' Dr Mary Hazell shouted at him.

He went through the door, finding Bronwyn, Rose Adler and Sally Cohen there.

He wiped vomit from his lips. 'Did I pass?'

Hazell strode past him. 'You surprised me, Mr Hook. I'll give you that.'

She went to a cabinet, opened it, and poured herself a large glass of whisky. Harry followed her and did the same. He took a generous swig and scrutinised the four women in the room. Then the false Hannah Rider walked in.

'How did you know it was fake, Harry?' Rose Adler said.

He finished the booze before pointing the empty glass at the pregnant woman.

'Is the baby fake as well?'

'No,' Adler said as Bronwyn ushered the woman out of the room. 'We knew you'd spot a fraudulent pregnancy from a mile off.' She watched her leave. 'We scoured everywhere for a Hannah Rider lookalike. I was sure she'd fool you.'

'Why all the smoke and daggers?' He glared at Hazell.

'I'm assuming what you told me was all a pack of lies about changing history numerous times?'

She poured them both another drink.

'Mr Hook, the question to ask is not if we can change the past, but should we? When Sally, Rose and I made this momentous discovery, we realised it would be the new Manhattan Project. Regardless of what you might think of us, and me in particular, we don't want to be the destroyers of worlds.' She moved away from the cabinet as Bronwyn returned. 'We couldn't just forget what we'd done, but also knew we couldn't expose the mechanics of it to the world. People have attacked and threatened us ever since that first TV interview, either to stop our research or to use it for their own ends.'

The chill of the glass ran through his hands and he realised Hazell hadn't put her glove back on.

Was that vague story about her scars true?

'Can time be changed?' he said.

'All will be revealed later, Mr Hook,' she said. 'As long as you want to join our little band of merry travellers?'

'I passed all the tests?'

Bronwyn stepped forward. 'Actually, you were below average for most of them.'

The pity in her eyes resurrected the excruciating throbbing in the pit of his stomach.

'So what does that mean? Did Ellie or the army man beat me to it?'

Rose Adler approached him. 'Nobody travels through time on their own, Harry. The Time Authority has a strict system of protocols, the first of which is teams of three for all our assignments. We had to make sure you, Ellie, and the Captain were compatible. That and the final test are the most important parts of the application process; all the rest of it is just window dressing we throw to the media when they ask too many questions.' She examined some-thing on her phone. 'Though we are concerned about your numbers for the physical tests. You're thirty-six years old?'

The last of the whisky settled into his blood. 'Yes.'

Mary Hazell laughed at him. 'Your results are worse than mine. It's a good job you won't be required to do any heavy lifting.'

He didn't know what time it was, but his body told him he needed rest.

'You're assuming I still want to join you lot.'

Ellie and Cronin strode into the uncomfortable silence the young woman broke.

'You better, Harry. I'm expecting you to take me to Studio 54, New York circa 1978.'

He ignored the fatigue coursing through him. 'Is there any reason to go there, Ellie?'

Her smile warmed the room. 'It was the greatest night-club of all time, Harry, the home of disco, and I love to boogie.' She winked at Cronin. 'And I don't think the big guy has the right moves for the dance floor.'

Ellie's enthusiasm sparked Harry's weary bones back to life.

'Who did they tell you to murder?'

'Hitler's pregnant mother, of course.' She shook her head. 'Needless to say, I didn't. I wouldn't kill an unborn child, even if it were a future mass murderer.'

Harry wondered if they'd played the same trick on her as Hazell had done on him, making her think she could kill someone who'd had a negative effect on her earlier life. He didn't ask and turned to the army man instead.

'What about you, Cronin?'

His face was like a block of ice. 'It doesn't matter, Hook. All that concerns me is the work we do going forward.'

He was right and Harry knew it.

Do they know about my assignment to discover Amy Croft's killer? The Crucial Three told me I'd have an experienced time travelling partner for that. And neither of these are that.

Unless it's all another subterfuge.

He returned the glass to the cabinet. 'What happens next?'

'Tomorrow, the three of you will visit the past to record an important historical event. So, we need to show you how the technology works.' Hazell smiled at him. 'And no, we won't be revealing any secrets to you, Mr Hook.'

She joined her colleagues and Bronwyn, exiting the room. Cronin followed behind while Harry and Ellie stood there. Then she went and he walked with her.

'What did you think of their fake killing Hitler as a baby scenario?' he said to her.

She shrugged, the two of them stepping into the corridor and following the others.

'I knew it was a test from the start. Did you?'

'The shaking lift and the sulphur made me throw up. I was too busy dealing with that to worry about what Hazell wanted me to do.' His legs continued to ache as he kept up with her. 'But once I realised it was a con, she threw another dilemma at me.'

'What was that?' Ellie said.

Harry told her. 'Did they do anything like that with you, something personal?'

She shook her head. 'No, it was just the Hitler thing.' They were fifteen feet behind the others, moving down an empty corridor. 'Did your sister disappear?'

They stopped walking. 'It was twenty-six years ago and I remember it as if it was yesterday. She was fourteen; I was ten.'

Ellie touched his arm. 'I'm sorry, Harry.' She glanced at the others waiting for them. 'Working for the Time Authority is the perfect opportunity to discover what happened to her.'

He didn't tell her what the Crucial Three had said about the limits to how close you could get to specific events.

'My father has dementia and the council has moved him into residential care.'

Harry didn't know why he told her that.

'Are you two flirting?' Hazell shouted at them.

They blushed together and Harry felt like a teenager again.

I'm ten years older than her. Maybe more.

Before he could reply, Adler spoke.

'Are you ready to see a time machine?'

Ellie and Cronin nodded while Harry peered at Dr Sally Cohen.

She hardly speaks compared to the other two. Is her shyness another part of the act?

Adler pushed open the door and everyone followed her inside. Harry was the last to step in, seeing a lot of computers and digital screens.

Hazell stood next to him. 'Did you really think you could travel through time in a lift?'

'Why not? It's no more unusual than using a chair, blue box, or a car.' He glanced at the equipment in the room, surprised there were no Time Authority employees there. 'Do you have staff for this?'

Adler joined them. 'Only the select few are allowed in

here.' She nodded at Cohen. 'Sally is our computer expert. All the data for our time trips go through her.'

Harry watched Cohen move to the closest machine and check the screen. He still couldn't see anything large enough to fit three people inside. She tapped a few keys on the keyboard before speaking to them all.

'Time travel produces paradoxical conditions, such as the possibility the traveller will encounter a younger copy of herself or that she kills her parents before they conceive her.' She peered at her colleagues. 'And we've dealt with situations where we've met different versions of ourselves.'

'Like on the TV show with the Secret Six,' Ellie said.

'Indeed,' Cohen replied. 'Meeting other versions of yourself is something that might happen to all three of you at some point. Bronwyn will show you the protocols we've designed to deal with such situations, but the main thing to remember is to be careful with what you tell the other you. One wrong word out of place could harm the whole time-line and not just your own.'

'Why?' Harry said. 'If you can't change history, what difference does one word make?'

Cohen reached into her jacket and removed a toy car. Harry smiled when he saw the DeLorean from the *Back to the Future* movies. She placed it next to the keyboard.

'We'll come to that later. First, however, there's another enormous theoretical difficulty that makes the invention of a time machine challenging: the problem of spatial precision.'

'Getting from one place to another,' Harry said.

She nodded. 'Moving through time is only part of the problem. There is a shift in space for every shift in time, which a time machine needs to calculate with absolute precision. This allows the traveller the opportunity to arrive at the same spot she travelled from, or, more importantly, to be in a different location and at a different time.'

She flicked at the car and it rolled down the edge of the keyboard.

'Each point in space is in constant movement. Therefore, even travelling back in time a single month can be an insoluble problem concerning the spatial coordinates that should be set at the start.'

Cohen stopped the toy DeLorean before it fell off the desk.

'I won't bore you with the problems of calculating the correct spatial positioning, but they proved as challenging as cracking the time travel code.' She smiled at Hazell and Adler. 'Thankfully, I had two of the greatest minds in the world to work with.'

Hazell picked up the car. 'To give you an idea of what Sal means, when I was a kid, I watched an old TV show where a group of people travelled back in time to live when the dinosaurs roamed the planet.'

'I remember that,' Harry said. 'It was mildly entertaining, but got cancelled early on.'

'Because of Earth's rotation,' Cohen said, 'and its revolution around the sun, calculating where to appear when going back in time is a dangerous thing. Missing the place of arrival in the past, even by a few feet, could mean reappearing inside a solid object, at the bottom of the ocean, or in space. If we wanted to travel to the age of the dinosaurs, it would become a huge and almost insoluble problem. A complexity of gravitational influences that cannot be reconstructed backwards with the necessary precision determines the variations of the planet's orbit over millions of years. The time machine would risk completely missing Earth's position and disaster would follow.'

'Are you trying to put us off?' Harry said.

Cohen smiled at him. 'No, Mr Hook. What my friends and I want you and the others to realise is that whatever notion any of you have about what a time machine might look like – likely based on TV shows and movies – will be wildly inaccurate.'

Ellie's shoulders slumped. 'So we won't travel inside a blue box?'

'It's something much more impressive than that, Ellie. The computers in this room and the rest in the building constantly calculate spatial coordinates in relation to time travel. And tomorrow, you'll experience it first-hand. But you must be aware of the risks involved.'

'So you are trying to scare us off?' Ellie said. She laughed, but Harry recognised the anxiety underneath her façade.

'Bronwyn will explain the legalities of what you are doing by working for the Time Authority. Then she'll tell you what you need to sign after she shows you to your rooms,' Adler said.

'We're not going home?' Harry said.

Adler shook her head. 'There's much you still need to go through and we have an early start in the morning.'

Hazell returned to the whisky. 'Don't worry, Harry. There's a minibar in each room.' She held a full glass up to him in a mock toast. 'Sleep well, because tomorrow, you're going to watch a lot of people die.'

12 CEREMONY

The room they gave him was better than most hotels he'd stayed in – a large double bed, en suite bathroom, big screen TV and laptop. Bronwyn went through the documents and left them with Harry to sign. If he didn't, he wouldn't be going anywhere in the morning but back home and to a failing business.

As well as the legal papers, she gave him a folder. Inside it was a brief history of Pompeii.

I guess that's what Hazell meant about watching people die.

He skipped through the information while he ate steak and fries, finished with half a bottle of red wine. Bronwyn had told him that not drinking alcohol twenty-four hours before travelling had been a joke.

Harry remembered little of what he'd learnt at school about Pompeii, apart from the fact it was an ancient Italian city buried under volcanic ash nearly two thousand years ago. He also knew it was a tourist attraction for those morbid enough to want to see the unfortunates preserved under the dust. He'd read in the papers that much of the detailed evidence of the everyday life of Pompeii's inhabitants was lost in the excavations.

Is that why we're going back there, to record what happened?

Observation only – that had been the TA's mantra since its formation. The Crucial Three were historians, nothing else. Yet, if that was the case, why hadn't they answered his question regarding saying something you shouldn't when visiting the past?

After the meal, he put the information aside and went to the door, hoping to find the others – Ellie, at least, since Cronin was hardly the talkative type – to ask their thoughts on this assignment to an ancient doomed city.

He wasn't surprised when he found it locked. Or by the fact he couldn't get a signal on his phone or the laptop they'd left him. But it had historical videos and reports on Pompeii, which he went through as he drank the rest of the wine and wondered what it would feel like to go back in time. He didn't think at all about the partner who'd got him into this and only had occasional thoughts about his father in that care home.

When he slept, he dreamt of his sister, of him standing outside their house as an unseen force snatched Lily from under his gaze.

Then that disappeared and all he saw was Amy Croft's murder on repeat.

BRONWYN DELIVERED breakfast to him at seven in the morning, leaving it on the table with a change of clothes. Harry rubbed at his cheek and stared at his new outfit.

'I never considered I'd need different clothes for time travelling.'

She picked up the papers he'd signed. 'You were probably more focused on wondering if you'll end up at the bottom of the ocean or on the moon.'

He couldn't tell if she was joking or not since she wasn't smiling.

'Tell me, Bronwyn; how many trips through time have you made?'

She shook her head. 'None. Only a rare few get to do that.'

Harry went to the table, naked apart from his underwear, totally unselfconscious and not bothered if she was disturbed to see him like that.

'Really?' He bit into a piece of toast and enjoyed the way the hot bread nipped at the back of his mouth. 'What about all the other TA staff I saw yesterday?'

'Oh, no,' she said. 'None of those travel through time.'

The beans smelt like Heaven to Harry as he shoved a forkful between his lips.

'So, apart from the Crucial Three and Amy Croft, who else has visited the past?'

'I believe that's it,' she said.

He sipped at the hot coffee and sat back in the chair.

'Then why do they allow the media and the public to believe there're hundreds of TA staff jetting off through time at the drop of a hat?'

She shrugged. 'I don't think they – the Crucial Three, as you and others call them – care what others say about what we do here.'

'That makes little sense, Bronwyn. People like Mary Boleyn and her Unity Group wouldn't have a leg to stand on if the truth of what goes on here was made public.'

But I still don't know what goes on here. And why was Croft the only other person given the privilege to travel through time?

Is that why somebody murdered her?

'I suppose you'll have to ask them, Harry. It's all above my pay grade.'

With that, she left him to get on with his breakfast. When he finished, he showered and scrutinised his new clothes: a tunic, which was a long white shirt; a green cloak; and brown sandals.

He put them on and peered at himself in the mirror.

I should be in a comedy show.

When he left the room, Bronwyn, Ellie and Cronin were waiting for him.

'Oh, my,' Ellie said. 'Don't you look grand?'

'You can talk.'

Her tunic was green and longer than his, and a dark cloth covered her hair.

She took his arm. 'Bronwyn tells me I'm to be your slave. So please be kind to me.'

Ellie was taking the whole thing so casually and it worried him. Then Harry turned to Cronin, amused to see him dressed like a Roman Centurion.

I guess he's going to be our security.

He walked arm in arm with Ellie as Bronwyn led them to the computer room from yesterday. Cronin didn't say a word.

Hazell, Adler, and Cohen were in heated conversation when they stepped into the room. Harry reluctantly broke away from Ellie.

'Has there been a change of plan?'

Cohen held up her hand. 'No, we were just going over the finer details before your journey.' She reached into her pocket and removed six small white pills. She gave two each to the travellers.

'What's this?' Harry said.

'That stabilises your body chemistry before the procedure, and it anchors you to this location and point in time. You must swallow the other pill just before you return as well.'

'Okay,' Ellie said as she went to pop one into her mouth.

Cohen stopped her. 'Only take it when you're inside the machine. It will cause some dizziness and you need to be strapped in before that happens.'

Harry rubbed at the pills between his fingers.

'Do we get invisibility shields for protection or a universal translator for the language?'

Cohen laughed. 'Don't be silly – we're scientists, not magicians. You're there only to observe, not converse with the locals. Captain Cronin speaks Latin if you need to communicate with anyone.'

Harry peered at the other man. 'What's with the military titles? Is the TA part of the army after all?'

Dr Hazell shook her head. 'Every organisation needs a hierarchical structure to function properly. So if you acclimatise to the journey with no problems, you'll be a detective in the Time Authority.'

Cohen led them beyond the computers and to the far end of the room, straight towards a large metal bell.

Harry didn't know whether to laugh or cry. 'That's it? That's your time machine?'

Dr Cohen narrowed her eyes at him, shedding any sign of shyness.

'It's the Time Authority Technology Phase Shifting Machine, Mr Hook. Now, if you and the others would step inside and strap yourselves in. Time travel can be a bumpy process.'

Cronin went first, then Ellie, then Harry.

'What happens to those who don't acclimatise to this?' Harry said.

He held his hand over the internal mechanisms of the bell, glancing at the wires and controls straight out of an old Buck Rogers movie. Hazell peered right through him, her eyes digging into his soul.

'Time travel can play tricks on the mind and the body. After a trip into the past, returning to your own time can be like a deep-sea diver coming back to the surface too quickly. So you need to take care of how you do it, and that only comes with practice.' Her gaze never left him. 'I've got great confidence in you, Mr Hook, to deal with anything you have to.'

Well, she's changed her tune since yesterday.

He fastened the belt around his waist, the cold biting through his flimsy Roman clothes. He reached out and ran his fingers over the metal rods sticking out of the chair.

'There were rumours on the internet of travellers never returning from the past, of them getting lost. How true is that?'

Especially if what Bronwyn told me is true and only four of them have ever travelled through time.

So why us now?

Hazell waved her fingers in the air. 'You should never believe what you read online.' Then she pointed at him. 'You should see what they say about you.'

Cohen joined her at the front. 'Remember to take your pill when the door closes.'

Ellie frowned. 'Can't we have a phone with us to record everything?'

Cohen shook her head. 'We can't risk leaving modern technology in the past. Find out what happened in the run-up to the volcano exploding. Then, when it explodes, return to the Time Authority Technology Phase Shifting Machine and take the second pill. And good luck.'

She closed the door and Harry took a deep breath inside his new environment.

'We need a better name for this piece of junk.'

'You think this is junk?' Ellie said.

He laughed. 'This is just another extension of what we went through yesterday, more smoke and mirrors. I think the Crucial Three and their Time Authority are the biggest hoax ever.'

'Take your pills.'

It took Harry a few seconds to realise it was Cronin who'd spoken. He twisted his head to look at the Captain and saw the burning determination inside his eyes.

They popped their pills together.

Harry waited for the same theatrics as yesterday: for the lights to go out, then the shaking and some gas pumped into the bell to further disorientate them.

As long as it's not that sulphur again.

The thought of it made him rub his throat. He turned to look at Ellie, surprised to see she wasn't next to him.

Did she get up?

Cronin was gone, too.

Harry tried to speak, to shout out for them, but his mouth wouldn't move. Neither would his hands as he attempted to remove the safety belt. A sudden pain stabbed the insides of his head. His eyelids flickered as his whole body felt as if someone was trying to stuff him inside a box half his size. A handful of cotton wool soaked in laudanum appeared to have been wrapped around his brain as dazzling lights danced before his eyes.

Then everything went dark.

However, he wasn't unconscious because the pain was keeping him awake.

A thousand tiny needles jabbed every muscle he had as the light returned and he could move again.

But he wasn't inside the time machine anymore.

Harry was standing in the middle of a long corridor with shimmering doors on either side of him.

Maybe I died and this is Heaven.

No, he didn't believe in an afterlife. And even if he did, he doubted he'd be welcome there. The light was a bright white that he had to shield his eyes from until it transformed into a rainbow and sparkled in front of him like fireworks on New Year's Eve.

The doors changed colours so quickly the movement hurt his head. His nose was blocked like he had the worst flu ever, and he had to breathe through his mouth. When he moved towards the nearest door, it was as if somebody had poured liquid metal into his legs.

As he trembled in slow motion, voices drifted around him like an out of tune radio. Harry placed one hand against a door, snapping it back as the heat seared his skin. He smelt his burning flesh as the voices came into focus and he thought he recognised them.

When he'd burnt himself on the door, he must have moved it as he saw it was open a little. This was where the voices were coming from.

Not voices, but a single voice.

His father's.

'Dad?'

He inched closer to it, but the heat forced him back.

The sparkling lights intensified around him and it was impossible to see the doors. He was on the verge of blacking out, but he'd heard one thing from beyond the door.

It had been his father saying something Harry would never forget.

'I know what happened to your sister.'

13 RUINED IN A DAY

An explosion of ringing bells invaded Harry's ears as he woke. The shimmering lights had gone, replaced by a perfect blue sky and the countryside.

Then he heard a voice again.

'Dad?' he said.

His hearing returned to normal as Ellie stood over him. 'Are you okay, Harry?'

She helped him up as he checked their surroundings. He saw the town nearby and the volcano a few miles away.

He let go of her hand. 'Are we in Pompeii?'

She nodded. 'It seems so. Cronin has gone to scout the area. If Cohen got her calculations right, we should have plenty of time before the eruption to make our observations of what daily life was like here.'

Harry stared at the buildings near them, watching as the sun turned the stone into a bright golden hue. His body was returning to normal and whatever had happened to him in that strange corridor was dissipating, but there was one thing missing.

'Where's the time machine?'

Ellie brushed the dust off her tunic.

'Cronin thinks it returns to our time until we pop the next pill, and then the anchor returns it to us. It makes sense because nobody will interfere with it while we're off exploring.'

Harry rubbed at the ache in the back of his neck.

'Okay, but you'd think Cohen or one of the others could have mentioned that.'

Ellie agreed. 'I suppose, but haven't you noticed that – even though they're three extremely smart people – they seem absent-minded?'

He hadn't, but he didn't tell her that. Something else occupied his mind.

'What did it feel like to you, travelling through time?'

Harry saw Cronin approaching from the direction of the town as Ellie spoke.

'It was like you said. The lights went out, everything shook, and I felt like throwing up. Then, when I could see again, I was sitting next to the Captain in this field. I thought we'd lost you, but you'd just got separated from us.'

He wanted to ask her about shimmering lights, transforming doors, and strange voices, but Cronin arrived before he could.

'It seems like a normal day in the town. We'll look around, but nobody speaks but me. Do you both understand that?'

Ellie nodded, but Harry wasn't in the mood to agree with the other man.

'Where's the machine?'

Cronin repeated what Ellie had said about it returning to their present.

'You don't have to worry about it, Hook. You're here to hone your observational skills and get used to what time travel does to your mind and body. You might see and hear strange things when you go back in time. Some won't be real, so you need to learn how to spot those. It could save your life.'

How does he know all this if he's a new traveller like us?

The whole thing stank to Harry, but something else was nagging at him. He removed the pill from the hidden pocket inside his tunic.

'What happens if I lose this?'

Cronin grinned at him. 'You'll be stuck here.'

With those charming words, he turned and headed into Pompeii. Harry and Ellie followed behind him. Harry had a thousand other questions burning through his brain, but he knew he couldn't speak while in town.

Was it all just a hallucination, brought on by what travelling through time did to my body? Did I only imagine my dad's voice?

He was only sure about one thing – visiting his father in the care home when he returned to the present to ask him about Lily.

They strode into the market square. A few people stared at them or said something he didn't understand, but Cronin handled everything expertly. Harry might have had his doubts about the other man, but he had to admit that sending him here in his centurion clothes with his ability to speak Latin was a masterstroke.

It would make sense for the TA to have specialists for different locations and times.

He glanced at Ellie as they stuck to Cronin's shadow.

I'm guessing the two of us are only here for a field training exercise, but Cronin must have done this before.

He watched the locals going about their daily business – the streets were crowded, the market full of life as sellers sold and citizens bought what they needed. In the forum, people walked and talked as few of them paid any attention to the strangers in their midst, and Harry's thoughts returned to Amy Croft and her murder. As much as he was fascinated by this Pompeii experience, he wanted to start his investigation into her death sooner rather than later.

I wonder who they'll give me as a partner.

They stopped as Cronin spoke to a man selling ornaments from a stall.

It will have to be one of the Crucial Three if there aren't any other travellers apart from us.

Ellie pulled on his hand. She didn't speak, but nodded towards the other side of the market where a group of people were arguing. Harry noticed other centurions nearby, realising the difference between them and Cronin in his disguise.

Harry sidled up to him. 'You don't have a sword.'

Cronin glared at him. 'I told you to keep your mouth shut.'

He ignored that. 'If they look over here and see you without a sword, won't they think that's unusual?'

As Cronin pulled him into the shadows, Harry's arm throbbed with pain. They were pushed together so close, Harry could smell the sweat coming off the other man.

'If they hear you speaking an unknown language, that will get them suspicious, you idiot.'

Cronin's nails dug into Harry's flesh, and he felt the blood trickling down his skin. Ellie intervened when he was about to wrestle the fake centurion to the ground.

'You two have got everyone staring at us.'

He wriggled out of Cronin's grasp and saw what she meant. Most of those in the market were staring at them.

The group who'd been arguing earlier were moving in their direction.

'Fuck!' Cronin said.

'That's not Latin.' Harry wondered if they could outrun those marching towards them.

Cronin pushed past him and Ellie and stood to face the mob. She dragged Harry further into the shadows as they listened to a conversation they couldn't understand.

She whispered in Harry's ear. 'I don't think they're too happy.'

He knew she was right. He might not have known what they were saying, but he recognised the anger in their eyes and their elevated voices. He felt in his pocket for the alleged anchor back to their time.

'Maybe we should take our pills.'

Before she could reply, one of the mob raised his sword to Cronin. What happened next was a blur to Harry, but years of watching action movies gave him a new appreciation for the third member of their team.

Cronin kicked the bloke in the knee, taking his sword as he crumpled to the ground. As he cried, the two men with him reacted to the event. However, they were slower than the fake centurion. He moved like a panther, hitting the closest in the face with his elbow. Then, as the other bloke struggled to get his sword free, Cronin stretched out his leg to push him over with his foot.

The three of them were lying in the dirt, nursing their wounds as the group of real centurions – at least six of them – withdrew their weapons and glared at the intruders amongst them. Cronin stepped back, so he was close to Ellie and Harry.

'Can either of you fight?'

She moved next to him. 'I've got a black belt in kickboxing.'

Cronin glanced at Harry. 'And you, copper?'

Harry rubbed at the bruise forming on his arm.

'Apparently, I'm out of condition, but I don't think it would matter.'

He pointed at the armed reinforcements rushing to join the centurions. The lead centurion spoke to them, and Harry asked Cronin what he said.

'He said they won't kill us if I lay down the weapon.'

Harry felt into his pocket, touching the pill and assuming it wouldn't help him. He was moving forward to speak when the ground trembled under his feet. He stumbled into Ellie. Then he glanced at Mount Vesuvius in the distance.

'Is it going to blow now?'

The earth shook again, knocking pots and pans off the market stalls.

'No,' she said. 'That's four or five days away.'

Harry watched people falling over as the tremors came again.

'You're assuming the Crucial Three got us to the correct time. Remember what Cohen said about how difficult it was to get the right spatial coordinates?'

'That was more about location,' she said as some ran for cover.

But not the mob in front of them.

Harry glanced across at the peak, seeing the smoke drifting out of it.

If they'd got the coordinates wrong, we could have landed in the middle of that.

He moved next to Cronin. 'Tell them Vulcan is mad at them and that's why the mountain is angry.'

He noticed the twitch in Cronin's face as he spoke Latin to the locals. Then, he turned to Ellie while the army man dealt with their situation.

But we've got another problem.

'That could erupt at any minute, Ellie. We have to leave now.'

'We're okay, Harry. Didn't you read the information Bronwyn gave you last night?'

'A little.'

She shook her head at him. 'This is the first lesson: never travel through time unprepared. This region had several minor tremors during the years building up to the eruption. There had been a powerful earthquake in the area in 62 AD. Wealthy Romans had used Pompeii as a holiday spot and purchased second homes as getaways. After the earthquake of 62 AD, many of them didn't return. By the time of the eruption, there were a substantial number of abandoned vacation homes. The warning signs increased as the day drew near and reports from eyewitnesses suggest the volcano began erupting a day before the deadly hot gas blast killed so many. Then, on August 20, 79 AD, small earthquakes occurred four or five days before Mount Vesuvius erupted. That's where we are now. It won't erupt.'

Harry nodded at the group Cronin continued talking to.

'They don't know that and convincing them it's about to blow might be the only way we get out of here.'

'It's not working,' Cronin said without taking his gaze from the men in front of him. 'They're going to arrest us to find out where we're from.'

Another tremor came, heavier and louder, and market stalls crashed to the ground. That didn't stop the centurions all pointing their swords at the travellers. The temperature rose around them as he watched the sweat rolling down Cronin's neck.

Harry pulled at the tunic, glad it was loose enough to let the air in, but feeling the heat wash over him.

I'm not sure I could run in these clothes, anyway.

The gang shouted at Cronin and inched forward. The big man stepped back, forcing Harry and Ellie to do the same. Smoke and heat drifted out of the volcano, matching what Harry saw in the eyes of those striding towards them.

Is this how it ends for me, killed by a mob thousands of years before I was born?

He reached again for the pill in his pocket as Vesuvius spat its guts high into the air.

14 THE PERFECT KISS

Many people fled, but Harry's feet were glued to the ground as he peered at the devastation filling the sky. A cloud rose high from the volcano in a trunk, and then divided into branches. He was mesmerised by it, unable to move.

Ellie grabbed his hand. 'Come on.'

The market was emptying fast, but some people were as frozen as Harry, standing as if nothing was happening. As Ellie dragged Harry through the streets, the temperature increased again. The buildings shook and tottered around them, shedding great stones that only just missed them as they ran. He hung on to her as they sped past startled women and children. He didn't see Cronin.

The heat clamped at his throat, his lungs struggling to breathe as his trembling legs moved forward. Smoke drifted out of the mountain as the tremors returned. People screamed as somebody ran into Harry and Ellie. He let go of her and crashed to the ground. His head hit the dirt as he rolled over into the side of a cart. The wood smacked into his hip and he bit his tongue. Blood trickled across his face as he got up, looking for Ellie, but not seeing her.

The screaming and crying continued, echoing through Harry's skull and setting his insides on fire as the temperature outside threatened to sear the flesh from his bones.

Then a great noise erupted from the mountain and the thick smoke increased. It was engulfing him, biting at his lungs and forcing Harry to double over in a coughing fit. Sharpened nails clawed at his guts, with long tendrils of searing smoke winding through his insides. He saw huge sheets of lightning flashing through the sky. Everything was dark, as if it was the middle of the night.

And everywhere smelt as if it was on fire.

Screaming and thunder filled the air as he shouted for the others.

'Ellie, Cronin, can you hear me?'

There was no reply as the oppressive heat settled on him like a smothering blanket. He removed the pill from his pocket and stared at it.

Maybe they've already taken theirs and are back home.

He held it to his lips, about to swallow when something smashed into his legs. Harry dropped the pill and crashed to the ground. Smoke slithered around him, filling the air as much as the sounds of the terrified people and the bellowing volcano. Harry's fingers were in the dirt when the smoke drifted away and he could see what was above him: an angry centurion with a sword pointing down. The man said something in Latin. Harry didn't understand it, but he got the gist of the meaning: he and the other strangers were to blame for what was happening. He tasted the blood in his mouth and the smoke in the air. Volcanic ash was drifting everywhere, but the blade pointing at his face was all he could see.

And he'd lost his return home.

What had happened to the pill?

That thought crossed his addled brain as the centurion plunged the sword at Harry's head. He rolled to the side and it missed him by inches. His attacker pulled the weapon from the dirt and tried again. Harry lifted his arm and the edge of the blade bounced off him.

Pain vibrated through him as the blood settled at the back of his throat. He coughed and spat into the dirt. When the centurion raised his blade again, Harry kicked his attacker's shins. He screamed in agony and buckled. Harry rolled over and grabbed the sword.

But the centurion held on to it.

They grappled in the dirt as death erupted everywhere around them.

The man was bigger and stronger than him, and Harry knew it would soon be over. So he released the weapon and went for the eyes. Harry dug his fingers into one of them, finding flesh and blood as he clawed away.

The centurion dropped the sword and screamed. He reached for his face to stop the bleeding and Harry let go. It was enough for him to get up and run.

He didn't look behind, ignoring the screams mixed in with the erupting thunder.

But now, he didn't have the others with him or his return home.

Hot ash was falling around and over him. He stumbled into a doorway, and then into a house. His breathing was heavy and his vision blurred, but he knew he wasn't alone. He saw the woman and children huddled in the corner when his sight returned to normal.

'You have to leave,' he said even though he realised they couldn't understand him. He pointed at the door and made a motion to run. They still looked at him with fear and confusion. Harry grabbed a rug from the floor and put it over his head and shoulders. Then he went to the door, turning to try one last time.

'Everyone has to go now. Or you'll die.'

They didn't move.

Despair settled into his heart as he left and draped the carpet over himself.

Then he ran.

Volcanic gas was everywhere as he stumbled through the streets and into the field where they'd landed not so long ago. People were crying and coughing around him, but there was no sign of Ellie or Cronin. Every part of him ached and he wanted to collapse, but as he gazed at the volcano spewing death into the air, he didn't think he was far enough away to survive the eruption.

I should have read all those papers about Pompeii that Bronwyn gave me last night. Then I might know where to go to be safe.

A thick black cloud of ash advanced behind him like a flood as he continued searching for the others. He heard women shrieking, babies crying, and men shouting. Some were calling for their parents, their children, or their wives. Others were so frightened of dying, they prayed for death. Many begged for the help of the gods, but even more imagined there were no gods left and that the last eternal night had fallen on the world.

Is this why the Crucial Three sent us here, to witness such terror?

He reached into his pocket, hoping he'd been confused about losing the pill, but unsurprised to find it empty.

Then he thought about the people he'd left behind in that house, and he put his head in his hands. The rug fell from his body as he wept and wondered what all this had been for.

'I thought we'd lost you, partner.'

Harry looked up to see Ellie and Cronin watching him.

He moved forward and threw his arms around her.

'I thought I'd lost you as well.'

Through the heat and the smoke heading towards them, she could smile.

'Not yet, mate. You still owe me a drink.'

He coughed and laughed at the same time.

'I'll buy you a double as soon as we get back.'

Then he remembered he couldn't go back.

I lost the pill.

He was about to tell her that when Cronin walked over and punched him on the chin.

Harry stumbled, crashing into the dirt and peering into the darkness surrounding them. He lay there as Cronin loomed over him.

'You nearly got us killed.'

Harry rubbed at the blood on his face, but didn't get up.

He'll only knock me down again.

'It wasn't me who dumped us into the middle of an erupting volcano, Captain.'

Cronin glared at him. 'You know what I mean, Hook. I told you to keep your mouth shut in that market, but you couldn't help yourself, could you? I said it was a mistake bringing you along.'

He turned away as Ellie helped Harry up.

'This is becoming a habit, Harry.'

His whole body shivered as he stood. Then he told her.

'I can't go back with you.'

'Why?' she said.

He licked the blood from his finger. 'I lost the pill in all that confusion.'

Cronin's laughter was nearly as loud as the roar of Vesuvius.

'Perfect. At least you didn't get us killed.'

He was about to reply when Cronin popped the pill in his mouth and disappeared.

'What?' Harry said.

Ellie pulled him further into the grass. 'The Captain has his uses, but he's hard work.' Other evacuees from the town joined them in the field as the volcano shrieked again. 'You were right; they got the coordinates wrong. Vesuvius is about to blow and kill thousands of people.'

He gazed into her eyes. 'Including me.'

Then he did something impulsive, leaning in to kiss her on the lips.

When she kissed him back, he didn't resist.

They stood like that for an age as the mountain roared and spewed behind them. When they separated, she was grinning at him.

'Well, it's certainly getting hotter around here.'

'I'm sorry,' he said. 'I should have asked you first.'

She pointed a finger at him and laughed.

'I'll let you off this time since you're about to meet your fiery and volcanic doom.'

Harry's legs gave way and he slumped to the ground. He sat there and watched the smoke cover Pompeii, knowing it was only a matter of time.

Ellie sat next to him.

'At least I'm glad I got to meet you, Ellie.'

She took his hand. 'Me too, even though you're older than me.'

Even with his impending death reaching out to him through dark smoky fingers, he could relax.

'I know. I'm a big kid at heart, though. When I'm not working, all I do is watch movies.'

Ellie squeezed his hand. 'Me too. What's your favourite?'

Harry pushed his shoulder into hers.

'It changes every day, but it's probably *Aliens* or *Blade Runner* right now.'

'Excellent choices,' she said.

It was becoming so hot, he wanted to take his clothes off, but didn't want to give her the wrong idea. He shut the screaming in the distance from his mind.

'What about you?'

She laughed. '*Looper* or *12 Monkeys*.'

He laughed with her. 'Is that what got you interested in time travel?'

Ellie nodded. 'Something like that.'

She removed the pill from her pocket and they both stared at it.

'If that's the secret of time travel, why did they put us into that machine?'

'I don't know,' she said, 'but I want you to have this.'

'What? No.' He moved from her and stood. 'You should take that now. I don't think there's much time left.'

She stood too. 'You could take the pill and return home to get more of them from Cohen or one of the others, and then come back for me.'

He shook his head. 'It doesn't work like that. They told me there are some points you can't travel to if it's too close to a violent event.' He glanced at the approaching cloud of death. 'And this situation covers that.'

'Okay. I'll sacrifice myself for you, Harry.'

'Why?'

'Because I'm in love with you.'

He stumbled away from her. 'You barely know me.'

'You don't believe in love at first sight?'

A great puff of ash erupted from the volcano and he knew the end was near.

'Take the pill, Ellie. There's no need for both of us to die.'

'You're right,' she said. 'But there's still time for one last kiss.'

He didn't argue with that.

Harry took her in his arms, knowing it would have to be brief. She pressed her tongue into his mouth, forcing it so far in, he could hardly breathe.

Then she pushed something from her tongue into the back of his mouth.

His reaction was involuntary, swallowing it before he had the chance to spit it out.

The pill.

Harry grabbed at his throat.

'What... what did you do?'

Before she could reply, he disappeared.

15 CONFUSION

Harry hit something hard.

His feet gave way under him, legs sliding and body falling, hands reaching out for support and finding damp wood hitting him. A thousand sirens shrieked inside his skull; his vision blurred as he opened his eyes. Darkness surrounded him as he lifted his head, his sight returning to see stars twinkling overhead. A seagull flew past him and drew his attention to the large object to his right: a sheer block of ice cutting the ship he was on in half.

He watched as the gulls were tossed in the storm, flashes of white in the grey, tumbling as they struggled against the gale. Beneath them, the sea rose over the iceberg and the vessel it had imprisoned in the icy water.

As the waves rocked the ship almost to a tipping point, everything Harry was, had been, or ever would be was concentrated into that moment.

The wind was strong enough to grab someone and throw them overboard. Harry's senses were maxed out, every muscle working beyond normal capacity, and still, there was no end in sight. He tasted the pill's effects in his mouth and smelt Ellie on himself.

Why did she do that for me?

The craft lurched to the side and he went with it, vomiting all over the deck. He had no time to wonder where he was before the crying and screaming started: he heard the sounds of people in distress, of women and children calling for help.

He placed his palm on the side of the ship, peering through the moonlight, searching for Ellie and Cronin, but he was the only one there.

As he struggled for breath, somebody dragged him up.

He recognised the gloved hand.

It was Mary Hazell.

'Where are the others?' he said.

She let go of him. 'Why aren't they with you?'

Harry wiped vomit and seawater from his face.

'You sent us to the wrong time. We landed in Pompeii close to the volcano erupting. We got separated in the confusion before I saw Cronin abandon us.'

He couldn't tell her about Ellie's sacrifice, not because he was ashamed – which he was – but because he didn't feel like telling this woman who'd caused all their problems what had happened in Pompeii.

The ship lurched to the side and seawater splashed through the air.

'The Captain wouldn't abandon you. He had strict instructions.'

Harry spat blood into the creaking vessel.

'You and the others are playing games with us, Hazell.'

She grinned at him. 'So it's only your training now.'

He leant against wet wood, twisting his head to stare down

the ship, watching people leap into the freezing water. Lifeboats were lowered through the waves battering the vessel, but there would never be enough for the huddled masses above.

'Where are we?'

She wiped saltwater from her face. 'We're witnessing the most famous sea disaster in history, Harry. You should feel privileged.'

All he felt were his feet lurching under him and his stomach turning into the insides of a demented washing machine.

'This is the *Titanic*?'

Hazell grabbed his arm and dragged him towards the stricken passengers.

'It is, and this is your chance to do some good.'

He wanted to resist her, but she was strong, or he was weak from what had happened in Pompeii. His feet slid through the water on the deck as the wailing grew closer and louder.

'What do you mean?'

She stopped dragging him when they were fifty feet from the closest passengers.

'You can save one of these unfortunate people, take them anywhere with you.' She glanced at them, and then back at him. 'Decide which person to pick, but be quick about it because there isn't much time.'

The thumping in his head grew louder as her voice punctured his brain. As he considered her words, two young boys staggered towards them. Moonlight flickered across their pale faces, the fear inside their eyes making Harry's stomach churn even faster. They appeared to be about three or four years old. One of them clutched a rag doll of a cat in his hands.

The wind and the rain swirled around Harry, matching the storm invading his head.

'You and the others, all of the Authority, said time can't be altered, so why are you doing this to me?'

The boys stopped a few feet from them, mouthing silent pleas to him. More seawater flew over the sides and they missed getting drenched by inches. Hazell held up her right hand, removed the glove and gave him a better view of her injuries. Even amongst the horror he'd been thrust into, it was a terrible sight: her fingers were twisted and bent as if removing them from the constraints of the leather meant they could now go back to their unnatural shape. Her palm was scarred, burnt black, and all the nails were gone. It appeared as if her whole hand had been through some torturous fiery mangle.

'Time can be changed, Harry, but only if you have a strong enough will to do it. I didn't and this happened to me.' Was she telling the truth? Or was this only another test? 'If you truly want to save one of these boys, you can. But choose quickly, or they'll both die.'

He looked up to see the *Titanic's* second funnel topple into the sea, creating suction that pulled the people who'd jumped overboard underwater. The ship sank further as a continuous wailing sound erupted from those still alive in the water.

As the *Titanic* lurched, the boys lost their footing.

Harry reached out to grab them, pulling them towards him. They shivered in his arms as he noticed one was older than the other, with dark curly hair to the other boy's lighter curls. They gazed at him and he wondered what had happened to their parents. His knees were touching damp wood when he turned to Hazell.

'That pill you gave me, you said that was an anchor back

to my present. How can I take one of these boys with me if that's the case? And how did I get from Pompeii to here without going through the time machine?'

Her smile reminded him of a hyena he'd once seen in a zoo. It was distracting enough he didn't see the syringe she took from her pocket until it was too late. She plunged it into the side of his neck as he let go of the boys.

The *Titanic* gave way below him, his body dropping down and down until Harry thought he'd hit the bottom of the ocean. But there was no water around him, only waves rushing through his head and crashing against the sides of his skull. It was as if heavy clawed fingers were exploring every part of his brain, digging nails into his synapses to tear everything from his head and scoop out his memories, his thoughts, and his entire mind.

Then he stopped sinking and hit the ground, cracking his elbow into thick concrete. Harry's eyes flashed open, his vision flickering through the dust and debris swirling around him. He'd left the ocean behind, was sprawling on his back across jagged rubble. He peered up through a broken roof and into another night sky; this time, the sounds were not of crashing waves and wailing people, but of diving planes and falling bombs.

'Dry land is much better than the sea, don't you think, Harry?'

Hazell stood opposite him, still flashing that annoying grin. He touched his neck, feeling the spot where she'd plunged the needle through his flesh.

'What did you inject me with?'

She dismissed the question with a wave of her fingers.

'All in good time, Mr Hook.' She glanced around the rest of the building. 'Where do you think you are now?'

'You mean when am I?'

He found the wall behind him and pushed his aching frame against it.

'Is this your war, Harry?' She peered into the hole in the roof. 'Is an eighteen-year-old you out there somewhere, following orders and doing your duty?'

He glanced across the rubble-strewn environment, searching for anything that would show when and where he was, but he recognised nothing beyond the broken walls and crushed concrete.

'I didn't go overseas until I was nineteen. So my first year in the army was all about getting ready.'

Hazell pointed a finger at Harry and winked. He was starting to think she was unhinged.

'Yes, preparation is everything. The others told me I was wrong about you. You may be a failed grunt and an ex-copper, but there is something about you.' He hoped her smile would fade and she'd disappear like the Cheshire Cat, but was out of luck. 'You're the perfect detective to discover what happened to poor Amy.'

If he hadn't been obsessed with a dead woman, he'd have marched out into wherever, or whenever, this warzone was and told Hazell to go fuck herself. But he was obsessed with a dead woman. He wanted to know more about her, never mind discovering who'd killed her and why.

'If that's so, why are you putting me through these stupid tests?'

'There's nothing stupid about any of this, Harry, believe me.' She held up her hands as the sounds of the falling bombs drew nearer. 'This is all for your own good; you'll realise that soon.'

He pressed his fingers against the concrete of the wall at his back.

'I get it. You want to prepare me for the perils of time

travel before I investigate what happened to Croft, but I've been to war. I've dealt with the worst kinds of human garbage on this planet. So I'm ready for the next step.'

She touched her chin and rubbed at her skin. 'Are you really, Harry?' She stepped towards him. 'Would you have saved one of those boys on the *Titanic* if you could?'

He didn't hesitate. 'Of course I would. If it was possible.'

He stared at her damaged hand, which was inside a glove again. Was that all another lie about trying to change the past, but the past bit back at her?

Hazell gazed at him through curious eyes. 'Which one would you have taken?'

'I'd have saved both.'

She moved closer to him and burst out laughing. It was only then Harry realised he was still wearing the clothes from Pompeii and the cold clawed at his bones. As he shivered and listened to the sounds of the warzone outside, Hazell leant into him.

And he was stupid enough not to stop her injecting him again, right into the same spot on his neck.

Electricity shot through Harry, starting near his throat and spreading through every sinew and bone, through blood and organs, before settling in his brain like a great cloud of pain. This time, there was no darkness, only bright searing light across his vision. He held one hand to his eyes for protection, but the illumination was so intense, it singed the hairs along his fingers.

When he removed the hand, he was back inside that long corridor with an infinite number of doors on either side of him.

From nowhere, Hazell stood beside him.

He rubbed at his neck. 'I swear if you do that again, I'll kill you.'

'Choose your final destination, Harry.' He moved from her, staring at her hands for that deadly syringe. She laughed at him. 'Don't worry; this is your last journey for now. But you have to pick the door to enter.'

All he wanted was to get away from this madness, to return home to his failing business. He scanned the unending rows of doors, wondering what it was she'd drugged him with, before pushing through the door in front of him. She followed behind and he waited for another trap. But he found himself in a room containing only a woman and a baby. She cradled it in her arms and smiled at him; they both did.

He turned to Hazell.

'What's the trick this time? Are you going to make me choose which of them to save?'

He'd had enough of her games, was ready to walk back through the door until he noticed it had vanished.

'There's no trick here, Harry.' She raised her arm and offered him a gun. 'You just have to kill the child and everything will be over.'

The woman with the baby kept on smiling. He didn't think she understood what was happening. But then, neither did he. Or maybe she couldn't see Dr Hazell because this was all in his mind, all part of the hallucinogenic she'd pumped into him.

'Is this your Hitler ploy all over again?'

She pushed the weapon towards him. 'Take the gun, shoot the child, and then we'll return to 2050 and start the investigation into the murder of Amy Croft. That's what you want, isn't it?'

'Why do you want me to kill the baby?'

Hazell wriggled the pistol at him. 'Because one day, sometime in its future, it will grow up and cause the death of millions of people and the untold misery of billions of others for generations to come. All you have to do is snuff out one life to save many more. Surely that's worth it?'

He pushed the gun away from him.

'You tried this trick on me before and it didn't work then, so what makes you think it will now?'

Hazell lowered the weapon and offered him a pill, which he took.

'Very well, Harry. Swallow that, then click your heels two times and you'll be back home.'

As he kept his eyes on her, watching out for the syringe again, she slipped the gun into her pocket and removed her pill. Then she swallowed it and disappeared. He stared at the baby in its mother's arms and lifted the pill to his mouth. As he put it between his lips, he wondered if Hazell had spoken the truth and that millions would suffer and die because of that kid.

No, all she's ever told me is lies.

He took the pill and vanished.

16 RESTLESS

Harry reappeared inside the alleged time machine at the Authority building. He stumbled out of it to see Cronin and Ellie in deep conversation. He embraced the pain in every part of him and lurched towards them.

Ellie slapped him on the arm. 'Well, that was exciting.' She removed her fingers from his clothes. 'Why is your top damp, Harry?'

He ignored Cronin and hugged her.

'Don't let the bosses see you two fraternising,' the Captain said.

Harry let go, his smile one of relief and confusion.

'I thought you'd sacrificed yourself for me, Ellie.'

'I would have if you'd let me.' She showed him the bunch of pills in her hand. 'Luckily, I had a few spares.'

Cronin grinned at Harry and went to the machine. Harry glanced between them both, wondering if there was no one left he could trust in this place.

Has Cronin been in on this all the time? What about Ellie?

He stared at the back of the former military man.

'Thanks for leaving us behind, Captain.'

Cronin ignored the dig as Ellie touched Harry's arm again.

'Why are you damp?' She grinned at him. 'Did you cry because you thought I was dead?'

He didn't tell her what had happened between him and Hazell.

'The volcanic heat must have made me sweat too much.'

'Nice.' She wiped her hand on her leg as Hazell entered the room.

'The others want to see you, Harry,' Hazell said.

He was tempted to question her motives there and then, but thought better of it. Cronin appeared to be only a TA flunky, but he didn't know what to think about Ellie.

Or how he felt about her.

He could still taste that kiss in his mouth as he followed Hazell. Harry glimpsed his reflection in a mirror as they strode down the corridor, grimacing at his wild hair and Pompeii garb. And his tunic stank of smoke.

'I need to change my clothes first.'

'Of course,' she said. 'Here's your room. I'll send someone for you in ten minutes. Does that give you enough time?'

'More than enough.'

He pushed the door open, stepped inside, and closed it on her. His body begged him to collapse onto the bed, or at least take a long shower, but he ignored it. Instead, Harry changed into his regular clothes, threw water over his face, and dragged a comb through his unkempt hair. Red eyes stared back at him from the bathroom mirror, his fingers running across lines on his cheeks that weren't there yesterday.

Was it yesterday?

How much actual time had he spent away from this place? The clock on the wall showed they'd returned ten minutes after leaving for Pompeii, but his body was telling Harry it was at least twenty-four hours. No wonder the Crucial Three were so obsessed with testing their travellers' emotional and psychological responses, but he considered how much it must take out of them physically as well.

He checked his phone for messages, surprised to see none from Chuck.

I thought he'd want to know how I'd got on. If we don't get this contract, we'll be out of business by the end of the month.

He sat on the bed, the muttering in his stomach telling him he hadn't eaten in a while. Then he looked at the clock again.

It's ten minutes after I left, but I spent hours away from here. If every trip through time is like this, the human body will collapse.

And what would it do to the mind and the brain?

Is this why only four of them, before me, Ellie and Cronin, had time travelled?

Harry gazed at the pictures on the wall of floral gardens and calming landscapes and touched the point on his neck where Hazell had injected him twice. None of it made any sense. They claimed they had a physical time machine, but the pills and other chemicals had transported the three of them into the past.

How was that possible?

The question irritated his brain as the knock on the door came. He expected to see Hazell when he opened it, but Bronwyn was waiting for him.

'Are you feeling better?' she said.

He peered into her eyes. 'Who told you I was unwell?'

Her cheeks reddened as she spoke. 'Well, I just thought travelling through time is always arduous on the body.'

Harry closed the door. 'How many time travellers have you met?'

She seemed confused by his question for a second before regaining her composure.

'Before yesterday, only three.'

'Hazell, Cohen and Adler?' he said.

She nodded. 'Yes.'

'And how long have you worked for the Time Authority?'

'Since they started the organisation, ten years ago.'

Harry studied her, checking for signs she was another who might be deceiving him.

But he couldn't find any.

'Did you know Amy Croft?'

Bronwyn shook her head. 'Only by reputation.'

'And what was that?'

Nervousness possessed her face. 'Well, she was the one the Crucial Three used for all their most important missions. Naturally, they were devastated when she was killed.'

'Are you taking me to see them?'

'I am,' she said. 'And you'll be glad to know there'll be refreshments available.'

She led him down the corridor and to the same place where he'd met the Crucial Three that first time. Bronwyn didn't join them as he headed straight for the food on the table in the middle of the room.

Cohen was sitting at a computer while Adler and Hazell talked near a large TV that had the sound muted. Harry drank a pint of water and devoured two ham sandwiches before anyone spoke.

He picked bits of bread from his teeth.

'I'm sorry to disappoint you, ladies, but I've decided that Hook Security and Detection will not be taking the offer of a contract from the Time Authority.'

All three of them looked at him with surprise.

Hazell grinned. 'Did we fry your tiny mind, Harry?'

He grabbed an apple and bit into it. 'You spent all that time playing games with me when I was supposedly getting ready to investigate a murder.' He glanced around the room. 'I think being stuck inside your ivory tower for the last ten years, cut off from the real world, has fried your brains.'

Cohen got up from the computer.

'Everything we put you through was necessary, Mr Hook. Yes, we lied and deceived you, but I promise you it was all essential to prepare you for what comes next.'

Adler stepped forward. 'How does your body feel, Harry?'

He put down the glass and peered at his hands. If he stared hard enough, he could have sworn his skin was shimmering.

'How long was I away?'

'Between ten and fifteen minutes,' Adler said.

'How long was I really away?'

The three of them looked at each other before Cohen spoke.

'Twelve hours.'

Harry sighed and sat down. 'It felt like it was a lot longer.'

Cohen pulled a chair up next to him. 'Different periods, locations and weather all have exacting effects on the human body. And then there are the psychological and emotional effects as well.'

Adler joined them at the table. 'When our discovery

was revealed to the world – unwittingly at first – the common consensus was there would be hundreds if not thousands of people travelling through time. But we knew early on through our own experiences such an undertaking would create massive negative consequences.'

Harry took another bite from the apple, chewing as he spoke.

'You realised only a small percentage of the population could deal with the harmful effects of time travel.'

Adler nodded. 'It was one of several reasons we had to keep our discovery from others, probably the most important. If a government or a big corporation got hold of what we'd discovered, do you think they'd be concerned with what it would do to most time travellers?'

Harry laughed. 'Of course not.' He scrutinised each of them, trying to find the deception behind their eyes. 'If all this is true, why don't you tell the world? Then the anti-travellers and people like Mary Boleyn and her Unity Group wouldn't be able to rile the public so much against you.'

Cohen replied. 'We have to limit what we reveal to the outside world, regardless of what problems it might cause us. It's taken us ten years to get to this point, and we can't throw it away now.'

'Knowledge is power,' Harry said as he finished the apple.

'Will you reconsider your decision?' Adler said.

He was considering it when he noticed something strange on the big TV.

'Can you turn the sound up on that?'

Hazell did as Harry got up and walked closer to the screen.

'Mysterious death on the London Underground,' the announcer said.

Harry staggered forward when the photo of Chuck appeared on the screen. He was frozen to the spot as it showed a video of the incident, of his business partner moving to the edge of the platform before the show stopped the clip.

The presenter continued. 'Eyewitnesses say there was nobody near Mr Connors before he stepped in front of the train.'

Lights flickered around Harry and blurred his vision. The sound of screeching tyres flooded his head and made his eyes throb. He staggered to the side and put his hand to the wall. Somebody spoke to him, but he didn't know who it was or what they said. All he could hear was Chuck's voice saying goodnight to his daughter.

Harry pushed himself from the wall. 'I have to leave now.'

He stumbled towards the door with a heart full of pain.

Hazell stopped him, putting her hand on his arm. 'I'm sorry about your partner, but we can help you.'

Something clutched at his chest as he faced her, this woman who'd done nothing but lie to him since he'd met her.

'How?'

She let go of him. 'You're ready now to investigate what happened to Amy Croft. Which means you can do the same with your partner. The Time Authority will provide you with the means to solve Mr Connors's death.'

He stared at her, fighting back the desire to flee the building and go to Chuck's wife and child.

It took him thirty seconds to decide.

'I'll do it. I'll work for you on these two cases, but you have to tell me the truth about the Time Authority first.'

'What do you mean?' Hazell said.

'I know that box with all the wires and tubes – that thing you called the Time Authority Technology Phase Shifting Machine - was a façade for the rubes. So tell me how you really do it, or I'm leaving and I won't be back.'

'Very well,' the Crucial Three said in unison.

Hazell smiled at him. 'Get ready for the true history of the Time Authority.'

17 SINGULARITY

Hazell gave Harry a large whisky. He tried to shake the image from his head of Chuck standing in front of that Tube train. It was impossible to forget what he'd seen, but he used the booze to calm his nerves and focus on what these three women were about to tell him.

Then he'd use time travel to save his friend's life.

I don't care what they keep telling me about time can't be changed – I know they're lying about that. I'll find a way to save Chuck and Amy.

And Lily.

'Sally and I were eighteen when we met at university, and Rose was nineteen. We became firm friends quickly, all of us studying to be physicists, but with an obsession with quantum mechanics.'

Harry sipped at his drink. 'Quantum mechanics?'

Cohen continued the explanation. 'It's the branch of physics relating to the very small. It results in what may appear to be some strange conclusions about the physical world. At the scale of atoms and electrons, many of the equations of classical mechanics, which describe how things move at everyday sizes and speeds, cease to be useful. For example, in classical mechanics, objects exist in a specific place at a specific time. However, in quantum mechanics, objects instead exist in a haze of probability; they have a certain chance of being at point A, another chance of being at point B and so on.'

Adler waved a hand in the air. 'You're boring him, Sally. Just tell him how it relates to theories of time travel.'

Cohen scowled through her freckles. 'For most of this century, studies on time travel were based upon classical general relativity. Coming up with a quantum version of time travel required physicists to figure out the time evolution equations for density states in the presence of closed time like curves.'

Hazell laughed. 'Yes, Sal, that's so much better.'

Harry took more of the whisky. 'Can't you give me the idiot's version?'

Hazell refilled his glass. 'Black holes, wormholes, loop quantum gravity, causal set theory, semi-classical quantum gravity, and string theory. In time – no pun intended – all had their champions regarding the possibility of time travel. The three of us decided it was our life goal to make it work.'

'And you found that one of them did,' Harry said.

'Quite the opposite,' Hazell said. 'None of them worked and they never will. In 2040, we knew that time travel was possible in theory, but impossible in practice.'

He put the glass down. 'Are you messing with me again?'

They acted simultaneously, reaching into their pockets and removing a pill.

'No, Harry,' Cohen said. 'Time travel is not only possible; it's real, and you're one of the few people to have done it. And it's all to do with what's inside these pills, the chemicals in your brain and chronoception.'

He shook his head. 'And this is the idiots' guide?'

Cohen continued. 'The study of time perception or chronoception is a field within psychology, cognitive linguistics and neuroscience that refers to the subjective experience, or sense, of time, which is measured by someone's perception of the duration of the indefinite and unfolding of events. The perceived time interval between two successive events is referred to as perceived duration. Though directly experiencing or understanding another person's perception of time is not possible, such a perception can be objectively studied and inferred through several scientific experiments. In addition, some temporal illusions help to expose the underlying neural mechanisms of time perception.' She moved closer to him. 'Imagine what it would be like if you could manipulate your sense of time perception to reach back into periods you've already experienced; not as memories, but as a physical experience.'

Harry rattled the ice around in the glass. 'Okay, I think I understand that, but surely if I could do that, I'd only be able to travel to stages in my own life. How could I go to Pompeii or stand on the *Titanic*?'

Even though I did both.

Cohen's smile accentuated those freckles again.

'Have you heard of epigenetics?' Harry shook his head. 'What about genetic memory?'

'Maybe,' he said. 'I think I saw a movie once about memories passed down through the generations where some kid was the chosen one to save the world from invading aliens.'

Cohen laughed. 'Epigenetics is based on the concept of changes in gene expression and of active and inactive genes.

Epigenetic scientists study how cells change to adapt to skin cells, liver cells, or even cancerous cells. They also study how genes are inherited and the changes to those genetics that we exhibit, even when those changes are not essential to our DNA. Our experiences, age, environment, and health can affect these changes. For example, studies by scientists and researchers have discovered we receive loads of genetic memories from our parents, grandparents, and further ancestors in an instinctive effort by their DNA to better prepare us for difficult experiences they faced, such as fear, disease, or trauma.'

'So,' Harry said, 'you're saying I could travel to Pompeii because the location has been passed down through DNA and still lingers in my mind somewhere?'

'That's the theory,' Cohen said.

He tasted the booze warming the back of his throat. Then he looked at all of them.

The Crucial Three.

'But you cracked that theory.' He stepped towards Cohen and took the pill from her hand. 'And you put it all into one of these.'

It sounded incredible, but he knew it was true because he'd experienced it.

'No,' Hazell said. 'We didn't do any of it.' Harry saw the shame in her eyes. 'The three of us are frauds. We didn't discover the secret of time travel.'

'What?' he said. 'So who did?'

Cohen took the pill from his hand. 'Ten years ago, a stranger turned up in our office and offered us the missing link to time travel. That link is the combination of the right chemicals connected to the correct parts of the brain. Therefore we use the pills or an injection through a syringe to travel.'

Harry rubbed at his temple. 'How did I get on the *Titanic* or into that warzone?'

'That was my doing,' Hazell said. 'The pill Ellie slipped you in Pompeii had the time and location programmed into the DNA. It was the same with the injections I gave you.'

Harry's brain felt as if it was inside a microwave turned up to full.

'Who was the stranger who gave you this secret?'

Cohen smiled at him. 'Can't you guess?'

He could. 'It was Amy Croft.'

All three women nodded together.

'It was Amy who supplied us with the pills and the chemicals to manipulate the brain,' Cohen said. 'And to manipulate time and space.'

Harry took a deep breath and moved to the window, his mind throbbing with what he'd heard. He gazed upon those moving around outside. London had a heart, a rhythm and a beat. It was a city of wide streets, hidden places, and joy and desperation in equal measure. There were places to sit and eat, to relax as people went about their day. Vast tall buildings were everywhere, unlike during his youth when they were the exception. Thousands of homes took up less ground space than a shopping centre. The rest was parks and wild spaces, a chance to walk among nature or enjoy the trails on bicycles or horseback while inside the urban jungle. He thought about his life in the city, of growing up there before needing to escape into the army. That hadn't lasted long and he'd returned to the place he'd missed. He'd seen so much of the world, but London was where he'd always wanted to get back to – inhaling the city's history because that's where his sister had taken him on their walks through the capital.

Lily had loved the city and the river, so Harry had

assumed his love for those things had come from her. That's why he was always desperate to return to London, but over time, he'd realised it was something different that drew him back to that place.

If Lily were alive, she'd be here.

There was little chance he could ever bump into her anywhere else in the world. Even now, as he looked out of the window, he imagined she was down there somewhere, waiting for him.

And now he could find her just by swallowing one of those pills.

But he couldn't get it wrong.

The tests were to prepare him for the Croft murder investigation. Still, at the back of his mind, Harry had known he was using his experiences with the Time Authority for something else: to go back in time and discover what had happened to his sister.

As long as he could get close enough to that day.

That conundrum, if what the Crucial Three had told him was true about some time points being off-limits, was enough reason to try it with Croft first before visiting Lily.

And now he had Chuck's murder to investigate as well.

He gazed across the capital, standing there as one of the few people who knew the world's greatest secret.

But he still didn't know enough as he observed Hazell cradling her drink.

'What happened when we arrived at the corridor of bright lights with all the doors?'

She smiled at him. 'All that glitters is not gold, Harry.'

Irritation grew at the back of his neck. 'What's that supposed to mean.'

'What Mary means', Cohen said, 'is that you have to be careful with what we call the Doors of Perception.' She held a pill out to him. 'As far as we can tell, when the chemicals Amy supplied us mix with the correct sectors of the brain, our minds take us to an infinity of doorways through time and space, and we choose one to travel where we want to.' She glanced at Hazell. 'But like any mode of travel, there are always risks involved.'

Harry rubbed his fingers together. 'I touched one of those doors and it burnt my skin.'

Cohen nodded. 'That was your mind warning you it was the wrong door.'

The memory was scorched into his brain. 'If I'd forced my way inside, what would have happened?'

Cohen shrugged. 'We don't know, but you wouldn't have come back.'

Harry examined their faces, convinced they still weren't telling him everything.

'What are you keeping from me?'

Cohen sighed and he saw the guilt consuming her. Guilt that wasn't apparent on Hazell or Adler.

'What we said earlier about the physical and emotional ramifications of time travel on the human body was true, but we didn't realise it until we were into the first two years of our experiments.'

The significance of what she meant stabbed at his heart.

'There have been other time travellers?'

Hazell spoke without a flicker of emotion. 'There were six we lost. We've always assumed they went through the wrong entrance at the Doors of Perception.'

His legs ached as he sat down. 'Who were they?'

'Volunteers,' Adler said. 'After our TV appearances, we were inundated with them, people desperate to do anything to travel to the past.' She looked at Hazell. 'It was a relative of one of the disappeared who tried to kill Mary.'

'You never searched for them, these missing volunteers?' Harry said.

Hazell laughed. 'You want us to search through all of time and space for them? You must be mad.'

He resisted the urge to throttle her. 'Was it worth causing so much pain and suffering just to be observers of history?'

Cohen sat next to him and touched his arm. The warmth in her eyes cooled his anger.

'What's the one thing you want most in the world, Harry?'

He smirked at her. 'To get out of here.'

She returned his smile and he hoped when he travelled through time again – as he knew he would – it would be with her.

'Be honest now. Before you came here and met us, if somebody had said you could go back in time only once and only to observe, what would you have chosen?'

He'd tried denying it to himself from the minute he'd first entered the building, but he knew it was futile to keep it from them.

'I'd see what happened to my sister.'

Cohen squeezed his hand. 'And you'll get the chance to do that once we know what happened to Amy, but what if every person on the planet was given that same opportunity to travel in time to see someone again? How do you think the world would receive that?'

Harry thought about it for ten seconds. 'To go back and see a loved one you'd lost? I guess it would be painful for some, but most would jump at the chance.'

She beamed at him. 'And that's what this is all about. Time can't be changed; the universe won't allow it.' She glanced at the others. 'We know because we've tried. So we came up with another purpose for time travel: to allow the world to see those they'd lost for one last time.' Cohen's smile lit up the room. 'Imagine if you could visit your parents when they were younger to see the things they did, or your grandparents or other ancestors?'

'It would be the greatest thing of all time.'

Cohen let go of his hand. 'So, do you see, Harry, what this is all ultimately about?'

He did. 'You don't have enough of the pills, do you?'

'No,' Cohen said. 'Only Amy knows the chemical composition of time travel.'

He gazed at her. 'Don't you mean she knew?'

Cohen stood. 'Harry, I'd like you to meet your partner for the investigation into the murder of Amy Croft.'

The door opened and he turned to see the person who strode through it.

Amy Croft.

18 ARE YOU READY FOR THIS?

Cohen stopped Harry from falling off the chair.

He wiped at his mouth. 'What is this?'

Hazell laughed at him. 'Your brain must be pickled. Don't you mean who is this?'

He gazed at the woman as she approached him, the murdered Amy Croft with the same blue eyes, sculptured cheekbones and dark bobbed hairstyle reminiscent of Louise Brooks.

She stuck her hand out to him and he noticed her perfect skin.

'Hello, Harry. I'm Amy.'

He gripped her hand, feeling the warmth of her touch increase the rapid beating of his heart.

Then it hit him.

'You're an earlier Amy, from before...'

He couldn't say the words, so she finished the sentence for him.

'From before my murder?'

He felt stupid doing it, but he nodded anyway.

'You know about that?'

Hazell laughed behind him. 'Of course she does. How are the two of you going to solve the crime if she's not aware of it?'

Once, a long time ago – after his sister's disappearance – his parents had taken him to the funfair. It was one of the few memories he had of his mother, of her golden hair and glittering smile, and the day had been great until he'd fallen from a ride and cracked his head on the ground. They'd rushed him to the hospital, where the diagnosis was a fracture with a light concussion. He'd bragged about it later at school, had shown the girls his scars as a badge of honour, but the whole of his skull had felt like it was inside a vice. He'd never experienced pain like that again, apart from his time in a war zone in a foreign field.

Until now.

It started in the back of his brain, travelled through every synapse until it settled behind his eyes and burnt his retinas like devils stabbing him repeatedly with tiny pitchforks.

He returned to the bottle of whisky, nudged Hazell out of the way, and filled his glass without water or ice. Then he drank it in one go, hoping its fire would quash the raging volcano inside him. Instead, his throat felt like the centre of the sun as he looked at the resurrected woman.

No, not resurrected – a different version.

'They went back in time and told you you're going to die in your future, and they need you and me to solve the murder. Is that right?'

Croft took the bottle from him and poured herself a small measure with ice. She held it to her mouth, but didn't drink it.

'Not quite. I said I'd only give them what they want if I discovered who murdered me.'

'What they want?' Harry said. 'You mean the secret of the pills and time travel?'

She sipped at the drink and he watched her lips glistening.

'Precisely. If it happened to you, Harry, wouldn't you want to know who'd killed you?'

He peered into her eyes, trying to discover who she was.

'I guess so. Which point of your timeline are you from?'

Cohen answered the question. 'We could only get as close as six months to Amy's death.' She stared at Amy. 'There's something in the time travel perception that won't allow travellers to get too close to some violent events. But we don't know why.'

All the Crucial Three peered at Croft as the tension in the room made the hairs on the back of Harry's neck stand on end. He put the glass down and resisted the temptation to have another.

'So you're the one who gave the secret of time travel to the Crucial Three?'

I guess they're not so crucial now.

Amy laughed and he felt a warm haze shoot through his body.

'Well, I provided them with the means to travel through time.' She smiled at the three women. 'But that is running out and they want me to get them some more.'

'Or you could tell us how it works,' Hazell said.

Amy shook her head. 'The fewer people who know, the better. I've already explained this to you, Mary, several times.'

Cohen moved closer to Croft. 'Yes, we understand your reasons, but it's been ten years now, and with what's happened, well, we might lose everything.'

'Your grief over my death is touching, Sally.'

'That's not fair, Amy,' Adler said. 'We were all broken up about it.' She glanced at her friends. 'We still are.'

Amy sat and nursed her drink. 'What was my funeral like? Where am I buried?'

Hazell slammed her hand on the table. 'We're getting distracted here. If you're refusing to tell us what we want, then you and Hook need to get on with your investigation.'

'Not yet,' Harry said.

Amy narrowed her eyes at him. 'Don't you want to solve my murder?'

He smiled at her. 'In time.' Then he pointed at the TV screen. 'I need to deal with that first.'

Amy looked at the rolling news story of the mysterious death of Chuck at the Tube station.

'You mean we need to deal with that?' she said.

'You'll help me?'

That smile nearly knocked him over. 'Of course, we're partners in time now. You'll help me and I'll help you. Plus, you can't go time travelling on your own.' She turned to the Crucial Three. 'It's against the rules.'

'What about Ellie and Captain Cronin?' Harry said.

'Who?' Amy replied.

Hazell spoke as if she was chewing a wasp. 'They were only here to aid you through your training, Harry. You don't need them now.'

Was that true? Didn't he feel something for Ellie?

Amy clapped her hands together. 'So when do we start?'

She seemed cheerful for someone who only had six months left to live in her timeline.

But was it only six months? Couldn't the Crucial Three keep returning to her past and plucking a different version of her from the timeline?

'Can the past be changed?' Harry said.

None of them answered.

So he asked it again.

'Why can't we go back and stop Amy's murder?'

Hazell shook her head at him. 'This has already been explained to you. It's impossible to get close to that point; six months out, that's the best we can do.'

'Okay,' Harry said. 'Let's say we investigate Amy's life as much as we can up to that six month cut off and we discover who it is who'll eventually kill her. Then, if we stop them before the murder, surely the crime won't happen?'

Cohen took a deep breath. 'How will you know that you've stopped them if you have no control of the time leading up to Amy's death?'

He scratched the back of his head. 'I don't know. Maybe we do something that makes it impossible for them to be at the crime scene in their future.'

Hazell smiled at him. 'Like what?'

'Like having them locked up in a prison cell beyond the murder date,' Harry said.

'How would you achieve that?'

He puffed out his cheeks and glanced around the room.

'I'm sure there are enough clever people in here to come up with something.'

Hazell slapped him on the shoulder, which caused a ripple of pain to sprint down his spine.

'I've got the solution for you, Detective Hook. You go back in time to when you were in the Met and use your connections to ensure Amy's future murderer is behind bars, like you said. You could even talk to a younger version of yourself and convince him of its merits, of which I'm sure there are many.'

She removed her hand and winked at him.

'What does that mean?' he said.

Hazell grinned. 'If you can change time and keep dear Amy alive, the two of you could have a great future together.'

From somewhere deep inside Harry, Pompeii's lava was threatening to reappear.

'What Mary means is that you'd likely have to frame this person for a crime to prevent them from killing Amy. Or maybe do something much worse,' Cohen said.

'I'd have to kill them,' Harry said.

Cohen nodded. 'It would be the only way to make sure.'

'Of course.'

Cohen's freckles appeared to shimmer as she spoke to him.

'Now do you understand why we put you through those tests of asking you to kill people to prevent future suffering for others?'

He did.

'You wanted to know if I could deal with the moral dilemma of killing one person to save the lives of many?'

'Yes,' Cohen said. 'You've been to war. We knew this and that you'd faced similar situations in the police. But they weren't the same; in those circumstances, you'd had no choice. So we had to give you a choice to see your reaction.'

And I'd thought they were only playing cruel games on me.

'Hitler as an unborn child; serial killer Rider's mother while he was in her belly; even the two boys on the Titanic. That was all to prepare me for this?'

Cohen nodded. 'They were part of your preparation, Harry, yes.'

He looked at her, reassessing his initial observation that shyness consumed her. That wasn't it. She didn't like to speak unless she had something important to say.

'And you all think I'm ready now?'

'You're as ready as you'll ever be,' Cohen said.

Amy sipped the last of her whisky. 'Are you ready to step through the Doors of Perception, Harry?'

He ignored the ache in his legs and peered deep into her eyes.

'I guess so.'

She reached into her jacket, removed a small box and handed it to him. When he opened, it he saw the pills.

'There are twelve of them, Harry.' She glanced at the Crucial Three. 'You should never travel through time without some spares, but there's been a shortage lately.'

He took a pill from the container, remembering the one Ellie had pushed down his throat during their kiss.

Then those feelings for her came rushing back.

Why am I thinking about Ellie when I know there's no future for us?

And that's even if she was interested in me.

And I'm obsessed with Amy.

No, not her – the person she resembles.

At least there could be something between him and Ellie, regardless of the age difference. But there could be no future with Amy.

And what difference does age make if you're a time traveller?

'How do the pills work?'

Amy seemed surprised by the question. 'Didn't the others explain it to you, Harry?'

He laughed. 'In a fashion, but what are the Doors of Perception?'

It was Amy's turn to laugh. 'Why, Harry, *The Doors of Perception* is an autobiographical book written by Aldous Huxley, published in 1954. The title comes from William

Blake's 1793 book *The Marriage of Heaven and Hell.* The singer and poet Jim Morrison also took part of the title for the name of his band, *The Doors.*'

Her smile influenced his. 'Yes, I'm aware of those, but you know what I mean.'

Amy held a pill up to the light so it glittered like a disco ball.

'Did they explain to you about time perception and genetic memory?'

'They did,' he said, 'though I'm not sure I understood it.'

She nodded. 'It doesn't matter. The human brain is a reducing valve that restricts consciousness and limits our perception of the external and internal world.'

'By the internal world, do you mean the past and our genetic memory of it?'

'Yes. And the chemicals in these pills allow us access to all that lies deep within us.' She lifted a pill to her lips. 'Once we take one, then the Doors of Perception grant us access to all the corridors of time.'

'Like Alice falling down that rabbit hole?'

She laughed. 'It's more like stepping into Wonderland.' Amy held the pill out to him. 'Are you ready for that?'

Even though he already had a box of pills, he took it from her.

After what happened to me in Pompeii, you can never have too many of these.

Amy grinned at him. 'Watch out, Mr White Rabbit.'

19 AS IT IS WHEN IT WAS

After slipping the box into his pocket, Harry hesitated with the pill close to his lips.

'So you'll see a corridor lined with an infinite number of doors when you take one of these?'

She narrowed her eyes. 'No. It's different for everyone, but most experience the glittering lights and the doors. When I succumb to the drug, I'm in a library surrounded by books. I find the one I want, open it, and get transported to that place and time. It all depends on how your mind visualises the trigger to travel in time. I guess for me, it's because I've always loved books.'

It all seemed fantastic to Harry. 'What would happen if you opened, say, a Stephen King or Agatha Christie?'

Amy laughed. 'I don't know. I've never tried. I go for historical books or geography close to where I want to be. I only need to think of the place and time, and I'll be led to a book on a shelf. Then I open it and I'm there. Finding the anchor which takes me back is as simple as visualising that book again and closing it. For you, I assume it's about stepping through the door again.'

He was about to put the pill into his mouth when he stopped.

'I need to know what happened to Chuck before anything else.'

'I understand. We can see if there's an entrance to that Tube station, but just like with my death, it might be closed to us.'

He nodded. 'I understand, which is why we have to stick to old-fashioned detective work for now.' He put the pill with the others in his pocket.

She seemed confused by what he'd said. 'You don't want to discover what happened to your partner?'

'I do,' Harry replied. 'But we need to visit his family before we do anything else.'

She agreed with him. Then they left the Crucial Three and made their way out of the Time Authority headquarters. Amy led him to the lowest level and towards a nondescript Volkswagen and unlocked it.

Harry got into the passenger seat. 'I need a change of clothes.'

He could still smell Pompeii and a raging sea on himself.

'Give me directions and I'll take you home.'

He checked his phone for messages while she did that, but found none. That meant he hadn't heard from Chuck since he'd left for the Authority building the first time. He tried to work out when that was, but travelling through time had messed up all of his perceptions.

The Doors of Perception.

Something that has always been inside the human brain allows us to travel to any point in space and time as long as it is encoded into our genetic memory through our DNA.

He glanced at Amy as she drove.

And this is the woman who discovered it. Or was it an invention?

He asked her. 'Was it a discovery or an invention?'

She slowed the car as the Thames appeared on their right.

'What do you mean?'

'Time travel through the Doors of Perception; was it a discovery or an invention?'

Harry peered at the boats on the river and got a sudden painful memory of being on the deck of the *Titanic*.

I wonder if those two boys survived the disaster.

'It was an accident.'

The smell of saltwater invaded his nostrils, but he knew it was an illusion.

'What happened?'

She looked at him as the car slowed in the traffic.

'Is this a ploy to get me to reveal my secret to you, Harry?' The glint in her eyes unnerved him. 'You're a charming man, Mr Hook, but did the Crucial Three put you up to this?'

She called me charming.

'We should stop calling them the Crucial Three, don't you think?'

'Why?' Amy said.

'Because they did nothing. You gave them the secret of time travel and they took the claim for that. There was hardly anything crucial about what they did.'

She reached over and turned on the radio, touching his knee as she did. His legs trembled as The Stones sang about not getting what they wanted.

'They spread the idea to the world, Harry. It was all about preparation. The Time Authority is still in its earliest stages, but you know their ultimate goal, don't you?'

'Yes, they explained it to me. They want to give people a chance to visit departed loved ones or ancestors they've never met. So it sounds wonderful in principle.'

'You don't believe in it?'

The disappointment in her voice upset him more than it should have.

'No, I think it's a fantastic idea in theory, but I see many obstacles along the way in practice.'

'So can they, and so do I. When I first approached Sally, Rose, and Mary, I explained the ultimate goal for time travel and how it would be challenging to get there. You might not look upon them too fondly, but they have achieved a lot in ten years. Now they have another stern test to overcome.'

'You're talking about your death?' He didn't want to seem insensitive, but he continued anyway. 'Why don't you just tell them everything?'

They were cruising by the river and thoughts of his sister occupied the back of his mind.

'I might be dead, Harry, but I'm not ready to relinquish my role yet.'

He didn't push the idea any further. 'What did you mean when you said time travel was an accident?'

A woman on the radio was singing about running up a hill.

Amy turned the volume up. 'Do you know how penicillin was discovered?'

'Vaguely.'

'One of the biggest medicinal breakthroughs in history came about entirely by accident. Sir Alexander Fleming interrupted his experimentation with the influenza virus for a two-week holiday. When he returned, he found a mould had grown which deterred the virus. Penicillin was born and is now used to treat everything from acne to pneumonia.'

'It was the same with Viagra.'

She laughed above the music. 'I'm surprised, Harry. You don't look the type.'

'Ha-ha,' he said. 'So you stumbled upon a method of time travel by accident.'

'Indeed.'

'You're not Louise Brooks, are you?'

'No, I just admire the way she looked and her life.' She drove on to the Strand. 'Time travel into the future is impossible, but why did you ask about Ms Brooks?'

Her eyes dazzled him and he thought it was a terrible idea sitting so close to her.

'Oh, I'm a film buff, especially old movies, and she's one of my favourites.'

'Me too,' Amy said. 'For the movies and Louise. What's your all-time favourite flick?'

He stopped himself from being dragged into the small talk, waiting for the music to finish.

'What year are you from?'

'What?' she said as a man with an impressive voice warbled out of the radio about the alcohol turning him blue.

'You must have come from the future with your secret, so what year are you from?'

Amy didn't answer as she parked near his flat. Instead, she stepped out of the car and he followed.

'Are you still trying to prise my secrets from me?'

'Hardly.' He removed the key from his jacket and marched up the steps. He opened the door and headed for the bedroom. 'Help yourself to anything,' he said as he got a change of clothes.

'Anything?'

Harry examined himself in the mirror, finding lines on his face that weren't there before he was dragged into this whole thing. He put his phone on the bedside table, wondering if he should call Chuck's wife, Sarah, before seeing her and Kelly.

'Within reason,' he replied.

He buttoned up his shirt while staring at his movie collection filling the bookcase. The hobby he'd inherited from his father was one of the few things he was thankful to the old man for. The discs were scarce nowadays since most people watched or listened to everything digitally.

Once all this is over, perhaps I can slip back in time and watch a Louise Brooks film when it was first released on the silver screen.

He sat on the bed and slipped on his socks.

Even better, I could go and meet her.

Next to his movie collection was his stack of books, biographies and autobiographies of the stars from the last century.

All I've got to do is flick through the books I have about her – ones I've read dozens of times – and I'll know the precise time and place to bump into her.

Once this is all over.

And after he'd discovered what happened to Lily.

Travelling through time might be worth all the hassle, after all.

He still had visions of Pompeii and the two boys he'd left behind on the *Titanic*, but there was nothing he could have done about any of that.

The past can't be changed; that's what they keep telling me.

He was dressed and ready to go, hearing Amy in the

other room, when a thought struck him like a bolt from the blue.

Time travelling into the future is impossible; that's the other thing they keep hammering on about.

So how could I have saved one of those boys?

He flopped back onto the bed.

I suppose I could have taken him into the past. Yes, that would have worked.

'Have you fallen asleep?' Amy shouted from the other room. 'Do you want me to come in and help you get dressed?'

He had to stop himself from telling her yes.

Harry smiled and got up, checking himself in the mirror. Even with his haggard face, he didn't think he appeared too bad. He stepped out of the bedroom to find her examining the Salvador Dali prints on the wall.

'How would you like to go back and meet the great man?'

He stood by her side and peered at an image he'd looked at hundreds of times before of watches melting in some strange faraway location.

'There are so many things I'd like to do, Amy.'

She smiled at him. 'Well, now you can.'

'Time travel is a dangerous thing, that's what the others keep on telling me. It's bad for the body and the mind, and the more you do it, the more strain you put on yourself. Isn't this why the Time Authority will only allow people one opportunity to travel into the past to see a family member?'

Amy shook her head. 'There are still plenty of practical problems we need to overcome for that, but, having met Mary and the others, do you believe they'll only give people one trip?'

'Why not?'

She laughed at him. 'Harry, think of all the money they could make with this once it's perfected.'

He inched away from her. 'What? They're only doing this for financial gain?'

'No, of course not, but it will come to them at some point, and it'll be a dilemma. Contrary to appearances, the three of them and the Time Authority do not have many financial resources. So if it becomes a choice between monetising time travel or letting big business or the government become a partner, what do you think they'll do?'

'I thought Adler had money through her family?'

'Had is the right tense, Harry. Most of it is gone, spent over the last ten years getting the TA to where it is now. That new building wasn't free, you know.'

He didn't want to think about it. His only concern was seeing Chuck's family and finding out what happened to him at that Tube station.

'We better get going. Chuck's place isn't far, so we can walk there.'

She moved away from the painting to the door, and Harry stared at the melting watches again.

Then a flash of inspiration sped at him and he wondered how he could have missed what had been in front of his eyes all along.

'How old are you, Amy?'

She let go of the handle and turned to him.

'Are you after more of my secrets?' She fluttered her eyelids at him. 'Or is this because you want to know if we're of a similar age?'

'What year were you born?'

She wagged a finger at him. 'You know I can't tell you that.'

'Okay, but you're a younger version of the Amy who was killed?'

'Murdered, Harry, don't forget that. But, yes, I'm a younger version of that Amy.'

'So, how did you travel to the future?'

20 EVERYONE EVERYWHERE

That's when Harry thought he had her.

But he didn't.

'What do you mean?' She moved near him and he got a whiff of her perfume, a hint of strawberries that played havoc with his senses. 'Oh, you think I've travelled to the future when that's impossible, right?'

'So, how did you do it?'

Amy grabbed his hand and pulled him to the sofa, where they sat next to each other.

'Time travel allows you to go back and forwards along your timeline or any that came before yours. For example, I died six months ago, but this is still my past. Does that make sense?'

It did and he felt like an idiot for bringing it up. So he tried to make light of it.

'Yes, but you still haven't told me how old you are.'

She pushed him gently on the shoulder.

'Age isn't important unless you're a cheese.' Amy got up. 'Are we going to see your partner's family, or do you have something else in mind?'

He stood, trying not to think of all the things running through his head. He locked the door behind them and they walked the route to Chuck's house. Technically, it wasn't his house since it was his late father's place, and from what Harry had gathered, the mortgage on it was beyond what Chuck could pay once his father's death was the inconvenience that stopped the mortgage payments.

He wondered what would happen with the property now Chuck had died.

As he strode next to Amy, the realisation his partner was dead struck home with him.

She must have seen it in his face. 'How long have you known Chuck?'

'Since primary school. We lost touch after I joined the army, but we were back in contact when I became a copper.'

'Sally told me you were in the Met, which I guess is why they chose you for this. What was it like working for them?'

They strode through the streets, past shops, restaurants and pubs. Harry knew there were two schools nearby for the kids from the estates.

'After leaving the army, the police was the only job I wanted. I started as a constable and worked my way up to a DI, a detective inspector, but I needed a change after fourteen years. Chuck had been badgering me for ages about us going into business, so it seemed the right time to do it.'

He didn't tell her that Chuck was the one financing the business and when his father died, all of his debts had tumbled into the open, so keeping Hook Security and Detection active was a constant struggle.

If it hadn't been for our desperate need for money, I wouldn't be walking with you now.

'What are the police like where you come from?'

'Oh, you know, all the detectives are androids dreaming of electric sheep, and every officer has a flying car.'

He glanced at her as they went, unsure if she was joking or not. They walked past a cinema showing the latest James Bond movie.

'Do they have cinemas in the future, or is everything digital with giant home screens and holograms?'

'Are you genuinely interested, Harry, or is this you still fishing for where I come from?'

They stopped at a crossing.

'Why aren't you bothered you're... well, you know?'

The light changed to green for pedestrians, but they didn't move.

'Dead?'

'Yes.'

'How do you know I'm not broken up inside and what you see', she pointed at her face, 'isn't just a façade?'

'I don't, but that glittering sparkle in your eyes makes me think you're enjoying this.'

She grabbed his arm and dragged him across the road, even though the lights had turned to red. A taxi beeped its horn at them as it swerved to miss Amy.

'Should I be worried you're looking into my eyes and seeing glittering sparkles?'

He didn't wriggle from her grasp, letting her hold him as they reached the other side with no more near misses.

'No, I'm just being observant, like a detective should. You were lucky with that car, so what would have happened if you'd died here, now, in this street?'

'The past can't be changed, Harry. I know this from personal experience.'

They got to the entrance to the Tube station as a crowd was leaving. People bustled in between them and they got separated. He saw Amy standing behind a group of teenagers. He didn't move, peering at her as he realised he didn't even know at which Tube station Chuck had died.

The throng split and he stepped through the gap towards her.

'Are you saying the taxi couldn't have killed you because time knows you're due to die in my past?'

'I'm unsure how it works, Harry, but Mary, Sally and Rose will tell you the past can't be changed, no matter how hard you try.'

'That's not true. Hazell told me if you have a strong enough will, then you can change history.'

Amy shook her head. 'I don't know why she said that, but I'd guess she was testing you again.' She watched the next group striding into the Tube. 'Look at these people, Harry. Each of them moves as if unseeing hands are dragging them this way and that, pulling their eyes to one thing, and then another. They respond in predictable ways, each with a goal to achieve, heading for a place to be. But underneath that is free will, the ability to choose their own path. We all have that, but if something that shouldn't be there tries to interfere with that free will, then a force greater than us will push back.'

'Are you saying you can't die here and now?'

'Do you want to test the theory and try to kill me?'

Harry grimaced. 'Of course not. I'm just trying to wrap my head around all of this. You mentioned free will, but the more you explain this, the more it sounds like fate or destiny, and not free will.'

'Mary tested you on the notion of killing one person in the past to save countless others in the future, right?'

'She did, more than once.'

'And she explained about how many times the three

of them had killed Hitler, but it never really changed history because it only altered the route to which his actions led.'

'I thought she was lying about that.'

'No, all of that was true. When we say the past can't be rewritten, we don't mean some invisible force will stop it from happening – though I'm not prepared to dismiss that possibility outright – but what was meant to be will happen. I'll be murdered on May 2 2050; nothing that happens to me here will prevent that.'

He thought he understood what she was saying.

'You'll die on that date, but it might not be how I witnessed it through the CCTV footage?'

'That's correct. Small modifications can be made to the past, but history's overall events can't be altered.'

Harry swatted away an insect and thought of something else.

'What about the Butterfly Effect?'

The crowd increased, so they continued their conversation as they walked.

Amy glanced at him as she spoke. 'Does the flap of a butterfly's wings in Brazil set off a tornado in Texas?' Then she stopped near an overflowing bin. It stank of rotten fish and Harry covered his nose. She lifted a spider from the top of the bin. 'Or if I killed this creature, would it cause devastating effects in the future?'

He watched the spider crawl over her hand. 'Yes.'

'Why would it do that?'

'A ripple effect through time, like that classic science fiction story by Ray Bradbury, where a character changes history by stepping on a butterfly.'

She let it move between her fingers. 'Do you believe if I kill this now, it might change the future?'

The spider stopped on her thumb and stared at him through its many eyes.

'Yes, I think it's possible.'

'Okay.' She moved to him and placed the spider in his palm. 'What about if you killed it?'

Harry felt its hairy legs crawling over his skin. Fighting the urge to swat it from his hand, he instead thought about her question.

'I guess not, no.'

'Why not?'

It settled in his palm and gazed at him. 'Because I'm from this point in time.'

'And I'm not, so me killing it would change the timeline?'

The way she said it made him realise it made little sense.

'No, that doesn't sound right when you explain it like that.'

He returned the spider to the top of the bin, where it continued to stare at him.

'But we're only talking about an insect here. You can't compare that to killing a person before history says they'd died.'

'Arachnid,' she said.

'What?'

'Spiders are arachnids, not insects. The term comes from Greek mythology. Arachne was a weaver who acquired such skill in her art, she challenged the goddess Athena to a contest. Athena wove a tapestry depicting the gods in majesty, while Arachne's showed the romantic adventures of the gods. Enraged at the perfection of her rival's work – or perhaps offended by its subject – Athena tore it to pieces, and in despair, Arachne hanged herself.

But the goddess, out of pity, loosened the rope, which became a cobweb. Athena changed Arachne into a spider, hence the name of the zoological class to which spiders belong, Arachnida.'

'I feel like I'm the spider in this conversation,' Harry said.

As they started walking again, he glanced around to look at the spider, still feeling its legs on his skin. As he did, a bird swooped down and snapped the creature in its mouth.

Amy saw it and grinned. 'Well, there you go. Is the future ruined now?'

He laughed with her, sensing everything would be okay, and no matter what they might do when travelling through time, he wouldn't be able to damage anything.

'No, I guess not.'

They walked for another fifteen minutes until they reached Chuck's house. It was two weeks since he was last there, popping over to drop off a present for Kelly's tenth birthday.

What would she think, or Sarah if they knew I could travel through time? Would they beg me to go back and save Chuck, and then I'd have to explain how that is impossible?

Seemingly impossible.

Amy whistled. 'This is an impressive house.'

'It was Chuck's father's. His dad left it to him in his will.'

'Wow. I wish my dad had been so generous.'

'It's not as good as it sounds. Old Man Connors also left his only child all of his debt, of which there is a considerable amount. Even selling this place won't pay it off.'

'Damn,' Amy said. 'I guess the debt passes on to his wife as well.'

Harry nodded. 'I suppose. It was Chuck who set up the meeting with the Time Authority, hoping it would prove lucrative and enhance our reputation enough to deal with our financial difficulties.' He looked at her. 'That was when I thought we were only going to be offered a contract for security at the TA building.'

'Solving my murder will pay a lot more than that, Harry.'

He felt guilty for laughing outside his dead partner's house.

'You know, I never asked the Crucial Three what we'd get paid for this job.'

She put her hand on his arm. 'Don't worry; I'll make sure Mary and the others amply reward you.'

He laughed even louder. 'You said they were running out of money.'

'That's true, but there are worse things than being skint, Harry. You could be dead.'

She walked up to the door and he followed her.

Or you could be dead and still alive.

21 SHELLSHOCK

Sarah opened the door, throwing her arms around Harry before anyone spoke. She didn't cry, but he could feel the well ready to burst as she held him. When she finally let go, he introduced Amy to her.

'Come in,' Sarah said as she took them into the house.

Harry remembered the laughter the last time he was there, but now it was as if he'd stepped into a funeral parlour. He stared at the family photographs decorating the walls as they strode through the corridor. The floor was contemporary wood made to look old-fashioned with a blend of deep homely browns. Sarah led them into the living room with expensive couches, a massive TV, table and bookcases.

'I'm sorry about Chuck,' Harry said as they all sat. Amy was next to him while Sarah took the couch opposite.

'The police came an hour ago. As soon as I saw them on the doorstep, I knew it was bad news.'

'I'm sorry for your loss, Mrs Connors,' Amy said.

'Do you want a drink?' Sarah said.

Harry did, desperate for some of that hard-to-get whisky Chuck had.

'No thanks, Sarah.' He looked around the room. 'Is Kelly here?'

'She's upstairs. She wanted a lie down after the police left.' She stood and went to the cabinet. 'Are you sure you don't want a drink? I'm having one.'

He watched her go, unsure of what to say.

Then Amy got off the couch. 'Why not, Mrs Connors? Let me help you.'

Harry observed the two women talking as if they were chatting about everyday events.

Death is an everyday event. You're looking at a dead woman, remember?

'Please, call me Sarah.' She looked over at him. 'Usual for you, Harry?'

Why not?

'Sure, Sarah.'

After the drinks were poured, they were all in their seats again. He only sipped at his, but the two women chugged theirs as if they were at a party.

'How did you find out, Harry?' Sarah said.

He didn't want to say he'd seen it on the TV by accident, so he lied.

'The police contacted me.'

As soon as the words came out of his mouth, he wondered if Agnes knew what had happened.

I should have called her.

Sarah put her glass on the table between them.

'Was he on his way to a meeting for the business?'

I don't know what he was doing or even at which Tube station he died.

As he struggled for a reply, Amy saved his blushes.

'We're not sure why your husband was in Brixton.'

Sarah reached for her drink again, but pulled back.

'Do you work with Harry and Chuck, Amy?' She realised what she'd said, and then corrected herself. 'Did you work with Chuck?'

Amy gave her that smile that melted Harry's heart.

'They took me on a week ago as a consultant.'

Sarah laughed. 'For a second, I thought you might be Harry's girlfriend.'

Harry blushed as he pulled at his collar, but Amy only joined in with the laughter.

'No, Sarah, he's far too young for me.'

He watched Sarah's lips tremble as she spoke.

'Or, you know, I thought maybe he'd brought you here so the widow could meet her dead husband's mistress.'

'What?' Harry said. 'Why would you think that, Sarah?'

She gulped down half of her alcohol. 'Chuck had been up to something for a while, Harry. I assumed you might have been in on it, you know, the boys sticking together while the wife is ignorant of what's going on.'

Amy leant over and touched Sarah's hand. 'What do you mean when you say he was up to something?'

'He was always late getting home, even though I knew the business had no work.' She looked at Harry. 'He couldn't hide the finances from me. The debt his father left him – left us – is considerable, so I could understand him staying out for a few drinks before coming back to us. Yet he never stank of booze, but I could smell perfume lingering on him.' She continued to stare at Harry. 'I could put up with it for a little, with all the stress he was under, but I wouldn't forever. I was going to have it out with him tonight, but... well, you know what happened.'

Harry was shocked. 'You believe he was having an affair?'

She grabbed her drink and finished it. 'I'm convinced of it. I'm surprised you knew nothing about it.'

'Well, I didn't, Sarah. I promise.'

What else don't I know about him?

'Do you think he might have been in Brixton to meet this woman?' Amy said.

'Why else would he be there?' Sarah replied.

This was just another in a long line of revelations where Harry thought his whole life had been turned upside down.

'What did the police tell you?' he said.

The way she slumped into the seat, he wondered if she'd had a few drinks before they'd arrived. Not that he'd blame her.

'Nothing much. They've got eyewitness reports and CCTV footage showing Chuck entering the station alone and walking towards the platform. Then, they said, there was nobody near him when he... when he...'

The tears came and Amy moved across to comfort the widow. Harry sat there, unable to move while considering the possibility his partner had been having an affair. While Sarah sobbed into Amy's shoulder, he thought of all the times when Chuck had behaved strangely around him.

Sometimes I'd get to work and see him whispering with Agnes.

Agnes. It couldn't be. Could it?

Sarah had asked him something, but he hadn't heard it.

'What?' he said.

'Did you notice him acting strange at the office?'

He shook his head. 'No, Sarah, I saw nothing like that.'

Amy let go of Sarah and asked the question Harry had considered, but didn't dare ask.

'Do you think Chuck might have killed himself because of this affair?'

Sarah jerked up so violently, Harry thought she was going to hit Amy. Instead, she stumbled away from them.

'I know nothing anymore. If he could do that to his daughter, then who knows what was in his brain?'

Harry got up and went to her. 'Did Chuck have any enemies?'

She stared at him and laughed.

'Wouldn't you be in the best position to know that, with your Hook Security and Detection?'

'I guess so.'

'You know he was upset because his name wasn't on the business with yours, don't you?' she said.

'No, I didn't. He told me he was happy to only have my name on the company because of my experience with the police.'

Sarah reached for the whisky bottle, clutching it in her hand like a weapon.

'Ah, yes, your precious work with the Met. Maybe some criminal you've upset over the years decided they'd get back at you by killing my husband.'

He didn't know what to say.

First, he heard Chuck might have been having an affair, and now this.

Was Chuck resentful his name wasn't next to mine on the business? He'd told me he wasn't.

Could some enemy from my police days have done this for revenge?

It was possible. He'd known criminals who'd done worse things for less reason.

'Dad was keeping something from us; I know that.'

Ten-year-old Kelly Connors had stepped into the room with none of them noticing.

Sarah ran to her daughter and hugged her.

Harry went to Amy and whispered to her. 'Maybe we should leave.'

She shook her head. 'No. We have to find out what the girl knows.'

When they turned around, mother and child had separated.

'What do you mean, Kelly?' Sarah said.

The newly fatherless child seemed to Harry as if she was still in a state of shock.

'I heard him on the phone a few times, whispering to somebody, saying he didn't want you or Uncle Harry to find out about it.'

'Find out about what?' Harry said.

Kelly shrugged. 'Don't know. He always looked scared when he finished those calls.'

He couldn't badger mother and daughter anymore. They had two leads to follow up without having to take a pill to go down the rabbit hole.

He smiled at Sarah. 'Thanks for talking to us.' Then he touched her on the arm. 'Do you have anyone to look after you?'

'We're going to my mother's later.' She glanced around the house. 'We can't afford to stay here anymore.'

Harry hugged them both as they said their goodbyes.

When they got outside, he was glad to feel the warmth of the sun on his face.

Amy had a pill in her hand. 'Should we take these now?'

'In the street? Are you crazy?'

She shrugged. 'There's no time like the present, partner.'

He moved from the house and she joined him.

'It's time travel, so what difference does it make when we do it?'

'You know why, Harry. As soon as we solve Chuck's death, we can discover who murdered me.'

'We might do it without using those pills, which are apparently in short supply.'

'How do we do that?'

'Sarah and Kelly gave us two leads: the possibility Chuck was having an affair and those phone calls.'

'Okay, I get you could probably trace where those calls came from, but if they're not from some mysterious woman, how will you track the caller down?'

Harry glanced down the street. 'We'll start in the office of Hook Security and Detection.'

22 ELEGIA

Harry took Amy on a different route back to the office. 'Do you want to show me the sights of the city?' she said.

They trundled past a shop selling fresh cakes, the aroma drifting out of it giving him a sugar rush, before turning a corner into a piece of theatre.

'Are you from London?' he said.

She laughed as they stopped in front of a group of hip-hop teenagers singing and dancing to a captive audience.

'You're still prying into my past, aren't you?'

He watched a young girl spinning on her back in the street. She was dressed in a multi-coloured jumpsuit, and the dizzying movements of her arms and legs resurrected memories of his time in that corridor with the shimmering rainbow colours.

The Doors of Perception.

'No, I only want to get to know you. It will help us work better together on our investigations.'

Amy spoke to a street trader and bought a fridge magnet of a London bus.

She showed it to him. 'Okay, fair enough, but it works both ways. You need to let me into your life.'

'That's why we're heading in this direction,' he said as they moved from the entertainers.

She held the magnet. 'Why this way? Is this where you grew up and you're going to reveal the secrets of your childhood to me?'

'Something like that. I'm assuming the Crucial Three told you about me before pulling you out of the past.'

She nodded. 'I know you were in the army for a brief time before returning to London to join the police. Then I looked at some of your case files for the Met.'

That surprised him. 'Did you find anything interesting?'

Amy grinned at him. 'Yes. You had the highest success rate of solving investigations of any Met officer. I could see why Mary and the others had chosen you to solve my murder.'

That was another surprise. 'Hazell picked me? She told me the opposite: the other two wanted me and she was against it.'

She slipped the magnet into her pocket, 'I wouldn't believe everything Mary tells you, Harry. She exaggerates.'

That was a polite description of lies and deception.

'I thought she didn't like me.'

'Don't judge her too harshly. She had a difficult childhood, which she overcompensated for at university. She still struggles with those memories.'

They walked past a garden of blooming flowers, the heady aromas making Harry slow his pace.

'I couldn't find anything about the three of them online between them leaving university and the announcement of their discovery, no photos or videos. Even when I tried to dig deeper into their childhoods, there was little to find.'

'Did you search for me on the internet?'

'Yes,' he said. 'There are plenty of Amy Crofts online, but you're not one of them. It was as if someone had wiped most of the details of all four of you from the world.'

'That's not a great conspiracy, Harry. Anybody can ask to have their information removed from the internet.' She glanced at him as they walked. 'If I wanted to see what you did during your three years in the army, would I be able to find it?'

'Of course not. The government doesn't release those details unless they're compelled to.'

Amy stopped and reached into the flowers, where she pulled a rose from a pot.

'That's stealing,' he said.

She placed the flower into her top pocket, so the petals peaked out of it.

'How can you steal from nature, Harry?'

'I don't believe those who planted them would think like that.'

Amy sniffed at the flower. 'Why are you people so obsessed with possessions?'

He laughed at her. 'You people? Is that an insult?'

She shook her head. 'No, only a confirmation that I am from the future.' She glanced around their surroundings, at the shops and market stalls. 'Owning things and keeping possessions isn't such a priority where I come from.'

'Yet you just bought a London bus fridge magnet.'

She removed it from her pocket and ran a finger over the surface.

'This is only a memento of our brief time together, Harry. Have you already forgotten about my impending death?'

Heat rushed through his cheeks. 'No. How could I?'

Amy put the magnet away and smiled at him.

'Great. So, where are you taking me on this journey through your life?'

He pointed down the road at the building he'd visited yesterday.

'There. We're going to see my father.'

'Ah,' she said. 'Is this about your sister?'

'It is. The Crucial Three told you about Lily?'

She nodded. 'I'm sorry you never discovered what happened to her, Harry.'

'Where you come from, in the future, do you know why Lily vanished?'

Amy shook her head. 'You know I can't tell you that.'

He didn't argue and continued walking, heading to the father he'd thought he'd never see again until yesterday.

Was it yesterday? So much has happened since and it feels like a lifetime ago.

She strode by his side into the Redhill Care Home. They waited at reception for two minutes before a staff member took them to Oliver Hook. Harry was unsure how he felt about his father, but as he went through the building, staring at the people looking blankly back at him, he knew this was no way to live.

'Just give me a shout when you want to leave,' the woman said as she left them in the room.

He nodded before seeing his father sitting in a chair, gazing into space.

'Why have we come here?' Amy said.

He took a deep breath. 'The Doors of Perception, or those books that you see after taking a pill. How do they work?'

'Well, you think about the place and time you want to travel to, and then, for the doors, you step through one.'

'But if you chose the wrong one, it can burn you?'

'Or worse,' she said.

'And it's the same with your books? If you pick the wrong one, you'll end up somewhere you didn't want to be.'

'That's right, Harry.'

He turned from his father's trembling, muddled face and stared at her.

'When you're in that library, do you hear voices from the books calling to you?'

She looked as confused as Oliver Hook as she replied.

'No, why do you ask?'

'Because on one of my visits, I heard a voice.' He turned to peer at his father again. 'It was his voice.'

Amy put a hand on his arm. 'That's normal, Harry. That would have been his voice talking to you through the genetic memory, speaking about things from before you were born.'

He shook his head. 'No, that isn't it. He spoke about Lily's disappearance.'

The sound of that name sprang Oliver Hook from his trance.

'Lily, is that you?' He twisted his neck around to stare at them. 'Oh, it's you, Anna. You shouldn't be here. Lily will never come back if you're here.'

'Who's Anna?' Amy said.

Harry stepped closer to his father. 'Anna was my mother. She died ten years ago.'

She reached a hand out to him. 'I'm sorry, Harry.'

He was grateful for her comforting touch, but he moved from her and knelt in front of his father.

'Dad, it's Harry, your son.'

Oliver Hook narrowed his eyes. 'Son? I don't have a son,

only a daughter.' He jerked his hand up and pointed trembling fingers at Amy. 'And she drove Lily away.'

He took his father's trembling hand into his own.

'What do you mean she drove Lily away?'

The old man turned his confused face towards the son he didn't recognise.

'I didn't know what was happening at first. Anna was angry at me because I was working so much, and when she hit Lily, it was where you couldn't see the bruises.' Tears streamed down Oliver Hook's face. 'Do you understand? I didn't know what was going on until it was too late.'

A cold sweat trickled down Harry's spine as darkness clutched at his chest.

'What do you mean, it was too late?'

'By the time Anna confessed everything to me, Lily was gone. I think she ran away.' He wriggled out of Harry's grasp and glared at Amy. 'And she won't come back while she's here.'

Harry got off his knees and stumbled into the sideboard, sending the tiny figurines of sheep tumbling over. He left them like that, peered at his father, and stepped out of the room.

Amy followed him. 'Is that the first time you've heard your father say those things?'

He rubbed at his throat. 'It is.'

'Do you think what he said is true?'

He shook his head. 'I don't know.'

She took his hand in hers, manoeuvring him so he gazed straight into her eyes.

'Do I resemble your mother?'

He gripped her fingers. 'No.'

They stood like that while Harry composed himself. Residents and staff were moving around them, stepping in and out of rooms with barely a word between them. Nobody looked their way or approached them.

How could I have not known what my mother was doing to Lily?

Guilt swept through him like a tidal wave and he thought he was back on the *Titanic*, waiting for the wind to toss him into the raging sea.

'Do you want to leave?' Amy said.

He nodded and let go of her, turning to get out of that place when a sight stopped him in his tracks: a woman he recognised stepping into one of the other rooms.

'Did you see who that was?' he said to Amy.

'No. Who was it?'

'Wait here.' He left Amy and went to that room.

The door was open, but he didn't enter, leaning against the wall and listening. The woman was talking, but he couldn't hear what she said.

That was until she raised her voice. 'Do you want to come in, Harry?'

He took a deep breath and stepped inside, looking first at the woman lying on top of the bed. Harry guessed she was at least ninety years old, with glasses and long, stark white hair that reached well below her shoulders. She was peering at the empty wall as if the most exciting thing in the world was happening there.

Then he switched his gaze to the other much younger woman. When she smiled at him, he didn't see the woman he'd seen on a computer screen not so long ago, but the one he'd watched in so many movies.

Mary Boleyn.

'Did you come for my autograph, Harry?'

The words tumbled out of his mouth. 'My father is a

resident here.' He glanced at the old woman again. 'Is that your mother?'

'It is. Her name is Elizabeth. How old would you say she is?'

He didn't want to guess, but did anyway. 'About ninety?'

Boleyn touched her mother's fingers. 'Her sixtieth birthday was last week.'

'Oh,' Harry said. 'Is it dementia?'

'That's what the doctors diagnosed, but we both know it wasn't that which aged my mother so rapidly and destroyed her mind. Don't we, Harry?'

He didn't know what she was talking about.

'How do you know who I am?'

She let go of her mother and got up. As she did, he had visions of all the movies he'd seen her in.

'Harry, my organisation watches everything the Time Authority does. The moment you stepped through that door to meet those three witches, I knew everything about you.'

'You don't know the truth about them and what they do.'

She laughed at him. 'Do you?'

He didn't want an argument, not there, so he turned to leave.

'I'm sorry about your mother.'

He was at the exit when her words froze his legs.

'My mother was one of their first volunteers.' He twisted around to see her. 'Once they'd been on that TV show, she became obsessed with them. She wasn't the only volunteer; there were dozens of them initially. She never revealed to me where they met – the Time Authority didn't have a fancy headquarters then – but she'd disappear for long periods. On the few occasions I saw or spoke to her, the changes were obvious. It started with the facial tics, and then gravitated to her trembling hands. Then came the memory loss and failure to recognise people and places. Especially me. Early-onset of dementia, the doctors told me – at fifty years old. But I knew better. Over time, I got some of the truth from her in my mother's rare lucid moments, of how Hazell, Cohen and Adler had sent her into the past; her and the others who never made it back.'

She moved towards him and all he could do was repeat those same words.

'I'm sorry.'

'You don't need to apologise for my mother's fate, Harry. But you will be responsible for what happens next if you don't expose those women for their crimes against humanity. You understand that, don't you?'

Before he could say anything, Amy grabbed his arm and hauled him from the room.

She dragged him out of the building.

He said nothing until they were outside. 'Did you hear any of that?'

'All of it.'

Harry leant against a wall before he fell over.

'Is it true what she said about her mother and the other volunteers?'

Amy put her hand on him, but he shrugged it off.

'Once I gave them the means for time travel, I left them to it. I had other things to focus on, but I'm aware they had some early setbacks.'

The anger rose in Harry like the lava exploding out of Vesuvius.

'Setbacks? People never came back.' He slammed his palm against the wall and the concrete cut into his skin.

'Look at Boleyn's mother. Will that be my fate if I continue with this?'

'Do you want to quit?'

Did he?

He watched his blood trickle down and into the grass.

'No, there's too much I need to do.' He turned his hand into a fist. 'But once I know what happened to Chuck, I'm going to reassess my working relationship with the so-called Time Authority.'

'What about my murder?' Amy said.

Harry pushed past her and away from Redhill's.

'We'll have to see.'

23 TIMES CHANGE

The office was empty when they arrived. Amy followed Harry inside as he went to his desk, finding a note there.

He picked it up. 'It's from Agnes.'

Amy slumped onto a hardly used sofa. 'Is it about your partner's death?'

He removed the phone from his pocket.

'No. The bookshop we came past on the way up here can't locate the book I'm after.'

She glanced at the bookshelf opposite her, staring at all the non-fiction titles about security and crime investigations.

'Is it to add to your private eye collection?'

He looked at her with a confused expression until he saw she was holding a Raymond Chandler novel in his hand, the one he'd left on his desk after rereading it for the umpteenth time.

'Not quite. I'd asked the woman who owns the place if she could find me a rare book published about the early days of the Time Authority.' He dropped the note into the bin. 'It looks like she can't.'

He watched her relax on the sofa and flick through the novel.

'You can always go back in time and get one, Harry.'

'Maybe.' He opened the contacts on his phone, found Agnes's number and called her. It rang for a minute before going to voicemail. He didn't leave a message.

Amy flicked through the pages as she spoke.

'You think Agnes was Chuck's mistress, don't you?'

He sat on the edge of the desk. 'Do they still use that term where you come from?'

She held the novel as she crossed her legs. She looked impressive in that suit, but he couldn't get the idea out of his mind of what she'd look like in a dress.

'What would you prefer, Harry? The other woman? The bit on the side?'

'I can't believe he was cheating on Sarah.'

She rested the book on the arm of the sofa. 'Why? Because he was your business partner and old school friend? I don't want to sound cruel, but Chuck was a man and they always cheat.'

'That seems harsh. Are all the men cheaters where you come from?'

'Are we back to that? Would it make you happy if I were to tell you I'm from five hundred years in the future where women rule the world, and we only keep blokes around for a bit of fun now and then?'

Harry grinned at her. 'That sounds like paradise. And wholly improbable.'

'Why? You don't think women can rule the world?'

'Quite the opposite. I'm sure they'd do a much better

job than what's gone before, but I know you're messing with my head again.'

Her smile increased the heat racing through him.

'Well, I enjoy messing with you. And it's such a pretty head.'

Amy laughed and the sound of it, how she moved in that seat, gripped his ribs as if she'd sent invisible fingers crawling through him, dragging their way over his bones until they settled into his heart.

She was giving him a hangover and he hadn't had enough to drink yet.

He was struggling to find a reply to her when his phone rang. It vibrated on the desk so hard, it knocked over the small plastic figure of a police officer Chuck had given him the day they'd moved into the building.

It rolled across the wood and onto the floor as he answered the call.

'Are you okay, Agnes?'

She told him she was. The police had given her the terrible news when she was at home. She was ringing to see how he was.

'I'm fine. When was the last time you saw Chuck?'

'Two days ago,' she said.

It didn't surprise Harry since both of them had been spending less time in the office once the work had dried up.

If it was true.

Could he ask her over the phone about Chuck's possible affair? Surely it was better to do that in person?

'I'll come over to see you soon, Agnes.'

She thanked him and ended the call.

'You never asked her if she was sleeping with her boss.'

He reached down and picked up the plastic police officer. He wore the traditional blue uniform of the British

Bobby, but part of his nose had broken off in the fall. Harry peered down, but he couldn't see the missing piece.

'I'll do that face to face while you wait here.'

Amy uncrossed her legs. 'Don't you want me with you?'

'It might be easier on Agnes just to have me there.'

'I guess you're right. A girl needs all the comfort she can get in her hour of need.'

'Will you be okay here?'

She nodded. 'Of course. When will you trace those calls Chuck's daughter overheard?'

'Good point,' he said. 'I'll do it now.'

He opened his phone again and called his former station.

'Sorry to hear about Chuck,' Detective Inspector Caroline Diaz said on the other end of the line. 'How are you holding up?'

'I'm fine, but I'd like you to do me a favour regarding calls to the Connors' house over the last two months. I could contact the phone company myself, but they'd only drag their heels getting me the information, and I need it as soon as possible.'

Diaz said she'd do it. They made more small talk for thirty seconds before Harry ended the call.

When he looked at Amy, she was flicking through the book again.

'It won't be long before I'm in the big sleep, Harry. We must get this done quickly.'

He clutched the plastic police officer in his hand.

'Why? My understanding is when this is all over, you'll return to the point the Crucial Three got you from, which was six months from your death.'

He'd stopped feeling terrible for reminding her of that every time he mentioned it.

'That's correct.'

'Doesn't that mean, in theory, you could stay here for months, even years, as long as you return to that point in time you originally came from?'

'I guess so.'

'So you could stay here, moving through this period, until you were, say, sixty, and then go back to that point. Right?'

'How many times did you watch the video of my murder, Harry?'

Too many.

'More than once.'

'So you had a good view of my face.'

'I did.'

'Did I look as if I was sixty in that clip?'

'No.'

'I won't live until I'm sixty, then?'

'I guess not.'

She got off the sofa and moved towards him.

'Never forget the lesson of that spider, Harry.'

Their legs were touching when he replied.

'I won't. The big bird swooped down and ate it.'

Amy's laugh returned like a hurricane, ready to take him off to Oz. Her body trembled next to his and her eyes lit up. Her face was near his, her perfume sweeping into his lungs like Viking invaders bent on conquest. He crushed the plastic police officer in his hands when the phone rang again.

She stepped away from him as he answered it.

It was Diaz. 'Only bad news, Harry. A week ago, the phone company's records were destroyed in a computer hack. So they've got nothing for Chuck's house or any of their other customers for the last two years.'

He thanked her and ended the call. Then he told Amy the news. He watched her reach into her pocket and remove a pill.

'This might solve all our problems, partner.'

Harry removed the broken bits of plastic from his hand and dropped them onto the desk, watching tiny legs and arms move in opposite directions. The head peered at him through empty eyes as he considered her words.

'Many people have claimed for years that pharmaceuticals solve all of our problems, but I'm not sure that's the case.'

Harry watched Amy roll the pill between her fingers as a long-forgotten memory rushed back to him: a recollection of his mother.

Since leaving the care home, he'd pushed what his father had told him to the rear of his mind, wanting it to be true and not true at the same time. If Lily had run away when she was fourteen, there was a chance she was alive somewhere. The other option – the one he hadn't stopped thinking about for twenty-six years – was she'd been abducted, and if that was the case then, no matter how much he'd wished otherwise, it was likely she was dead.

So he wanted what his father had said to be true while still not believing his mother could have been capable of abusing her daughter.

But now, a memory had returned. It was of him and Lily coming home after a walk by the river and the look he'd seen on his mother's face when they'd stepped through the door. Her eyes had been large and burning when she'd told him to go to the neighbours while Lily and she prepared the food for later. He'd done it without a second thought, only thinking of next door's dog.

Harry had forgotten about the rest of that day until now,

the image of it flooding back to him: how red Lily's eyes were as they'd sat around the dinner table; how her voice trembled when she'd told their father about their walk.

Did my mother hit Lily while I was out of the house? And if so, how many other times did it happen?

Guilt washed over him until he drowned in it as Amy kept rolling that pill.

Why Lily and not me? Why didn't she hurt me?

He pushed aside any desire to discover who'd killed Chuck and Amy. All he wanted was to grab that pill, swallow it and find the door to take him back to when he was ten and see what he'd missed in his family.

'Do you want to know what happened to Chuck?'

He took the pill from her and watched as she got one for herself.

'Can we travel to that Tube station just before his death?'

Her eyes narrowed until they were shadows creeping out of an ominous alley.

'We'll try, Harry, but I doubt we'll be able to get that close. We need to think of being in the station ten minutes before the tragic events.'

He nodded. Then they took the pills.

Everything went dark for him before it transformed into a blinding light. He shielded his eyes from it until the illumination lessened, and he was in that corridor again.

The Doors of Perception.

They shimmered around him, but Amy wasn't there.

She must be in her library.

There were too many doors to count, but he felt the heat coming off them. He moved towards the closest and stretched out his arm, moving his hand to push it open.

But he couldn't. The temperature forced him away.

It was the same with all the others. He had no sense of time there as he travelled along the corridor, trying to get close to each door, but failing.

So he gave up.

He closed his eyes and thought about being back in the office.

Amy was sitting on the desk when he opened his eyes.

'I couldn't touch any of the doors, never mind open them.'

The heat was inside him now, burning his blood to near explosion point.

'It was the same for me,' she said. 'All the book covers were blank. I was thrown back before huge shadows slithered into the library when I tried to touch one. That's when I returned here.'

'What does that mean?'

Amy reached into her pocket. She removed a handkerchief and handed it to him for the blood dripping from his palm.

'It means it's impossible to get close to the event. So we need to look at the CCTV footage in more detail. Do you think there's a better version than the one shown on the TV?'

He wrapped the cloth around his hand.

'Yes. And I know exactly where to find it.'

24 YOUR SILENT FACE

The air was thick when they stepped outside, heavy with the type of fog Harry hadn't seen in years. Then the rain came, a great slanting sheet that hung on the wind like the blade falling onto the executioner's block. He zipped his jacket up as far as it would go, looking at Amy in her thin suit and wondering if they should head to his flat for sturdier clothes.

But she didn't seem bothered by the conditions.

'This is time pushing back on us because we tried to get close to your partner's death.'

Water dripped down Harry's forehead as he spoke.

'What?'

The weather chilled his skin, but it wasn't as cold as the look she gave him.

'I told you the elements wouldn't let us get near to what happened to Chuck.'

His mouth was open so wide, the rain was gathering under his lip.

'You're saying time is a force that will push back against

any changes?' He peered at her through the fog. 'And it's causing this bad weather? Is that because you're someplace you shouldn't be?'

She grinned as she slapped him on the shoulder.

'I'm messing with you, Harry.' Her dark hair glistened in the rain. 'This is just bad weather. Where are we going?'

'To the Met,' he said. 'They should have the CCTV footage of Chuck's death.'

'Why would they give it to you?'

He was surprised at the question. 'Because I was his business partner.'

'Indeed. But if they don't think it was an accident or suicide, they might consider it was foul play. So then they could wonder if you're in the frame for that.'

He thought about that. 'I'll tell them it's connected to a case I'm investigating and I'd like copies of both videos.'

Amy narrowed her eyes at him. 'Let me guess – the other investigation is my murder?'

Harry nodded. 'A former partner owes me a favour. She'll do what I ask.'

'Okay.' She pointed across the road. 'Are you taking me on another walk?'

He glared at her as he made a phone call. 'No. We'll take a taxi.'

Thirty minutes later, they were walking into the headquarters of the Met Police at New Scotland Yard. Harry glanced at his reflection in the glass as they stepped into the reception. He'd dried out during the journey, but there were still drops of rain lingering in his ears. And some of that fog appeared to have taken up rent inside his skull. He shook his head to clear his mind as he went to a familiar face at the desk.

'Hi, Jodie,' he said as he smiled at her through damp lips.

She returned his grin. 'Hooky, you old dog. Have you come crawling back for your job?'

They laughed together and he found it hard to believe it had been six months since he was last in this building.

'Maybe next week, Jodie. Is Caroline here today?'

Harry hadn't seen Caroline Diaz since he'd left.

'I'll check for you.' She picked up a phone, but didn't dial it. 'I'm sorry about Chuck, Harry. Such a terrible accident.'

Accident? Do they know something I don't?

He moved from the desk and sat with Amy in the reception.

'Your old colleagues have a high definition copy of my murder?'

'Yes,' he said.

'Okay, but you haven't thought this through, have you?'

'What do you mean?'

She leant in close, her cheek brushing against his and making Harry's chest feel as if it was full of candy floss.

'Why does Jodie keep glancing at me?'

He looked up at his former colleague just as she turned her head from them.

'She probably thinks you're my new girlfriend.'

Amy touched his knee. 'Well, as flattering as that is, I don't think it's the reason.'

'She's on her way down to see you, Harry,' Jodie shouted.

'What's the reason, then?'

She sighed. 'For a clever man, you can be dumb.' She put her hand on his shoulder and turned his face to hers.

'This former colleague of yours coming here to talk to you; I assume she's watched my murder several times.'

Icy fingers clutched at Harry's heart as he realised what she meant.

'Christ, when Caroline sees you....'

She let go of him. 'We'll tell her I'm my sister.'

Harry rubbed at his chin. 'Hang on; she knows you're a time traveller, so it shouldn't be confusing.'

She laughed so loudly Jodie looked over again.

'Are you sure?'

'No, I'm not,' he said. He touched her arm. 'There's a pub around the corner. You wait there and I'll meet you when I leave here.'

The disappointment in her eyes stabbed him in the heart.

'Okay, if that's what you want.' She got up. 'But don't take forever. I'm easily bored and there's no telling what I'll do if I'm left on my own for too long.'

He watched Amy wink at Jodie as she went. His breathing was just about returning to normal when Caroline stepped towards him.

'Is this about Chuck?'

That was it – no warm greeting or asking Harry how he was.

It was to be expected.

'Sort of. I need a favour from you, Caroline.'

Diaz glanced across the reception as if she was working undercover and didn't want anybody seeing her talking to Harry.

'Favours are in short supply around here at the moment.' She didn't add the words, *especially for you,* but Harry knew she was thinking them. 'The politicians are calling for reform in the Met again and it hasn't gone down too well.'

'It needs reforming, Caroline. You know that.'

'Bad apples are everywhere, Harry, but they're in the minority.'

'The majority protect the minority.'

DI Caroline Diaz looked ready to leave. 'What do you want?'

'Is the Amy Croft murder case still open?'

'The so-called time traveller?' She laughed. 'It's not on our priority list. We've got terrorists, agitators, serial rapists, drug gangs, people traffickers, and all the random murders and petty crimes to deal with.' Caroline scrutinised Harry. 'And SD deal with alleged temporal crimes.'

Harry offered her his phone. 'Can you put a copy of the CCTV footage on there for me? And the video from Chuck's death at the Tube station?'

Caroline laughed at him. 'Is this entrapment? You want me to commit a crime?'

'You owe me a favour, Caroline.'

His former partner glared at him for a full forty-five seconds. Then she snatched the device from Harry and returned from where she'd come.

Harry watched her, wondering how long it would take to transfer the files and scrutinise everything on Harry's phone.

It took twenty minutes.

Diaz threw the mobile at him, Harry catching it in one hand.

'Thanks, partner,' he said.

'Don't come back, Harry,' Diaz said as he left.

Harry said goodbye to Jodie and went to the pub.

When he entered, Amy was sitting in a booth with a pint of cider waiting for him.

He sat and took a large gulp from it. 'You know what I like to drink?'

She sipped at her drink. 'Mary Hazell told me. I think she'd studied you for months before you got the invite into the TA.'

The place was busy, with people standing at the bar while others dropped money into flickering glittering machines. Amy leant towards him, the flick of her hair distracting Harry from what he was going to say. Blood burst out of his heart, speeding through his veins like a cheetah chasing an antelope.

I'm trapped inside my own Pandora's Box.

'Studied me how?'

Her eyes sparkled with the knowledge he was desperate to acquire.

'I guess she searched for you on the internet.'

She settled into her seat and he felt the pressure in his bones lessen.

'Why would she do that when she could have gone back in time and watched everything I've ever done?'

Amy nearly spat cider all over him. 'I'm surprised you got through the door with such a big head.'

'You know what I mean. Instead of staring at bland details about me, all she had to do was take two or three trips into the past to see what I'm like.'

She raised her pint to him. 'You don't have any bland details, Harry, and who's to say Mary or one of the others didn't take a pill or two to spy on the younger you?' The bubbles in the glass rose to the top. 'I'm tempted to try that myself.'

He downed half of his cider before removing his phone.

'Are you going to watch this with me?'

Amy moved over to sit next to him. 'Scrunch up, partner.'

Her body leant into his and he knew he'd be on his second pint in about five minutes. He found the footage from the Tube and prepared himself for watching Chuck die again. There was no sound to the clip, which lasted one minute and twenty seconds, from Chuck entering the station to him jumping onto the track just before the train arrived. Even though it was mute, Harry could hear the screech of the wheels and the cries of the other passengers echoing in his head.

They watched it six times before he'd had enough. He dumped his mobile on the table and finished his drink.

'He killed himself; it's clear as day on there.'

She grabbed his phone. 'Can you send the clip to my phone?'

'Sure,' he said. 'Does it have a wireless connection?'

She grinned at him as she took the mobile from her pocket.

'It's from the future, Harry. It can get you to the moon and back.'

Amy placed both phones together and he watched her press something on her device. While the data transfer was happening, he went to the bar and got two more pints of cider. By the time he'd returned, the transfer was completed and she had her face pushed into the screen.

He sat and put the drinks on the table as music erupted behind him. It took him a few seconds to realise it was some bloke murdering a version of *Lucy In The Sky With Diamonds*.

'Did you watch the clip again?' he said to her.

'Three times. I ran it through special software I have;

it's much better for slowing down individual frames than anything you have now.'

She held the phone out to him, but he left it hanging there.

'What you're doing here: sitting in this pub, running the video through software which shouldn't exist at this time; aren't you changing the past by doing that?'

Amy pulled the mobile from him and put it on the table. Then she drank from her second pint.

'Do we need to talk about spiders again?'

Harry shook his head and sipped at his drink.

'I'm just trying to get my mind around this whole can't change history thing.' He wiped cider from his lips. 'You must admit it hurts the noggin' just thinking about it.'

'Noggin? I don't think we have that word where I come from.'

'Maybe you'll take me there sometime,' he said.

'Maybe,' she said, 'maybe. Now, do you want to see what I've found?'

Of course he did. This time, he went and sat next to her, squeezing against her so he could feel the heat coming from Amy's body.

Then she showed him the clip again. Harry had seen plenty of death up close and personal in his life, but repeatedly watching Chuck jumping in front of that train left a gaping hole in his chest.

'I see nothing different.'

'Yes, but look what happens when I slow it down and run it through the software frame by frame.'

He did, and it didn't take long to see what she meant: in the frames just before Chuck jumped, there was a sparkling blink of light in each one.

'Is that a lens flare or a fault on the camera?'

Amy stopped the clip. 'It could be, but I don't think so. I believe it's the reason your partner died.'

Harry tore his gaze away from the final image of Chuck. 'What is it?'

She pointed at the light on the frozen frame.

'That's a time traveller appearing and vanishing in an instant. They pushed Chuck onto the track: this is murder.'

25 GUILTY PARTNER

They sat in silence while they finished their drinks before Harry put his glass on the table.

'Are you sure?'

Amy nodded. 'That blinking light is moving so fast, you can't see it in the video. That's because it's a traveller phasing in and out of time.'

'You've seen this kind of thing before?'

'Not the murder, but yes. One of the first experiments I ran with Mary, Sally and Rose was to observe how many times we could travel between short points. We called it phasing, but we never got it to be that precise where it worked between seconds.'

He didn't look at her, only at the picture on her phone.

'If this is true, you know what it means, don't you?'

'Yes. A time traveller murdered Chuck Connors.'

He shifted in the seat, pushing his legs into hers and enjoying the feeling.

Until he looked at that image again.

'Not just a time traveller, Amy – it has to be one of the Crucial Three.'

Her head was next to hers. 'Why would they kill your partner?'

'I don't know and we need to find out.'

'When was the last time you saw Chuck?'

'Before I set off for those tests at the TA building.'

'What did you do after you saw him?'

'I had another case.'

'Okay. We can't get close to the murder, so we have to go further back and start from that point. Let's travel to the morning of your TA tests and meet outside your office. Will Chuck be at work then?'

Harry nodded. 'He pops in first thing every morning to check the mail.'

She offered him a pill with another in her hand. 'Let's see how near we can get to that time.'

He took the pill from her while watching more people flood into the pub.

'Shouldn't we do this somewhere else?'

'It makes no difference, Harry. Whoever sees us will think they've had too much to drink. I already have the location of your office. Focus on the park opposite and the time you gave me.'

They swallowed the pills together just as Johnny Rotten was singing there was no future on the jukebox. Everything around Harry shimmered, a haze drifting over his eyes before vanishing to be replaced by those familiar rows of doors on either side of him.

Amy wasn't there, but he'd expected that.

Before taking the pill, he'd thought of Chuck and their last meeting together, visualising the calendar on his desk and the clock on the wall. It was different from the other times he'd travelled: the doors in the corridor were changed, which was perhaps to do with how he'd focused on Chuck and the office. Each door had a date and time on it. One of them displayed the exact point he'd sat in the office when Chuck had mentioned working for the Time Authority. In theory, from everything he'd experienced so far, if he went through that door, he'd find Chuck with his younger self. Amy had told him to think about the park opposite the building so they could discover what happened to Chuck, not save him.

But he had to try, at least.

And there was no overpowering heat coming off the doors.

Harry placed his hand on the door and pushed.

Nothing happened.

He tried again, harder this time, but with the same results. Finally, he put his shoulder to the door and used both hands. Even so, it wouldn't move. After two minutes of fruitless effort, he gave up and took a step back.

Was it closed to him because something, Time itself with a capital T, recognised what he'd do if he got through? Was this what Amy had meant when she'd said the past couldn't be changed? Was Time an entity a living, conscious being which would push back at human efforts to change it? Hazell had implied something had happened to her hand when she'd attempted to alter her past. She'd also hinted at worse things that had happened to others who'd tried the same thing.

He didn't care. He wanted to change Chuck and Amy's fates and, no matter what everyone had told him, he had to try.

Harry reached into his jacket and removed the container of pills Amy had given him earlier. Did they modify the human brain to allow the taker to bend the perception of time and space to step through a door into the past?

Or were they just another bluff like the lift and the Time Authority Technology Phase Shifting Machine had been?

Harry considered this conundrum as he glanced at the doors, finding the one for the morning of his TA tests. Then he pictured the park opposite his office.

He pushed it open, stepping through it and straight into a bunch of rose bushes. The door disappeared behind him as his legs brushed against crowns of thorns.

'You took your time getting here.'

He turned to stare at Amy. 'What?'

She grinned. 'It's a traveller joke. I just got here as well.'

'Were you inside your library again?' She nodded. 'What book did you see to bring you here?'

'There was a photo of this building on the front and the date and time. So it was an easy pick.'

'What would have happened if we'd picked different times?'

'Then one of us would have been waiting around for the other. But, thankfully, we both chose the right time.' She pointed across the road. 'Look.'

Harry did and saw Chuck leaving the building.

'Is your car here?' Amy said.

'Yes, I drove to the office, and then took the Tube to the TA building.'

'Good, then we can follow him.'

Chuck turned the corner and they moved after him.

'We always park our cars in the same spot, on opposite sides of the street next to our office. We have to let him pull out first.'

They watched him step into the car before Harry led Amy into the other vehicle.

Chuck set off and they followed.

'Don't get too close to him,' Amy said. 'I'm assuming a security expert will know when he's being trailed.'

He laughed. 'Chuck's no expert. He provided the finances for the business, while I brought the security and deduction expertise.'

'It's a shame his money didn't last so long.'

'Indeed,' Harry said. 'I'll need to return the car to the office in less than an hour, or Chuck will notice it missing if he returns.'

He kept away from Chuck, but still in the line of sight. Wherever he was going, it wasn't home to his wife and daughter. Chuck stopped at a red light, so Harry did the same as he glanced at Amy.

'There are two versions of me at this point. Me in the car here and a younger version on the way to the Time Authority building.'

'You're correct in that there are at least two versions of you at this point.'

The light changed to green and he followed Chuck again.

'You mean there could be more?'

'Of course, Harry. There could be infinite versions of you all over the place at this very moment. Especially if this gets messy in the next fifty minutes.'

He wound down the window to ease the pressure on his brain. The car slowed a little as Chuck approached a junction. An aroma of fried chicken drifted in through the window and Harry's stomach groaned. He couldn't remember the last time he'd eaten, and those two pints of cider were playing havoc with his guts. He turned right and followed his partner.

Then he asked another question, one he'd mentioned to the Crucial Three before.

'Do travellers continue to age at the same rate when they move through time?'

She turned the radio on and someone was singing about the last night at a fair. 'Absolutely. The human body still ages as normal.'

'So, if I spend a year in the past, and then return to a minute after I originally left, I'll have aged a year in mind and body, but only one minute in real physical time?'

Chuck parked outside a coffee shop, so Harry pulled up on the opposite side of the street.

'The question you have to ask yourself is what do you mean by real physical time?'

He rubbed his temple as Chuck got out of the car and entered the coffee shop. He ignored her impossible conundrum.

'Do we follow him and go inside?'

'There's no need.' She reached into her jacket for her phone. 'This is all we require to discover what he's up to.'

She tapped on the screen to open the camera app and pointed the mobile at the front of the building.

'Unless he takes a window seat, you won't be able to see him with that. And even then, you'll need a powerful zoom.'

She patted him on the knee like he was a child. 'Don't you worry about that.'

Amy moved her arm to the right and adjusted the aim. He watched the screen as she did so, amazed as the lens went into the coffee shop, and then swept around the corners as she modified the direction until she found what she wanted – Harry's partner at a table with someone he knew: Dr Rose Adler.

'What's Chuck doing with her?'

'Let's find out, shall we?' She changed a setting on the device and sound bounced into the car. Adler's voice was so clear, it was as if she was next to them.

'Did you convince him?'

'He took little convincing, Dr Adler. He wants the business to be as successful as I do.' Harry stared at the screen, watching as Chuck placed his hands on the table. A server brought glasses of water to them. 'Though I still don't see why we can't tell him the truth.'

Adler put her hand on his. 'What we're doing here, Charles, will change history.'

Charles? Even his wife didn't call Chuck that. What was going on between them? What had Harry's old friend got him into? He was close to Amy as they gazed into the screen, his leg pushed into hers, taking in the aroma of her perfume, watching her flesh move as she breathed. His mind drifted away until he remembered she'd be dead soon.

Adler continued. 'You're both playing a part in saving humanity from itself. Harry will learn the truth in good time, but we have to make sure everything is on course before that. You said yourself if he knew the details of what we're about to do, he'd put a stop to it.'

Harry watched Chuck try to pull his hand away, but she wouldn't budge. She ran a finger over his skin.

'I feel guilty, though.' Harry heard that guilt in his voice. 'I don't like keeping secrets from Sarah and Kelly.'

'It won't be long now, Charles, and then you'll all be able to start new lives together, wherever and whenever you want.'

Harry rested his head against the seat.

Is that what this was all about: Chuck taking his family to live in the past? But what was he helping the Crucial Three with and how was I involved?

Adler took her hand away and Chuck stood. He pulled at the top of his shirt and drank the water. Then he nodded to her and left.

Amy turned to Harry. 'I think you need to have a word with your partner.'

He wiped the sweat from his forehead. 'Okay.' He watched Chuck leave the building. 'Should we do it now?'

Chuck got into his car and drove off.

'There's no time like the present,' Amy said.

They followed Chuck to his home. Sarah and Kelly greeted him at the door with hugs and they went inside.

'You stay here,' Harry said.

She didn't protest as Harry strode towards the house with only one thought in his head.

Can I prevent Chuck's murder?

Chuck looked surprised to see Harry when he opened the door.

'Hi, partner.' He scratched at his wrist, nervousness wearing him like a jacket. 'Didn't you go to the meeting I arranged with you at the Authority building?'

'I need to speak to you, Chuck.'

He glanced over Harry's shoulder, his eyes darting everywhere.

'Sure, Harry, of course, of course.' He stood to the side and let Harry in before ushering him into his study. There was no sign of Sarah or Kelly. 'Do you want a drink?'

He went to the cabinet and removed a bottle of bourbon.

'Not for me, Chuck.'

He shrugged, but poured himself a large one, neat. Then he checked his watch.

'We need that contract, Harry. I worked hard to get you into the Authority building as well.' The ice cubes in the glass rattled as it shook between his fingers.

'Don't worry, partner, I got the job.'

His eyes sparkled as he gulped down half of the bourbon. 'That's great, Harry.' Then realisation sank into his brain along with the alcohol. 'So, how can you be here now when you should be there?' He looked at his watch again. 'The tests won't have started yet, unless...'

'I told you, I got the job. Then I travelled back in time to see you.'

Chuck bit into the top of the glass. 'But why would you do that?'

'Because I discovered something important, something you need to know. So I came here to visit you.'

Chuck finished the rest of the drink and shook his head, his eyes cradled in confusion.

'You've travelled back in time instead of talking to me in your present? Why, Harry?'

Harry ignored his question. 'I saw you with Dr Adler in the coffee shop.' He didn't reveal he'd heard their conversation. 'What were you doing with her? Why did the Time Authority come to you to get to me?'

His eyes darted everywhere, searching for something or other in the room. Then he poured himself another bourbon, without offering Harry one, and slumped into the chair behind his desk. Papers were spread across much of it, and a glance told Harry most of them were bills.

Chuck saw Harry looking at them.

'Understand, partner. I was swamped in debt with no way out of it. It was only a matter of time before I'd lose this house, and then the business – our business – would be gone as well.' He rifled through the papers in front of him, clutched a few, and squeezed them into his fist. 'If it hadn't been for my father and the crippling debts he left me, we'd have been okay, I'm sure of it. But no matter what I did, no matter how many times I tried to find more work for us, things only got worse and worse. And then Adler came to me and said she had a proposition which would eliminate all of our problems.'

The sparkle returned to his eyes and Harry needed that drink. He strode across to the cabinet and poured himself a double.

'What proposition?'

'They wanted you to help them find out who killed their colleague, Amy Croft. Adler believed you were the best person for the job and I agreed with her. And then there was a bonus.'

Harry bit through a piece of ice and water slipped from his lips.

'Tell me about this bonus, Chuck.'

He jerked out of his chair, finding a paper on the desk and grabbing it. He held it towards Harry.

'Here, look at this.' Harry took it from him. 'I thought it was great they wanted you in their organisation. I mean, what a privilege that is, but, to be honest, this was just as important to me.'

Harry sipped at his drink and read the paper: a Bill of Sale for the factory Chuck's father had left him that was adding to his growing debt every day.

'Why does the Time Authority want this?'

Chuck grinned and shrugged. 'I don't know and, to be honest, I don't care. It just means I can be free of the debt my father burdened me with. It also means we can concentrate on the business with nothing else to worry about.'

'There's something not right about this, Chuck.'

Is this why he was murdered? Why would a time traveller kill him at the Tube station? And should I tell him what is coming?

'I was going to tell you all of this, Harry, once you

passed the Authority's tests. I had no doubts you would. But why aren't we having this conversation tomorrow? Why did you travel back to see me?'

He must have read my mind.

Before Harry could reply, Kelly burst into the room.

'Uncle Harry!' She ran forward and threw her arms around him. She let go after squeezing for a minute, her father's eyes never straying from Harry's. 'Did you get me a present from the future?'

I don't know if she overheard us or Chuck told her what I was doing with the Authority, but her question has unnerved me. And Chuck as well, I think.

Harry winked at her. 'Maybe I'll bring you a baby dinosaur tomorrow, kid.'

She screamed with joy as her mother walked into the room.

'You'll have to go through me first, Hooky.'

All the family was there now, Kelly bouncing up and down as Chuck and Sarah held each other. How could Harry reveal what was waiting for them in the near future? Before he could say anything, the doorbell rang.

'I'll get it.' Kelly ran from the room as Chuck continued to stare at Harry.

'I hear you're about to become an agent of the Authority,' Sarah said.

Harry tried to smile. 'I'm not sure that's what they call them.'

Call us.

Kelly shouted, 'Dad! There's a woman here to see Uncle Harry.'

Harry guessed Amy had grown impatient waiting outside. At least it gave him an excuse to leave.

'I'll see you at work tomorrow, partner,' Chuck said as Harry walked past him and headed for the door.

Will this be the last time I ever see him, or will I travel through time again to visit him before his murder?

Amy was standing away from the house. Harry assumed this was to avoid worrying Chuck too much if he saw her.

'Did you miss me?' he said to her.

'Did you get anything useful from him?'

He told her what Chuck had said about Adler and selling his factory to the Time Authority.

'We should visit that place and see what the Authority wants it for,' Harry said.

She didn't appear too interested in that. 'Do you think it will help in discovering who murdered your friend?'

'It might. What other options do we have?'

'We have to find my killer, remember?'

Of course. I still have the video footage imprinted inside my head.

As they walked to the car, Harry's mobile rang.

He let it ring and looked at Amy. 'If there are two of me – or at least two – in this time, are both versions of my phone ringing at the same time?'

'Just answer it, Harry.'

So he did. 'Hello, Agnes.'

'I've found your missing girl, Harry.'

He was confused about who she meant with his mind full of time travel and death.

'Which girl?'

'Christine Kerr. You promised her parents you'd find her and you've come up with zilch in a week. You're slipping, Harry. Don't make me look for another job again.'

'I remember her, Agnes.' According to her parents, Christine was a sixteen-year-old runaway they wanted back and, having gone to the police, they were getting nowhere in finding her, which is why they'd gone to Harry. They never said why she ran away, but that wasn't his concern until he located her. 'You say you've found her?'

'Ten minutes ago, she was spotted going into Madame Tussauds. My contact keeps me updated by text and the girl is still inside. So get yourself over there.' She hung up before Harry could reply.

'What now?' Amy appeared bored, her gaze focused on Chuck's house.

'I've more than one job to do, and surely a time traveller can be flexible in what they do and when.'

She pouted at him. 'I guess so, but I'm coming with you.'

'No problem,' Harry said.

They got into the car and he drove away, his mind packed with what Chuck had told him. His partner's unusual behaviour was driven by the debts he'd inherited from his father, so pushing Harry into the arms of the Time Authority to remove the financial albatross of that factory hanging over him made sense.

But there was something niggling away at the back of his mind.

'What's bothering you, Harry? If we're going to work together, you can't keep things from me.'

Harry kept one eye on the road as he answered.

'There's still so much I don't understand with time travel and it's interfering with my focus. You're an expert in this, so maybe you could help me.'

She stretched her legs and raised her knees to be up against the front of the car.

'Fire away, partner. I promise to try my best.'

She flicked at that distinctive hair of hers and he felt like he'd stumbled into a 1920s jazz bar.

'Okay, take that call I just got from Agnes. Why didn't that go to the phone of the other me in this period? This is my past. So I shouldn't have received that call, should I?'

Amy raised her finger and wagged it at him. 'You must be confused, Harry. The other you, the younger you, is going through the Authority tests at the moment.

'Didn't you leave your phone in a TA locker?'

'I did, but which of us would have received that call?'

She ran the finger over her perfect cheek and considered the question.

'I don't know, Harry. It's a puzzle.'

It wasn't the only one, but there was no time to ask any more questions as they approached Madame Tussauds. Harry parked on Great Portland Street and they walked the rest of the way. Agnes continued to send him texts to inform him Christine was still inside. There was a small queue outside and he considered what their next move should be. It would be full of tourists, so trying to get the girl and bring her out without a commotion seemed unlikely. It would be better to wait there for her.

He turned to Amy. 'Have you ever been inside?'

She peered at the front of the building, its green dome stretching into the sky.

'Have they replaced the wax figures with androids yet?'

'Androids? What do you mean?'

She smiled at him. 'Haven't you heard? They're going to update the attractions, so they move around and interact with the public.' She turned her back on Tussauds. 'Why don't we wait in that café opposite? I can't remember the last time I had something to eat, which can be tricky when you're jumping between different periods.' Her grin grew wider. 'I assume you know what this girl looks like and will recognise her when she leaves Tussauds?'

Harry's hunger clawed at his guts. 'Of course I do.' Plus, he had photos of her on his phone. 'Come on. I'll treat you to something to eat.'

He glanced at his phone as he went, wondering if Agnes's texts had also gone to the other phone in the TA building.

If they had, wouldn't I have seen them before this?

27 SOMEONE LIKE YOU

The café was only half-full, so they took a table near the window with a perfect position to see the building. Agnes's contact must have been following Christine inside as Harry was getting constant updates to let him know the girl was still there. Amy ordered a coffee while he went with green tea and lemon. She got a burger, fries, and salad with her drink. His hunger had lessened, so he settled for a grilled chicken wrap.

They sat in silence while they waited for the food, with Harry pretending to check the messages on his phone. Amy spent the time watching the clip of Chuck's death again, seemingly fascinated by that blip of light frozen in each frame.

She was quick to identify that as a time traveller.

Maybe too quick.

He scrolled through the photos he had of Christine Kerr. He'd accepted the case as a favour to her parents, people he'd met when investigating a random attack on the father. Harry and his Met colleagues had never discovered who the attackers were, and he always felt guilty when that happened. This was why he'd taken no fee from the Kerrs to look for their daughter, which hadn't gone down too well with his business partner.

'Are you sure you're not doing it because of what happened to Lily?' Chuck had said during their disagreement.

Harry wasn't sure. Thousands of teenagers went missing in the UK every year, hundreds in London. So what were the odds he could find this specific one?

He thought about that as their food arrived and Amy dived into hers.

Bits of beef dripped over her lips as she gazed at him, slurping coffee into the meat sticking between her teeth.

'Go on then, Harry. While we're here, I know you want to quiz me some more.'

It was an invitation he couldn't resist.

'I don't believe you, Hazell, and the others. I think you can alter history. The Crucial Three and you have tried to hammer it into me since the beginning, but I'm convinced that has been another of their deceptions.'

Amy removed a slice of tomato from the bun and dropped it on the table.

'The past can't be changed, Harry. I thought you understood this by now.'

'All I know is I've been told that many times, but I've never seen it in action. Even with what Mary Boleyn said at the care home, I don't think she told me everything that happened to her mother and those early TA volunteers. There's a bigger reason than wanting justice for her mother that has driven Boleyn to lead the protests against the Crucial Three. She knows Adler and the others have been lying to the world since the beginning.'

Amy's eyes narrowed. 'You think they're lying to you and the world? Why would they do that?'

Harry pushed his plate away, losing his appetite.

'When people realised time travel was possible, apart from seeing what the future holds, altering the past was the only thing anyone was interested in. All across the world, governments, organisations, businesses, and individuals desired the ability to go back and alter what had gone before. And the only thing standing in their way were three women who said yes, we can travel in time, but no, we can't change anything. I'm guessing most people thought they might be lying about that.'

She waved a fry at him. 'Why would Rose, Sally, and Mary do that?'

Harry dropped two sugar cubes into his tea to erase its bitterness.

'I can think of many reasons.' He glanced across the road to see the queue had increased outside Tussauds. He hadn't had a message from Agnes in five minutes. 'The main one is the panic it would cause if it were possible to interfere with history. Every nation on the planet would scramble to get their hands on the Crucial Three and their technology. I assume most would do anything, would sink to any levels, to control that amount of power.' Harry let her consider what he'd said. 'But if all time travel could do was go back and record history, well, there's limited use in that for the power grabbers in the world. Sure, we could discover if President Kennedy was assassinated by Oswald or what happened to the Lindbergh baby or Lord Lucan, but if that's all it could do, then time travel wouldn't change anything, would it? So the Crucial Three wrapped themselves in Rose Adler's wealth and bought the protection they needed, and then apparently spent a decade recruiting a few people to become time travellers in the Time Authority.

'And while they were telling the world they were only observers of history, they were working on offering people one chance to see again someone they'd lost in their lives. It all sounds wonderful and altruistic, but I'm not buying it.'

Tomato sauce glistened on Amy's lips.

'I told you, Harry, I'm sure at some point they'll monetise the technology. They'll have to since they're running out of money. But if you still don't believe me, what do you think is really going on, especially now you've been invited inside the hallowed halls of the Authority?'

'I believe we can change time, and you're with me so we can go back and prevent your death. So I don't know why we're messing around trying to discover your killer when we can stop it from happening.'

Amy finished her food and reached for the salt and pepper pots. Then she took another two from the next table and placed them on top of the others, where they wobbled until she steadied them with her fingers.

'Look at what happens, Harry, when you try to put the same items into the same spot.'

She let go of the top pots and they fell off, discarding bits of salt and pepper everywhere. He stared at the mess and knew what she was getting at.

'The TV interview where there were two versions of Adler, Cohen, and Hazell, the so-called Secret Six, proved that to be untrue. And even if that were the case, it wouldn't prevent me from going back and stopping your murder because I wasn't there in the first place.'

Amy sipped at her coffee. 'Many people think the whole TV thing, also known as the Sinister Six in some quarters, was faked using doubles or doppelgängers.'

He laughed at her. 'You'll be telling me that time travel is a fake as well next.'

She returned his grin. 'No, Harry, time travel is real. I understand that better than anybody. The ability to change the past is what's impossible. I also know this to be true from bitter experience.'

'So, sometime soon, you'll leave me and journey into the past, to the point you came from, and wait for your death. You'll wait to be murdered?'

Her hands were in the air, her expression a mixture of resignation and frustration.

'What else can I do? Time can't be changed.' She said it with such conviction, yet he still had his doubts. 'And now I have to pay a visit to the little girls' room.'

Amy got up and left while he considered her words, gazing out of the window, watching Kerr leaving Tussauds. Christine lingered outside as if waiting for someone. Harry wouldn't drag the girl back to her parents, but he needed to speak to her, tell her how worried they were, and perhaps hear her version of events. Then he could decide on telling her parents, and maybe the police, where she was. He could get Diaz there in fewer than five minutes, and it would be easy enough for the Met to detain her until her parents saw her again. Then they could sort the whole mess out themselves.

Harry had decided he'd speak to her when he saw a woman approaching Christine. He couldn't see her face since she wore a large hat, but recognised something familiar about how she walked. There was a swagger and confidence in her which nipped at his brain.

She must have been the person Christine was waiting for as she waved at the woman. Dread rushed through him as the woman got closer, her jacket and jeans as stylish as anything from Bond Street.

What if this woman is one of those who befriend young girls with the promise of expensive gifts and clothes, only to procure them for trafficking gangs?

Harry had seen plenty of that during his time in the Met.

He kept scanning the surrounding area, checking if anybody else was approaching Christine, maybe hired thugs to drag her into a vehicle.

He was ready to rush out at any second.

Then Harry focused on the woman in the hat.

His nails bit into the table as she removed her hat and threw her arms around Christine. Even before she pulled away from the girl, he knew who she was. He continued staring at her as Amy returned.

'Are you going to tell me about that?' he said.

They gazed at Christine and her companion.

'Well, I never,' Amy said as she stared at another version of herself.

'Why is there another you talking to Christine?'

Amy threw up her hands. 'I don't know. That's obviously a later version of me.'

He glared at her. 'How many more of you are going to turn up?'

She played with the salt and pepper pots, rolling them between her fingers.

'Who knows? Maybe dozens of me will come down the street, and dozens of you will confront them, the mood you're in.'

Harry smashed his hand against the table, forcing the sauce bottle to fall over and spill its contents. Pain rippled up his arm.

'I'll tell Christine who you really are.'

Amy dismissed the idea with a wave of her fingers.

'Maybe she already knows. Perhaps she's with the other me because I'm going to take her through time so she can get away from her abusive parents. Maybe she was inside Madame Tussauds to check out where she wants to go in the past. Have you thought about that?'

Despite all the things racing through his head, that wasn't one of them. So he got up to leave.

'I'm off to see Chuck and tell him to stay at home for the rest of the week, to keep away from Brixton Tube station and stay alive.'

'You can't do that, Harry. You've no idea what terrible events you'll cause. You can't change history.'

Christine and the other Amy continued to talk across the road. He glanced around the café and saw a flaw in her constant insistence that the past couldn't be changed.

He sat back down. 'If the past can't be changed, then how come I'm here now?'

She played dumb. 'What do you mean?'

'This is the past for me, right? I didn't come to this café originally because right now, I'm over at the Authority building going through those time travel tests. So I've changed the past by coming here, haven't I?'

She lifted one hand to her face, a finger caressing her skin.

'You've altered nothing significant, though, have you?'

Harry slapped his hand on the table again.

'But you must admit I've changed something.' She didn't reply. 'And who's to say this isn't significant?' He glanced around the café. 'The money I spent in here could change someone's life.' He stared at the server. 'I may have annoyed someone so they leave here and do something stupid. That woman watching me lose my temper might get agitated by my actions so much, she'll walk across the road without looking and cause an accident that kills several people when she leaves here. Or she could get into her car and drive carelessly, again killing others.'

He was convinced the past had been changed, but Amy wasn't.

'It doesn't work like that, Harry. I told you the Butterfly Effect is meaningless.' She glanced through the window at her other self. 'Nothing significant is different because of our trip here.'

He got up. 'I'm going to see Chuck. You can do what you want.'

'If you do that, you'll put his family in danger. Maybe all of his neighbours as well.'

'What are you talking about?'

'If you tell Chuck about his death, Time will push back on you. The consequences could be terrible for anyone close by.'

He shook his head. 'That's nonsense. You're doing this to scare me.'

'Think of the spider, Harry.'

He waved his hand at her. 'Insects aren't humans.' Then he grinned. 'Sorry, arachnids aren't the same as humans.'

She got her phone, found something on the screen, and placed it on the table.

'Do you want me to prove it to you?'

Harry looked at the device, peering at the news story. It was from a week ago, another school shooting in America.

'What are you suggesting?'

Amy picked up the mobile and held it towards him.

'How would you like the chance to go back and save the lives of five people?'

'No sane person would turn that down.'

If I could save them, then I could save Chuck. And maybe save her.

And find Lily.

He tapped on the window. 'What about those two?'

'Don't worry, Harry. They'll be there when we return.'

She handed him a pill and the phone. 'Take a good read through that and memorise the time it started. I'll meet you opposite the front of the school half an hour before.'

Amy grabbed her mobile, swallowed the pill, and then disappeared. The server behind Harry screamed and dropped a plate.

He didn't turn to look at the commotion Amy's sudden disappearance had caused.

That poor woman will be traumatised.

And that is the two of us changing our past and the server's present.

He was convinced of it now. All the times Amy and the Crucial Three had strained to persuade him that history was irreversible were for nothing. But why had they tried?

Harry put the pill on his tongue and peered out the window. As he did so, the other Amy – the one outside with Christine – glanced at him and smiled.

All the other times he'd seen that smile, it had warmed his heart.

Now it sent a chill trickling down his spine.

He took the pill and travelled to the Doors of Perception.

The corridor went on forever as he stepped towards the doors. They shimmered with light and heat, the hottest being the door with the precise location, day and time when the shooting began. The others had different times on them, reducing by minutes on each, fluctuating between one, two, and five minutes.

He moved along the corridor and found the door thirty minutes from the start of the tragedy. It was cool to the touch as he pushed it open.

The smell of gasoline settled over him as he stepped through and on to the grass.

Amy was sitting on the bench nearby. 'Is this your first time in America?'

He went to her. 'We only have half an hour to stop the shooting.'

She showed him her phone. 'The shooter, James David Addison, lives behind the school, which is across the road from here.'

He stared at the building. 'Okay, let's go to his house now.'

'Why don't we call the police? There's time for them to get here.'

'No; even if they believe us, many things might stop them from getting here on time. So we have to do it ourselves.' He moved closer to see her phone. 'How do you have the details of the tragedy on that mobile if the information is from the future? The internet can't show you that.'

'It's not from the web, Harry, not the one here anyway. I have the reports of the event recorded on this, along with many others from my past. My past, which is in the future for you.' She got up. 'It helps a lot when you're jumping in and out of different periods regularly.'

He stepped into the road. 'We need to talk about that device later.'

Amy pulled him back. 'Are you going to confront Addison?'

'Yes, and we've already lost valuable time standing here.'

'Do we have a plan?'

He thought about it for a second. 'You'll distract him while I disarm him.'

'That sounds simple. And after that?'

'Then you call the police on that fancy phone of yours. Now, how do we get to his house?'

'Follow me.' She headed towards the front of the school.

Harry strode by her side, scanning their surroundings. 'What do you know about the boy?'

'He lives with his mother. His father died two years ago. Reports after the shooting said he struggled with his father's death.'

They reached the other side of the road and the school entrance. The outside of the building looked as if it would fall apart in a strong wind. Amy nodded to the right and led him that way.

Harry searched his memory for what he'd read about the tragedy.

'He kills four, including a teacher who throws herself in front of one of her students, then takes his own life when the police arrive.'

She stopped at the end of the building. 'That's correct. His house is in the middle of that bunch on the other side of the field, 22 Oak Road.'

He glanced at the school. 'Addison gets in through an entrance at the rear; I remember that bit. So they have cameras, but no security personnel and no metal detectors?'

'Not at the moment,' she said.

He checked for movement as they went, watching a black cat run across the top of a fence as they entered the housing estate. It was eight-thirty in the morning and teenagers were making their way to school. None of them gave Amy or Harry a second look as they stepped on to Oak Road.

'Do we know what the motivation was?' he said.

She was glancing at her phone as they increased their speed. Harry guessed they had five to ten minutes to get to the house before Addison left.

'There's nothing that stands out with him. According to

his mother and teachers, he wasn't a loner and had many friends and a girlfriend. He wasn't socially awkward and was involved in student activities. The police didn't find any notes or social media posts to indicate why he did it.'

Kids hurried past them in the opposite direction as they reached number 22.

Harry peered at the house. 'Is his mother at home?'

Amy shook her head. 'No. She left for work an hour ago.' She turned to him. 'How do you want to do this?'

'I'm guessing we've got five minutes until he leaves, so there's no time to mess about. So I'll knock on the front door.'

'Okay,' she said. 'What about me?'

'You go around the back in case he comes out that way.'

'You're not worried he might kill me?'

He smiled at her. 'The past can't be changed, remember? You won't die today, Amy.'

She returned his grin. 'But you can, so don't be reckless just to prove a point.'

He didn't reply and strode to the house. He walked up to the porch and knocked on the door. Amy went to the rear as Harry waited.

He didn't check the time on his phone, but he knew it was ticking down.

If we've got both the exits covered, we'll know if he comes out.

Unless he'd already left.

Harry lost patience and pushed the door open. It swung wide and he peered inside, seeing a narrow corridor and stairs. He didn't call out as he stepped into the house. Instead, he left the front door open as he moved forward, catching an aroma of burnt toast as he reached the living room. He watched for any sudden movement as he went in.

Old magazines and newspapers covered the carpet, with an empty birdcage at the end next to a small TV.

We got here too late. He's already gone.

Then something flew at his head.

He threw his arms into the air as protection, expecting a gun or fist into his face.

Instead, the exotic bird clawed at his hands and drew blood from his fingers. He waved his arm at it and the bird fluttered out of the room. Then he took a step back, his feet finding a glossy magazine. The momentum dragged him down and he crashed into a coffee table, spilling cups and glasses everywhere.

He rolled across the floor until his shoulder hit the bottom of a sofa. A stab of electricity shot through his bones and jerked him up. When he looked to see where the bird was, James David Addison loomed over him with a gun in his hand.

'Who are you?' the teenager said.

Harry pushed his spine into the furniture and peered straight down the barrel.

I can die here. But wouldn't Amy know that if she's got details from her past recorded on that future phone of hers?

'I'm a friend, James.'

The kid grinned at Harry. 'That's funny, mister, because you don't look like any friend of mine.'

'I'm here to prevent you from doing something terrible, James.'

Addison pushed the gun closer to Harry's face.

'Stop calling me that.' He glanced around the house. 'Did Benny tell you about our plan?'

'You're going to your school to kill people, kid. It doesn't matter how I know, but I do.'

'You're right, old man; it doesn't matter.'

Harry watched him squeeze the trigger and waited for his death.

Then the bird screeched into the room and clawed at Addison's face. The teenager jerked around to protect himself, giving Harry enough time to jump up and grab the gun. He got hold of the handle, forcing Addison back until they fell together to the floor. They skidded over magazines and newspapers, grasping for the weapon as the bird shrieked above them.

He was bigger and stronger than the teenager, but he couldn't get the proper leverage because of the rubbish under them. Then he thought he had the right angle to grab the weapon from him. That was until the bullet exploded from it and the noise was like a bomb going off near his head. His ears were still ringing when he staggered up and saw the hole in James David Addison's chest.

He dropped to help the kid, but realised it was no good. The gun lay at his side, but he didn't reach for it.

'I knew that stupid bird of Ma's hated me,' were his last words.

Harry watched him die as Amy ran into the room.

'What happened?'

'It was an accident, but at least I stopped him.'

He slumped onto the sofa and stared at the kid's blood on his fingers.

'Addison died then and he died now,' Amy said.

'I understand,' Harry said. 'We didn't change his fate, but we did for the others.'

Amy's face darkened. 'You didn't, Harry.' She nodded to the door. 'Go and listen.'

The whole of his body ached, telling him not to stand, but he did.

He followed her outside, his pain increasing as he heard the gunshots coming from the school.

He placed one hand on the door to steady himself. 'How?'

Amy held a pill out to him. 'We need to go back, Harry, to your present and your office, five minutes after we left to see Chuck. You'll get your answer then.'

She took her pill and he watched her vanish.

I could just stay here and never return.

When the gunshots stopped, he swallowed his pill.

29 FINE TIME

Harry went straight to the drinks cabinet when he arrived at the office. Addison's blood lingered on his fingers when he gulped at the whisky. It warmed the back of his throat as he turned to see Amy at his desk, staring at the computer.

'Did you break through my password?'

She smiled at him. 'I hope you don't mind. I'm reading the reports of the shooting. Addison's death was registered as a suicide.'

He never took his eyes from her as he slumped onto the sofa reserved for clients.

'What happened at the school?'

'A student, Benny Smith, killed himself and two of his peers, plus a teacher. The authorities still don't know why.'

'Addison mentioned someone called Benny. It must have been him.'

Amy got up and handed Harry her phone, showing him the recorded details of the original shooting.

'All five people who died when we were there have the same names as in this report.'

'Including Benny Smith?'

'Yes.'

He pressed the glass against his cheek, wanting the chill to unfreeze his brain.

'We changed the past, but we didn't change it; that's what you've been trying to tell me all along.'

She sat in the single chair opposite him.

'Yes. Small things can be altered, but not the major events they lead up to. You could go back and tell Chuck or me we're in danger, but it wouldn't change the outcome.'

'When Hazell and the others kept on killing Hitler, all they did was alter the way in which his actions caused so much death, destruction and misery.'

'That's right,' she said.

'Okay, you've finally convinced me, but I still need answers to difficult questions: is that a version of you with the missing teenager, Christine Kerr? Who murdered Chuck and why?'

'And who killed me and why?'

'It has to be one of the Crucial Three who killed you,' Harry said.

She didn't seem convinced. 'I don't think so.' She removed a pill from her pocket. 'Without me, they don't have these.'

He put his drink on the table. 'Maybe one of them snapped. I saw it happen in the army and the Met. If you push people too far, they'll eventually break. Perhaps you should tell them your secret and you'll live.'

Amy shook her head. 'Or once they get what they want, they'll no longer need me around.'

He stared at the dried blood on his fingers and knew she was right.

Harry finished his drink and got up. 'Do you need to rest or eat something before we go again?'

'You want to time travel now?'

Harry's grin masked the pain in his heart. 'There's no time like the present.'

'You don't have any side effects from your recent trips? Nothing unusual happening to your body or your mind?'

He stretched out his arms and stared at his hands.

'Nothing more than usual. If I stay here and do nothing, it will only fry my brain so it's even more mixed up. When I was in the Met, I couldn't wait around before doing anything.'

'Okay. Do you want anything to eat?'

Harry rubbed his stomach. 'I'm still digesting what I had in that café.'

'You had little. This is one of the physical side effects of time travel Mary and the others discovered early on with their volunteers. Jumping rapidly between different periods messes with your body clock and too much of it can create negative consequences.'

While he listened to her, he thought of Boleyn's mother in the care home.

'I'll be okay for now. If I turn into Mr Hyde, I'll let you know.'

She removed two pills from her pocket and he wondered how many she had left.

'Fine. You're the detective in charge, so where are we going?'

'I want to know why there's another you with Christine Kerr outside Madame Tussauds.'

She handed him a pill. 'That makes both of us. How do you want to do this?'

Harry rolled the pill between his fingers and considered how much he trusted her.

'We'll arrive at the museum just after Christine gets there – do you remember the time she was there?' Amy nodded. 'Good. Aim as close as you can to before she goes inside. I'll stay back as you talk to her. She'll think it's the other version of you, and hopefully, you'll get some useful information from her.'

'And then?'

'I'll step in and tell Christine how much her parents are worried about her. Then she can decide if she wants to go back to them or not.'

'That sounds like a plan, partner.' She put the pill in her mouth. 'I'll see you with the waxworks.'

Harry watched her disappear. Then he reached into the box she'd given him earlier and counted the pills inside: twelve.

Good. These are my emergency backups as long as she keeps giving me some from her stash.

He thought about his plan, and then swallowed the pill.

The doors shimmered before him and he was getting used to the heat. He moved to the one closest to Christine entering the museum. Harry put his head near the door and listened in case he could hear anything on the other side, but all he got was the buzzing from the vibrating light around him. Then he looked down the other doors, moving beyond them until he saw the one ten minutes before Christine entered Madame Tussauds.

He stepped out on to a busy Marylebone Road. Nobody screamed or shouted as he appeared out of thin air. Instead, a few kids eyed him as he crossed over to observe the entrance to the museum from the other side. He didn't know which direction she'd come from, so he twisted his head right to look everywhere.

Two minutes later, he saw her striding towards the distinctive green dome on the front of Tussauds. He ran across the road, dodging the traffic and the blaring horns of angry drivers. She was about to go inside when he called her name.

'Christine.' She turned to stare at him. He realised she didn't know who he was as he approached her. 'Your parents sent me to look for you.'

Harry recognised the fear in her eyes and the eagerness to flee, but there was no quick escape through the people surrounding them.

'Who are you?' she said.

He tried his best smile. 'I'm not here to take you back, just to let you know they're worried about you.' He delved into his pocket and found the last of his money. 'They wanted me to give you this.'

She snatched the forty pounds from him. 'Okay, you can go now.'

Harry held up a hand, aware that some people waiting to get into Madame Tussauds were watching and listening to them.

'I will, Christine, I promise. I've just got one question for you if you don't mind.'

She stuffed the money into her pocket and narrowed her eyes at him.

'What question?'

Harry showed her the photo on his phone. 'Do you know this woman?'

She hesitated for a second before nodding.

'That's Beth. Did she send you? I'm supposed to meet her around here.'

He continued smiling. 'Yes, she sent me to tell you she's going to be a little late, but please wait for her. Will you do that?'

Christine moved between people and stepped near him.

'Yeah, I can do that, especially after what she's done for me.' She checked Harry from top to toe. 'You say my parents sent you to find me?'

He resisted the urge to drag her from the entrance.

If I stop her from meeting Amy here later, will that mean I'll never see the two of them together? But I'm only here now because of that.

He ignored the electric pain shooting through his body and answered her question.

'Yes, I'm a private investigator. They wanted me to make sure you're okay. I'm not here to take you back to them. Do you understand?'

'Sure,' she said as she seemingly saw him as no threat. 'Tell them I'll be home soon once I've finished this job for Ms Grey.'

He didn't need to ask who Ms Grey was. 'Okay.'

'It's funny you being a private investigator,' she said. 'Because that's what I've been doing for Ms Grey and Mr Connors.'

Harry nearly fell over when she mentioned Chuck's name.

'Right. Is it something exciting?'

She grabbed his arm and pulled him from the front of the building.

'Ms Grey found me living under the bridge – I don't know how – and gave me money to pass messages on to Mr Connors. She couldn't do it herself because his wife was jealous and thought they were, you know, knocking each other off.' She laughed as Harry dug his nails into his skin.

'That's why I'm here today, to get another message. I don't have a phone, so I always meet her here.' Christine peered at him. 'But I guess you already know that.'

He moved away from her. 'That's right. Anyway, she said she's running late, and you might as well have a look inside Tussauds, and she'll meet you out here later.'

Harry didn't wait for a reply, turning his back on her and heading down Marylebone Road. The place was a bustle around him, full of tourist chatter and the noise of the buses and cars. He was looking for a pub to throw himself into, but couldn't see one.

He turned on to Baker Street and saw what he needed between two fast-food joints. Harry slipped into the Moriarty Bar and Grill and went straight for a drink. He bought a pint of cider and headed for the most secluded booth he could find. Once he was sitting, he tried to process what Christine had told him.

Chuck and Amy were working together.
Both of them kept that from me.
Both of them are dead.
Why did they get Christine involved?

He stared at the people having a good time around him, watching them relax without a care in the world. But he knew that wasn't true, that it would be a façade for most of them, hiding their worries beyond a joyful exterior dulled by booze, drugs, sex and anything else that worked.

Harry watched the bubbles in his pint streaming up from the bottom, then popping out of existence, only to start the same process all over again. He grabbed his drink and helped those bubbles on their way. The cider was dry and bit at the back of his throat and sank into his gut. He put the glass on the table, reached into his pocket, and removed the pills.

What do I do now?

Twelve pills mean twelve trips through time, six return journeys or eleven points along the highway and one way back to my present.

He moved the box from side to side and the contents rattled like the thoughts rattling inside his head.

I can't trust Amy or anyone at the Time Authority.

He glanced around the pub as the noise increased, wondering if there were any time travellers in there with him.

Did he believe what he'd been told that the TA only had a few travellers?

The Crucial Three.

Cronin and Ellie.

Amy and me.

That gave him a suspect list of six people, unless there were others he didn't know about.

There was a large TV in the corner, switched on but with the sound off. Harry watched the text running across the bottom of the screen saying how there would be a Unity Group rally in London tomorrow.

Maybe I should go and speak to Mary Boleyn.

He considered that as somebody slipped into the booth opposite him.

'I knew you'd be in the first pub I found.'

He stared at her. 'Are you Amy, Ms Grey, or someone else?'

She grabbed his pint and took a drink from it.

'I was waiting for you inside Tussauds, Harry. When you never showed, I had to get out before the other me turned up.'

He pushed his back into the booth and the leather itched at his spine.

'What would have happened if you'd met the other you? Would the world have exploded?'

Amy laughed at him. 'No, but maybe the heads of all those around me would have gone up like Vesuvius.'

Harry moved his drink to the side. 'Tell me where you're from in the future and why you gave the gift of time travel to Hazell, Adler and Cohen, or I'm leaving right now, and you'll never see me again in any timeline.'

She picked up his glass and drained it. Then she wiped her lip and waved at a server.

'Okay, Harry, but it's a long and tragic story and you'll need something stronger to drink to make this go down smoothly.'

He watched her ordering a round of double gin and tonics.

Then he listened to her tale.

30 LOVE VIGILANTES

Harry glanced through the ice in his glass at this strange, infuriating woman who made his heart beat faster than any person ever had.

He listened to her speak.

And what a story it was.

'I travelled here from a hundred years in the future, from 2150. I don't want to brag, but I was the foremost biochemical engineer of my time.' She looked around the pub, at the noise and the happiness. 'I'm a Londoner, born and bred, but it's a lot different now to my time.' Her voice dropped a level. 'It's worse all over the world.'

'Climate change?' Harry said.

Amy nodded. 'That was the spark. But, even with the measures humanity implanted in the early part of this century, it wasn't enough to stop the catastrophe. Average temperatures increased about ten degrees across the globe. This created more extreme heat days and regular heat-waves. It's also meant sea levels rose by thirty inches or more in most of the world's oceans.

'Increased rainstorms become more intense, wreaking

havoc through flooding and erosion. Stronger hurricanes, longer droughts, more and wetter thunderstorms brought disaster to communities all over the globe.

'But the worst was to come. If humanity had stood together against this devastation, then we might have come out of it okay, and I wouldn't be sitting here with you now.'

'War?' Harry said.

Amy nodded. 'When resources dried up and people rioted, some governments panicked and reacted in the worst possible way. If you don't have the resources you need and your neighbours do, what do the desperate resort to but trying to take what isn't theirs?

'So this brought localised conflict, which quickly spread worldwide. 2140 saw the first nuclear bombs dropped in anger, and they weren't the last. It wasn't long before most of the world was uninhabitable and unable to support any life.'

The sounds of people enjoying themselves were everywhere around Harry as he listened to this tale of the end of humans a century hence.

But did he believe her?

'What did you do?' he said.

'Do you remember me telling you that my discovery of time travel was an accident?'

'I do.'

'Well, it wasn't just me. My husband and I worked on chemical experiments to ease memory loss in the human brain. We'd been up for eighteen hours and Jack had gone upstairs to make the coffee. Unfortunately, I made a mistake with the solutions, mixing a combination that should have been discarded, and injected it into a mouse we used. I knew I'd made a blunder as soon as I did it, but I didn't have time to chastise myself before the mouse vanished in front of my eyes.'

'You must have thought you were hallucinating from lack of sleep.'

Amy nodded. 'I did. I was still staring into the spot where the mouse had been when Jack returned with the coffee. When I told him what had happened, he didn't believe me.'

'That's understandable.'

She reached into her jacket and removed her phone.

Her future phone.

'Luckily, I had it on video.'

Amy handed it to him and he watched the clip, stunned by what he saw with the mouse vanishing just like she'd described.

'I guess he believed you then,' he said.

'Even more so,' she replied, 'when the mouse reappeared an hour later.'

She played him another video, where he was more focused on staring at her husband than waiting for the mouse to return. He smiled when it did and returned the phone to her.

'And you repeated the experiment?'

'Yes, once we had enough of the same chemicals to make the right amount of mixture.'

'How did you know the mouse had travelled through time?'

'We didn't at first. It took us two years of animal experiments to tell us we'd only understand the full truth by testing it on humans.'

'Is that allowed a century from now?'

'No, not without government intervention, and we

weren't prepared to let them know what we'd discovered. So we had to find another solution.'

'You experimented on yourselves?'

'We did. Small steps initially, until we tried to move forward in time, but couldn't go into the future. So we travelled to a point in our past, to when we first met, watching from a distance. This was when we decided to change history, to stop the nuclear Armageddon before it started.'

'The past can't be changed,' Harry said.

Darkness swept across her face. 'Months of research through travelling to the past led us to discover where the first missile blasted off from to start the war. This was at an American nuclear station in Alaska. We'd mastered the time travel technique of having the solution inside the pills you're familiar with. Jack saw the Doors of Perception while I had my library. We didn't know how we'd stop the attack, but we knew we had to try.'

She paused for breath and Harry recognised the pain in her eyes.

There is no deception here.

'The two of you went there?'

'We did. We travelled into the bunker in Alaska, getting as close as we could to the missile leaving the silo.'

'How were you going to stop it?'

'We weren't sure, but it didn't matter. Our lives weren't important; we just had to prevent it.'

'Did you?'

'We appeared in the launch room, Jack first and me about twenty seconds later. When I got there, he was grappling with a soldier who shouted that it was only a training exercise.'

'What?'

'We'd made a terrible mistake, but it was too late by

then.' She took another sip of her drink. 'I hadn't realised it, but Jack had tried to get to the exact point where the launch was instigated, so he'd swallowed more than one pill.'

Amy stopped talking and shook her head.

'He told you this?'

'Not to my face. It was in a video he'd left behind for me.'

He felt the gin sink into his guts. 'Then...'

'My escape pill was already in my hand when I watched Jack shake and the lights seep out of his skin. The heat was intense, worse than any fire, and I saw the blood boiling in his eyes. The last thing he said to me was *go*.'

She'd had no choice.

'Shock froze me to the spot when I got back to the lab. I don't know how long I stood there without moving. I think I was waiting for him to appear at any second. Eventually, I moved and went to the computer. Do you know what I found when I checked the historical beginnings of the nuclear war?'

'You'd changed nothing?'

'There was a meltdown at that bunker which set off all the missiles, firing them at their prearranged destinations. Whatever had happened to Jack started that tragedy.' She reached over to him. 'We didn't change the past, Harry; we caused it.'

They sat there in silence before finishing the drinks.

Then they ordered more.

'What did you do next?'

Amy took a cube from her drink and rubbed it across her lips.

'I lost track of everything, of the times I went back to stop Jack and me going to that bunker, but nothing ever changed.' She swallowed the ice. 'I was the spider over and over again.'

'You realised you couldn't change anything?'

'I understood I needed a bigger web.'

'What does that mean?'

She smiled at him. 'You can't alter the ultimate events, Harry. I think you understand that now, but you can change smaller things that lead up to those actions. That's why I travelled back a hundred years to here, why I gave Mary, Sally and Rose the ability to travel through time and let them run with that. I didn't care what they did with it; they were only the distraction.'

Something dark gnawed at his heart. 'Am I part of that distraction?'

Amy shook her head. 'No, Harry, you could never be a distraction to me.'

'Okay, so what is the Time Authority distracting people from?'

She removed a box of pills from her jacket. 'Have you kept all of yours?'

'I have since you keep giving me ones from your stack.'

'Not any more. I'm running out, as is the TA. I travelled back to this century to make more. The destruction to the environment in my time has meant there isn't enough left for what I have to do.'

'What's that?'

Amy placed the box on the table. 'The future is dying, Harry. Within twenty years of where I left, little of humanity will remain. That's why I must rescue as many as I can.'

Her words sped through his brain. 'You want to remove people from your present and take them back in time?'

'That's the plan.'

He got his drink, letting the gin and ice trickle down his throat.

'That's a massive undertaking.'

She shook her head. 'Once I have enough chemicals, I'll only need to explain to the refugees how the pills work with the Doors of Perception or whatever visual representation they see. Some will likely be lost, but I should save the majority.'

The enormity of it weighed heavily on him.

'What if your refugees don't want to leave?'

Amy sat back in her chair. 'That's up to them. Of course, nobody will be forced to leave, but given the choice of staying on a dying planet or travelling to a better time, what would you do?'

'Where will they go? Where and when will they travel to?'

She shrugged. 'Does it matter? They can't change the past, so it makes no difference. I'll leave the choice up to them.'

'It's a nice story, Amy, but I still have several questions.'

'No problem, but can we order some food because I'm starving? Recounting how your husband died and how humanity is on the verge of extinction works on the appetite.'

The rumbling in his stomach meant he didn't argue with her. Instead, he ordered steak and chips while she got the fish of the day.

With another round of gin and tonic to go with it.

'I thought you would have gone for something more exciting than the fish.'

Amy smiled at him. 'Fish is exotic in my time, Harry, since there's hardly any of it left.'

'What you've just told me, how much do the Crucial Three know of that?'

'Most of it. I only tell them what they need to know.'

'Did you push them into speaking to Chuck about his father's factory?'

'No, that was their own doing. They're trying to reverse engineer what's in the pills. That's why I used Christine as a go-between, so neither Chuck nor them would know I was involved.'

'You want that factory for your own manufacturing process?'

'Yes, it's perfect, and it stops them from progressing.'

Harry heard the worry in her voice. 'You think they've cracked your code?'

Amy sighed. 'I believe one of them has; probably Rose, since she was the one we caught talking to your partner. I'm not sure if the other two are involved. Not being able to get too close to specific events is an annoyance, especially when I'm running out of pills.'

He analysed what she'd said. 'If that's true and Adler has cracked your code, and she got Chuck to sign off on the sale of the factory, then she wouldn't need you or him.'

The food arrived before she could reply.

Harry watched his steak sizzle as he ate a chip. Then, she bit into a large chunk of fish and her face lit up.

'When this is all over, I'm going to settle somewhere on the coast with the perfect climate. Do you have any suggestions?'

He ignored her question. 'Did you hear what I said about Adler?'

Amy chewed as she spoke. 'Yes, Rose wouldn't need your partner or me anymore. So therefore, she's probably the one who killed us both. But I guess she couldn't stop

Mary and Sally from bringing you and then me into this investigation.'

She picked a bit of food from her teeth and grinned at him.

'So what are you going to do about it, Harry?'

31 SHAME OF THE NATION

Harry's head was buzzing with the alcohol and the thought of what he had to do next.

'We must visit Hazell, Adler, and Cohen separately to talk to them.'

Amy peered at him with startled eyes.

'They won't tell you the truth, Harry. It's not in their nature.'

He agreed with her. 'You know them better than me. So what do you suggest?'

'We need to stop Rose.'

'Stop her from doing what?'

'She must have got my formula somehow before she killed me. I doubt she'll use it for good and certainly not for that nice dream the Crucial Three told you about helping people visit their loved ones in the past.'

'Don't take this the wrong way, Amy, but since you're dead, why do you care anymore?' He watched the fire spark into life in her eyes. 'Yes, I know, I'd be upset if somebody had killed me – and I realise how stupid that sounds – and

I'd demand justice, but I'm not sure what you want me to do.'

'Rose is a murderer twice over, Harry, including your best friend, so I'd expect you to be more interested in seeking justice than me. Also, don't you think she's probably committed those crimes because she's got a bigger one brewing?'

'What do you mean?'

'Harry, think about it. She wants to use the time travel chemicals for some ulterior motive other than the Time Authority's alleged benign gift to humanity. We need to find out what that is and stop it.'

He grabbed her arm. 'What aren't you telling me, Amy?'

The pub was full now, crammed with loud people and a continuous noise coming from the jukebox. He recognised it as Motörhead as she wriggled from his grasp.

'I haven't told you the whole truth about time travel and the reason I came here, a hundred years into the past.'

The combined buzz of the booze and the crowd made his head spin.

'Call me shocked.'

'Rose discovered the one thing I kept from the Crucial Three and the world.'

He knew what her secret must be and said it for her.

'History can be changed.'

Amy nodded. 'But it takes a huge amount of the chemical to allow the human brain to have the strength to force it through, and the sacrifices needed to do it are too terrible to contemplate.'

'Show me.'

She turned her head from him so he couldn't see her face. He thought she'd leave for a second until she faced him again.

'Do you trust me, Harry?'

'No.'

She laughed. 'Fair enough.'

Before he could say or do anything, she moved forwards and kissed him.

The shock of it forced his mouth open, but not in protest. He'd been thinking about kissing her long before he knew there was a version of Amy Croft still alive.

He was considering how wrong that was when she stuck her tongue down his throat. It was difficult for him to breathe and his instincts took over; grabbing her hips, he tried to force her away.

But it was too late.

The pill hit the back of his mouth and he had to swallow it.

'I'll see you on the other side, Harry,' she said before she disappeared.

And then he vanished.

There were no Doors of Perception this time and no library either.

He reappeared five feet in the air and fell to the ground. Harry's face hit cold concrete and the blood came out of his nose. He fumbled for leverage, his trembling finger finding a large barrel so he could pull himself up. The blood trickled on to his cheek as a familiar, but long-forgotten odour invaded his senses.

He was about to step forward when somebody pulled him into the shadows. He twisted on his heels, ready to punch them, only stopping when he saw it was Amy.

'What did you do to me?'

'I kissed you into the past, Harry.' She let go of him. 'You'll thank me later.'

He wiped the blood from his face, tasting it on his lips.

'You passed a pill to me through your mouth; I get it.' He glanced around his surroundings, recognising them as a large factory or warehouse. And part of him – a younger buried version of him – recognised the place. 'But why didn't I see the Doors of Perception? Why wasn't I given a choice?'

Amy leant against the wall behind her, lounging as if she was waiting for a train to arrive.

'Couldn't you taste the difference in that pill?'

He ran his tongue around inside his mouth.

'I thought that was your lipstick. It tastes of almonds.'

She shook her head. 'No, Harry. What I gave you – what I gave both of us – is a stronger version of the pill, with added chemicals. It allowed me direct access to your synapses; direct access to your memories.' She peered over his shoulder. 'Don't you realise where you are?'

He turned, gazing at the end of the warehouse and the door in the far wall.

Do I know this place?

'I'm not sure.'

She took his arm and led him out of the shadows.

'Shall we have a look? It's early days, so they haven't increased the security yet. If we keep to the sides, I don't think anybody will see us.' She looked up at the rafters. 'Because of the sensitive nature of this operation, they've installed no cameras. I'm sure you'll understand why.'

Part of his brain told him to get away from her, to flee this place.

But something stronger in him wanted Amy to keep holding him; he needed her to want him.

'What operation are you talking about?'

They were halfway to the door, moving past stacked boxes and broken pieces of machinery. An aroma of chlorine lingered in the air and he wondered if there would be a swimming pool beyond the entrance.

Amy answered his question when they reached the door.

'Operation Cerebrum, Harry. Remember?'

She pushed the door open and he peered inside, staring at the dozens of bodies lying on tables.

No, not bodies. Living, breathing people, strapped down against their will and injected with something Harry had hidden in the back of his mind for twenty years.

But now he remembered.

His legs nearly gave way as she hauled him inside, dragging Harry behind a pile of boxes and out of sight of the soldiers and medics at the rear of the building.

'Cerebrum,' he whispered.

He watched, unable to tear his gaze from the doctors injecting chemicals into the prisoners' brains.

Amy pushed her face close to his.

'Do you know where the nineteen-year-old version of you is in this circus of horrors?'

Harry lowered his head, struggling to control his breathing. He saw a spider crawl into its web as he spoke.

'I'm at the far end, one of the security detail guarding the serum.'

'Serum?' Amy said.

He glared at her. 'You know what this is. That's why you brought me here.'

'You're right.' She watched syringes going into heads. 'I understand why you wanted to forget this.'

'I can never forget this.'

'Did you know what was in the serum?'

He shook his head. 'I only knew what they told us. I was

a grunt. The top brass and the scientists didn't tell us what they were doing, only why they were doing it.'

'To hasten the end of the war?'

'That's what they said.'

'To save lives?'

Harry's face was as dark as the shadows that consumed him.

'I guess so.'

'You must have heard rumours about what this was.'

He nodded. 'They were trying to manipulate the brain, using chemicals as mind control.'

'Indeed,' she replied. 'Your government wasn't the first or the last to attempt such a thing.'

'Nothing changes,' Harry said.

'Sacrificing the few to save the many.' She put a hand on his arm. 'You could have protested.'

He shrugged her off. 'They forced me to do this. I wanted to run, but couldn't.'

'Ah yes, you were only following orders. But, of course, that's always the way of the military, isn't it?'

'What could one person do against all of them?'

He nodded at the people in the warehouse, the guilt that had never left him growing by the second.

'One person can change the world, Harry.'

'But not history?'

'How many times were you involved in this?'

'Too many.' He turned his head to the shadows. 'Can we go back now?'

'It was worth it, though, wasn't it, Harry? All these experiments hastened the end of the war and saved thousands of lives.'

'By murdering innocents.'

'Everything for the greater good. Would you rather this didn't happen and more people died?'

'I'd rather not be here at all, then and now.'

'Then is now, Harry. What do you want to do next?'

'I want to see what Adler and the others are using Chuck's factory for.'

A blood-curdling scream erupted through the place before she could reply.

Harry didn't need to look where it came from, but he did. The memory played out inside his head as he lurched forward to see the commotion.

'Be careful,' Amy said, but his mind was too far gone to heed her warning.

He stumbled out of the shadows, seeing his younger self struggling with a "patient" who'd jumped from the bed. The anaesthetic hadn't been strong enough to keep him subdued as a doctor attempted to inject the chemicals into his brain.

But he'd been too slow and the big bloke – he was over six feet tall – had grabbed the syringe and thrust it into the doctor's throat. The younger Harry was the only soldier there and he fought for his life while trying to disarm the enraged man.

'We have to go,' Amy said.

Yet the older Harry couldn't move, watching the teenage version of himself while reliving the events in his head. It was surreal, like seeing the same actions from two different viewpoints. Although he knew how it would end, he was worried for the other him.

Yet there was something else he should have remembered. It was on the edge of his memory, but not quite there.

He hung on to Amy's arm as the younger him crashed to

the ground and the big man climbed on top of him with the syringe about to rip his throat open.

He knew the gunshot was coming. Even so, it hurt his ears. Harry gazed at his hands and remembered how the other man's blood had turned his flesh red.

Then it came to him.

Just after I'd killed him, there was a commotion across the other side. Screams and shouts I thought had come from a woman.

Amy shouted as someone shoved her into him.

They crashed into the wall behind them. Harry's shoulder cracked as he hit the concrete, his legs buckling as he went down and she fell on top of him. He glanced up to see the soldiers approaching, men from his old unit.

No, men from my unit now.

Amy pushed her face into his and he opened his mouth, desperate for her lips on his for more than one reason.

Then she kissed him like he'd never been kissed before.

For him, it seemed to last for an eternity – he wanted it to last forever – but it couldn't have done as they reappeared on top of each other in the bar.

People jeered and shouted at them as they lay there. He was under Amy and in no hurry to go anywhere. The memory of where he'd just been, the old one mixing in with the new, left Harry with no desire to do anything but gaze into her face.

Perhaps she doesn't have to go back to the past to die. She said it was possible to change history with a more potent chemical solution in the time travel mixture.

Amy crawled off him and the spell was broken.

She reached out a hand to him and he took it, accepting her strength as a counterbalance to his weakness as she lifted him from the floor.

Their drinks were still on the table as they sat opposite each other. Harry drank the gin and tonic as if it was water. He wanted more, but knew it was foolish to get drunk with what was coming next.

'I'd pushed it all into the darkest reaches of my mind, letting it fester there for all these years, but it's back now, and I can't deny what I saw and did anymore.'

'You were a soldier in a war not of your making, Harry, following orders you could never go against.'

She was right. Even so, it pained him.

And there was that other thing nagging at his tired brain.

'We created a paradox.'

'How?' she replied.

'My time in the army – most of it – I'd locked away in a box stored in the deepest part of me. It all came back today, all the terrible things I did or witnessed.' He peered at his clean hands, seeing the blood under his skin. 'I killed that man because I had no other choice – it was him or me once he put that syringe to my throat. But one thing I'd forgotten was the commotion I'd heard over the other side of those operating tables.'

'When those soldiers confronted us?'

Harry nodded. 'Yes. I didn't ask anybody about it. I was still traumatised by what I'd done and what was happening around me. But I heard rumours from others in my unit of how they'd caught two intruders – a man and a woman – but they'd got away. They'd just vanished, some said. It wasn't reported to our superiors, for who wants to admit to letting enemy agents get into the building, and then escape? So it was never spoken about again, and I forgot about it along with everything else.'

'Until now.'

'But it was a paradox, wasn't it, me travelling in time to create an event the younger me would witness before the older me went back to create it?'

'Yes, Harry, it was a temporal paradox, a causal loop; something that occurs when a future event causes a past event, which causes the future event. Both events then exist in space-time, but their origin cannot be determined.'

He laughed. 'Well, I won't ask how it originated, then.'

She got up and went to sit near him. Her body was pressed against him; her legs pushed into his. He was intoxicated and it wasn't from the booze, or the paradox, or the time travel.

Amy took his hand. 'What do you want to do next?'

He let her warmth flow through him.

'Was it true what you said about the possibility of changing the past?'

'Yes.'

'So I could save Chuck?'

'Yes.'

'And I could save you?'

'Yes.'

He put his other hand on hers.

'Then that's what we'll do next.'

32 TRUE FAITH

Memories of Harry's complicity in the army's horrific experiments threatened to overwhelm him as he staggered out of the pub.

Amy grabbed his arm before he fell into the road.

'Do you want to rest before we do anything else?'

He shook his head. 'No, I can't wait any longer. We need to find out what Adler is doing at Chuck's factory.'

'Do you have the address?'

He removed his mobile from his jacket. 'He mentioned it in several texts, always complaining about the debt his dad had left him.'

Amy let go of him. 'How did his father die?'

Harry dragged his thoughts away from following orders and teenage atrocities and remembered the funeral.

'I never pressed him on the full details, but he said it was an accident, his dad falling from a balcony while on holiday in Portugal.'

'It was definitely an accident?'

'I think so. Why?'

'Would your business have been in so much financial trouble if Chuck's father hadn't died?'

'Probably not, no.'

'Would Chuck have needed to sell this factory if his father was still alive?'

'What are you getting at, Amy?'

She dragged him from the people heading into the pub.

'Think about it, Harry. You're only involved with the Crucial Three and the Time Authority because of that death. Everything that has led you to here started with that.'

'You think Adler or one of the others killed Chuck's father?'

She shrugged. 'I wouldn't put anything past them. Where is this factory?'

'It's in an old abandoned industrial park in the middle of nowhere. That's why Chuck could never sell it.'

'Until Rose bought it for the Time Authority. It's the perfect place for her to reproduce my experiments.'

He removed a pill from his pocket. 'Let's go there now.'

She put her hand on his. 'Don't waste that, Harry. I've got less than a dozen left, and there's an easier way to get to the factory.'

He moved closer to her. 'Okay, but I need to do something first.'

'What?'

He leant into Amy, his intentions as clear as day. He waited for her to pull away from him, but she didn't. Instead, she pushed her lips into his, and when they kissed this time, there were no pills passed between them.

He was flushed when he pulled away. A crowd of people jeered at them, but he couldn't keep the smile from his face.

He took the phone from his pocket. 'We'll get a taxi to

the factory.'

Amy grabbed the mobile from him. 'I've got a better idea.'

Twenty minutes later, she was dragging him into the bedroom of his flat.

THEY DIDN'T REAPPEAR for two hours.

'I hope you've got food here, Harry. I'm starving.'

'There's pizza in the fridge,' he said through a smile wide enough to swallow the horizon.

'How long has it been there?'

He laughed. 'I didn't realise that time was so important to a time traveller.'

She shook her head. 'Laugh it up, laughing boy, but getting proper refuelling is important for time travelling; otherwise, your body might give up on you.' She grabbed his arm and dragged him on to the sofa. 'And I don't want your body giving up on me now.'

Harry gazed into her face. 'No regrets, then?'

Amy narrowed her eyes at him. 'Of course not. You?'

He laughed again. 'Yeah, can't you see it in my eyes?'

She pushed him back and climbed onto him.

'I can see lots there, Harry. Most of which my mother would never have approved of.'

He relaxed. 'Maybe I'll get to meet her.'

She slipped off him. 'No travelling to the future, remember?'

He didn't move. 'Perhaps you can bring her here.'

The smile disappeared from her face. 'If I can't access more of the chemicals I need, then neither of us will travel through time much more.'

Harry jumped off the sofa and took her arm. 'What you said about creating a formula to change the past. Is that possible?'

'Yes, as long as I can increase the dose with the right combination of ingredients.'

He let go of her. 'It sounds like a recipe.'

Her grin returned. 'I guess it kind of is.'

He hugged her. 'Then we have to do it.'

She didn't pull away from him. 'It will involve some difficult choices.'

He squeezed her harder. 'I'll do anything it takes, Amy, I promise you.'

'Time to visit Rose Adler at the factory, then.'

Harry nodded and rang for the taxi.

IT DROPPED them at an industrial wasteland.

There was a vast expanse of gravelled paths. Some bizarre concrete blocks remained, covered in graffiti, which Harry guessed was over thirty years old considering the names of the pop groups on it. Derelict abandoned warehouses filled the landscape like biblical pyramids reaching into a sky that no longer wanted them. A lingering stink of pollution hovered in the air as they strode through the rubble and fossilised bits of metal.

'Where now?' Amy said.

He checked the directions on his phone. 'It should be behind that big water tower.'

They headed for the looming construction, dodging the rats and the rubble.

She saw it first, the dilapidated sign for Connors's Clothes.

'Great. I need some new trousers.'

Harry pushed through the rusted metal gate. 'I doubt they've made anything in here for a long time.'

She followed him through. 'Apart from whatever Rose is making inside.'

The chill of the air bit at Harry's face as he reached the entrance, finding the lock broken. He went in with Amy by his side. They stepped through the reception, glancing at abandoned offices still littered with the remains of crushed furniture, filing cabinets and dead computers.

At the far end was a large door, and beyond that, they found machines in the hundreds, all covered in dust with an aroma of decay everywhere.

'There's nothing here but industrial entropy,' Amy said.

Harry pointed to the back. 'There's another entrance, probably to the warehouse.'

They went to it, striding between machines that had been used to create things, but were now only skeletons; fossils to a once productive part of the city.

She stopped at the entrance. 'What do we say to Rose if she's in here?'

'We ask her why she killed you and Chuck.'

Then he pushed open the door.

And froze on the other side.

Harry clutched at his chest, desperate to stop his heart from bursting through his ribs.

Then he stumbled into the wall, his eyes scanning everywhere.

It was as if he was inside that military facility again. He struggled for breath as he looked for the nineteen-year-old version of himself, wondering how he'd gone back in time again without taking a pill.

Did Amy do this to me?

He pushed that thought from his head when he saw the tables, about a dozen, all with people strapped to them. The words wouldn't come from his mouth as the shadow stepped from behind the bodies and he waited to shout at Adler.

Only it wasn't her.

It was Cronin who walked towards them.

Harry pressed at his throat as a single word crept from between his lips.

'What?'

Amy answered the question.

'I'm afraid I haven't been completely truthful with you, Harry.'

She went to Cronin as Harry watched the former army man cradle the rifle in his arm.

'What is this, Amy? Where's Adler?' He pointed a shaky hand at Cronin. 'And what's he doing here?'

'Would you like to see Rose?'

She moved towards the bodies before he could reply. He stumbled after her, ignoring Cronin's stupid grin. He looked at the people tied to the tables, seeing drugged, confused faces that brought back all the memories from those army experiments on the other side of the world so long ago.

But still, only a few hours ago as well.

'Who are these people, Amy?'

She stopped at the end of the row, running her fingers through the hair of an unconscious woman: Rose Adler.

'It's a long story, Harry. Where would you like me to begin?'

He glanced around the room. 'This is all your doing?'

She let go of Adler. 'Well, some of it is yours, too.'

'Mine?'

'Operation Cerebrum, remember?'

His legs were about to give way until he grabbed the table containing Adler. He peered into her glassy eyes before turning away.

'What's this got to do with Operation Cerebrum?'

'Did you think the government had stopped its experiments after you left the army?'

'I tried to forget about the whole thing.' And he had done an excellent job until now. 'Are you saying they continued Operation Cerebrum for another hundred years, right until the nuclear war?'

She nodded. 'Yes, it continued until the war, but it's not a hundred years from now, Harry.'

The reality was dawning on him.

She's lied about everything.

'Tell me where you're really from, Amy.'

'Perhaps you should sit down before you fall.'

He lifted his arm and smashed his hand on to the table next to Adler's head. Harry's body throbbed as Cronin pointed his weapon at him.

'Tell me.'

She sighed. 'Okay. My future is not a hundred years from now, but twenty.'

Harry gasped. 'Twenty?'

'Yes; two decades from now, the world and humans will be extinct. Climate change starts the process, but the radioactive Armageddon finishes everything once and for all.' She nodded at Cronin. 'The Captain was one of the military personnel at the facility where Jack and I conducted our experiments. We were the only ones who escaped into this time.'

'What you told me about your husband and the nuclear

silo, of trying to change the nuclear attack but instead causing it; that was a lie?'

Sadness covered her face. 'It was, Harry. But, unfortunately, Jack was already dying when we had our time travel accident.' She glanced over the tables. 'But he would have been proud of how far I've come.'

Harry laughed. 'You went from killing mice to experimenting on humans. So yeah, I'm sure he'd be ecstatic about that.'

Amy shook her head. 'Oh, Harry, there were never any mice involved. Robert and I were experimenting on live human brains when we discovered the magic hidden inside them.'

He dug his nails into the table. 'You experimented on living people?'

'We had to, Harry. Time travel won't work with dead tissue. We conducted experiments using brain tissue from cadavers, but they never worked.' She ran her fingers over Rose Adler's forehead. 'The tissue we need has to come from active brains; the younger, the better.' She glanced across the other tables. 'These homeless people won't be missed and they'll do for creating more pills, but I need something different if we're to create a pill strong enough to change the future.'

The bile rose out of his gut and sped up his throat. He stared at her before swallowing it.

Harry glanced over the bodies. 'You want to do this with children?'

The terrible taste in his mouth swept through him and settled on his brain. Then he stared at Amy and knew she was insane.

33 THIS TIME OF NIGHT

'I have to, Harry, don't you see?' She reached for him, but he flinched backwards. 'There'll be no more life on this planet within twenty years. I've seen it with my own eyes.' She nodded at Cronin. 'So has he. But we can change it if we're willing to make the right sacrifices.'

'The past can't be changed; that's what you've been drumming into me.'

Amy removed a pill from her pocket. 'Not with these, no. I need stronger, healthier brain tissue, something with uncontaminated DNA. Using babies might do it.' She gazed across at her victims. 'I need enough to change your present to prevent my future. To prevent humanity's terrible future.'

He stared at Adler. 'Is she one of your experiments?'

'Rose got too close to the sun, but Operation Cerebrum proved useful in that respect. Her memories of what she did for me will only linger in her head like butterflies drifting in the wind.'

Harry gathered his thoughts. 'You came here from 2070?'

Her smile unnerved and excited him. 'That's correct.'

'So, even with the war, you and the world must have been aware that time travel was real, of the work Adler, Hazell, and Cohen had done.'

'Ah, yes, the greatest of temporal paradoxes. I knew time travel existed before I accidentally discovered how it works, and then went back in time to reveal it to the people who claimed they'd created it before I discovered it.' She laughed out loud. 'I think I need some of that Cerebrum juice to heal my aching brain after all that.'

'You know what I mean, Amy. You were aware of Adler and the others before you travelled back to hand them your time travel pills.'

'Yes, the Crucial Three are famous twenty years from now, but mainly because they all disappear from history in 2050.'

'What?' Harry said.

Amy touched Rose's head again.

Then Adler vanished.

'I thought it might have happened sooner, but I guess the injection worked slower because of her sleeping mind.'

He rushed to the empty table. 'What have you done?'

'I do what's necessary. I needed Rose and the others to get you to me, and because history says they all disappeared this year, that had to be done as well. So I wiped all their minds and sent them to different time zones. I'm sure they'll be fine.'

He resisted the urge to strangle her. Instead, he looked at Cronin.

'You're forgetting there's still another time traveller out there who can undo all your plans.'

She narrowed her eyes at him. 'Another... oh, you mean Ellie.' That laugh unnerved him again. 'I thought she would

be the one to give everything away, but I guess your love –
or lust – really was blind.'

Harry's legs ached. 'Ellie is in on this as well?'

'Sort of,' Amy said. 'You didn't recognise her?'

'What?' He stumbled forward.

Amy caught his arm. 'You don't know who she is?'

'Lily?' he said. 'It was you who stole Lily from us?'

She let go of him. 'God, no. Do you think I'm a monster,
Harry? I never stole your sister from time. I don't know
what happened to her, but we can check together once we
sort this out.'

'Then... who?'

Amy tapped the side of her head. 'Those memories still
haven't returned. I thought they would have by now.' She
glanced at Cronin. 'I've had to rely on the Captain's
account of what you did at Pompeii.'

Harry stumbled from the table. 'Ellie is...?'

'The younger me, yes.' She gazed deep into his eyes. 'I
assumed you'd see the resemblance when you met her, even
with the twenty years difference.'

'Why... why did you bring her into this?'

She laughed. 'Who wouldn't want to go back in time
and meet the teenage version of themselves? Not that I met
her – I only observed from a distance and let Rose and the
others deal with Ellie, because trying to explain to her who I
was would have been too complex at that stage in her life.
And anyway, Harry, wouldn't you say the person you are
now is completely different from who you were at
nineteen?'

He dug his nails into his skin. 'I don't know if you're
lying to me again or not. Why do you have different names?'

'Amy is my middle name and Croft my married name.'

Harry gazed at her. 'In the future – in your present –

did you remember what Ellie, you, did here with me and the others?' The paradoxical nature of it all fried his senses.

'No,' Amy said. 'Cronin wiped all of Ellie's memories with the TA before she left here.'

The blood trickled across his palm. 'Did you kill Chuck?'

She shook her head. 'No, that was Rose. I'm not sure why she did it. Perhaps the solution I injected into her hippocampus, neocortex and amygdala tipped her sanity over the edge.'

He watched Cronin cradling the weapon in his arms.

'What happens now, Amy?'

She went to him and grabbed his hands. Her touch excited and repulsed him at the same time. When he gazed into her eyes, he only saw suffering.

'That's up to you, Harry. We can take the next step and improve the time travel solution. Then we'll rescue Chuck, change the future and save humanity.'

'And stop your murder?'

'Yes.'

He continued to hold her as he stared at the bodies strapped to the tables.

'How do you do it?'

She let go of him and he remembered how close they'd been in his flat.

'Come, I'll show you.'

Amy dragged him to the nearest table. His legs told him to flee, but his brain wouldn't let him.

And Cronin has that rifle.

She let go of him and grabbed a scalpel from a tray next to the homeless man.

He saw the man's eyes flicker into life. 'He's still awake, Amy.'

Her smile didn't warm his heart this time, instead turning it into a slab of ice.

'They have to be, Harry. The brain needs to be stimulated as I cut into it and remove the tissue.'

'Stimulated?'

'Fear, Harry. The synapses that produce fear are essential for creating the chemical I require.'

She took the scalpel and sliced it across the man's scalp. Harry's instincts were screaming at him to stop her, but Cronin's gun kept him frozen to the spot.

Blood seeped out of the skull, with the man unable to move his head because a vice-like structure secured it. Harry watched the man scream with his eyes. He opened his lips, but nothing came out.

'You removed his tongue?'

Amy ripped the scalp from the silently screaming man and dropped it into a bucket at her feet.

'It makes things easier. Early on, Jack and I discovered that covering the mouth wasn't helpful because the patient would bite through the tongue when the pain became too much. Then they'd pass out and there would be no more fear and we'd have to start the procedure all over again.'

Harry glanced at Cronin, calculating if he could grab the weapon from him and end this horror show once and for all.

But he had to keep her distracted.

'How many of these procedures have you done?'

Amy stopped slicing into the man's skull. 'One brain produces one pill.'

She's done this hundreds of times. Maybe thousands.

'Did the Crucial Three know about this?'

She shook her head. 'No. They kept badgering me to

tell them the secret, but I wouldn't. I don't believe they would have been able to deal with this.'

Amy removed a piece of skull and moved the scalpel to the brain.

'And you think I can?'

She nodded. 'I do, Harry. That's why I brought you into this. I can't save humanity by myself. But, with your experience in the army, especially during Operation Cerebrum, and your involvement with the police, I believe you have the perfect mentality for this.' Amy pointed the bloody scalpel at him. 'Your reaction here – or the lack of it – proves I was right.'

She returned to the procedure, removed a small part of the brain and held it up so Harry could see it.

'We can get as many infants and young children as we need. Kids go missing all the time and there are plenty of them homeless in this city. With the babies, we might have to visit some of the more remote places on the planet, so we don't attract too much attention.' She placed the brain tissue into a glass tube. 'But I'll harvest these brains first, so we have enough pills to move to the next stage.'

He stood there, transfixed by horror, his hands deep into his pockets. Then he turned from her and buried his head in his fingers. He didn't move, but felt the rifle barrel pushed into the back of his neck.

'I don't trust him,' Cronin said.

Harry waited for him to squeeze the trigger, knowing the bullet would be a blessed relief.

And it would prevent what he knew was coming next.

'But I do,' Amy said. 'So leave him and check on the others.'

Harry felt the gun pulled from his neck and she grabbed his hand.

He turned around to face her. 'Others?'

She smiled again, but it meant nothing to him now.

'Yes, we have more subjects in the basement.'

An abyss of despair and terror surged through him. 'Children?'

Amy shook her head. 'No. You and I will lead that process. Then, once we have the stronger chemicals for the pills, we'll travel back and you'll stop my murder. It may take a few attempts before we get it right, but I'm convinced we will.'

'Who do you think killed you?'

'It has to be Rose during one of her manic periods.' She laughed. 'It's ironic, really. The injections I gave her alerted her brain so much, it drove her to kill me. Or perhaps she got sick of me refusing to reveal my secrets and she'd had enough.'

He dragged a smile from somewhere deep inside his shrivelled heart, leant forward and kissed her. Amy's arms were around him, squeezing the life from Harry as he found the back of her throat. Then he released the pills from the side of his mouth and swallowed his own.

I hope I get this right.

They disappeared together.

There were no Doors of Perception for him, only his feet landing on the spot he'd seen many times before. But this time, he had a wide-screen view and not the limited one he'd had while watching that CCTV footage.

The river shimmered in front of him and the moonlight bounced off its dark surface.

Amy's laugh was of shock, not of joy.

'You? It was you all along?' He turned to peer into her sparkling eyes. 'You're my murderer, Harry?'

'I don't have to be, Amy. We can change everything

now, right here, the two of us. All you have to do is promise you won't hurt anybody else.'

She put her hands on the railings. He watched her do it, seeing it from a new angle now, different from what he'd observed on the video when it was impossible to see who she was talking to off-screen.

And he knew what was coming next.

It was me all along.

'I can't, Harry, you know that. The fate of humanity rests on my shoulders, on our shoulders. Are you prepared to sacrifice the future of humanity to save a few people here and now?'

He thought about arguing with her, but realised it was pointless.

The past can't be changed.

He moved forward and put his hands on her, knowing they would be the only part of him visible on the CCTV.

Then he pushed her off the bridge and into the river.

As he heard her body hit the water, he took another pill.

Harry appeared outside the factory sixty seconds after he'd left. Once more, he'd bypassed the Doors of Perception, wondering if he'd see them again or if he'd evolved past that stage. Then he removed his phone and called Caroline Diaz.

Once he knew the police were on their way, he checked the pills in his pocket: he had four remaining.

Enough for what he needed to do next.

34 DREAMS NEVER END

Harry sat on the bench opposite the house. He had been there for three hours, longer than he'd ever spent on that spot as a kid. Then he was too busy to sit and do nothing, too distracted to take time to appreciate the world and what was around him.

He embraced it now, the sun on his face, wind in his hair and the aroma of the trees. Harry let it all wash over him as he waited, the time ticking down more slowly than he'd expected.

Then she ran out of the house, her eyes bulging and cheeks flushed. He could hear her swearing from where he was, see the way she turned her hands into fists.

He wanted to shout out to her, but didn't.

Kids shouldn't talk to strangers.

Yet all his years in the police, all the things he'd experienced had taught him it was the people closest to you that inflicted the most hurt.

How had I been so blind?

Harry wasn't sure how he'd do this, but he didn't have to

worry. She'd seen him staring at her and marched across the road towards him.

Lily's anger seeped out of her as she spoke.

'Are you spying on us?'

'No.' He couldn't say her name. 'Don't worry; I'm just leaving.'

She reached out her hand and stopped him.

'Harry? Is that you?'

Her smile warmed his heart. 'It's a long story, Lily.'

She let go of him. 'It's okay. I know I'm dreaming again.'

'What do you mean?'

She rolled up her sleeve to show him the bruises covering her arm. Monstrous invisible fingers tore at his heart as she stared at him.

'Sometimes she misses, and instead of this, she hits me in the head. There's been a few times where it's happened and I've blacked out. Then I fantasise like this.' She rubbed at her forehead. 'I guess you're the Ghost of Christmas Future.'

'That movie frightened me as a kid.'

Lily sat next to Harry and punched him in the arm.

'You and your obsession with movies. I keep telling you to read books; they're so much better.'

She rolled down her sleeve so he didn't have to look at those bruises anymore. He wanted to ask about their mother, but was too scared. So he said something else.

'Have you told Dad what's happening?'

She pulled back her shoulders and scrunched up her face.

'I'm not telling anyone. I'm only saying this to you, Future Imaginary Brother, because you're not real. And even if I told someone, what would they do? The coppers would split us up and we'd probably end up in different care homes. So I'm not having that.'

He wanted to discuss it with her, but couldn't.

The past can't be changed. Little things, but not the major events.

He understood that now.

'What will you do, Lily?'

She glanced across the road at the house.

'I'm going to run away.' She grabbed his hand. 'Do you remember all our walks along the river?' He nodded. 'Well, now I know loads of places where I can stay, hideaways where I can wait, bide my time, and come back here in six years.'

'Six years?'

Lily squeezed his fingers. 'For when you're sixteen, little brother. I'll be twenty then and be able to look after you, especially as I'll have a job and a place to live.'

Harry wanted to sit there forever, but knew he couldn't.

'What job will you have?'

Her grin made his heart expand. 'I'll have my own bookshop. I might even keep a space for you and your ancient movie collection.'

He let go of her hand and reached into his pocket. He removed a pill and held it out to her.

'If you take this, all your dreams will come true.'

She snatched it from his hand. 'Oh, is this for a trip to Wonderland or Oz?'

Harry laughed as he took a pill for himself.

'Where we're going will be much better than that.'

THANK YOU!

Thank you, dear reader for purchasing this book.

Many thanks to my wonderful wife for all her support and patience.

The Time Traveller's Murder edited by Alison Jack.

Extra special thanks to Karina Gallagher for being a dedicated reader of my work.

Cover design by James, GoOnWrite.com